Little Girl Lost

Janet Gover

Book 4 – Coorah Creek Series

Where heroes are like chocolate – irresistible!

Published 2016 by Choc Lit Limited
Penrose House, Crawley Drive, Camberley, Surrey GU15 2AB, UK
www.choc-lit.com

A CIP catalogue record for this book is available
from the British Library

ISBN 978-1-78189-322-7

Printed and bound
by CPI Group (UK) Ltd, Croydon, CR0 4YY

This book is for John, of course.
And for my nieces, Kate and Emma. Love you girls.

Acknowledgements

Whenever I stop to think about the process of
writing a book, I almost quiver with fear. It's
such a daunting thing, and I am so very grateful
for the help and love I receive along the way.

In researching *Little Girl Lost*, I was fortunate to
make contact with an amazing woman who, like Tia,
drives a big open cut mine truck. Thank you, Mel
Harrison for being willing to answer my questions.
Any errors in the book are my fault entirely.

Thank you, Rachel Summerson for reading those
first few chapters and being honest with me. As
always, you helped me find the right path.

I started working on this book while on a retreat
in an old pub on a wild headland in Devon with
a group of fellow writers whose support and
love never wavers. The Quayistas Rule!

In the difficult bits, I turn to my friends in the
Romantic Novelists' Association, and my fellow
Choc Lit authors for everything from spelling and
punctuation hints, to a glass of wine and a shoulder
to cry on. Thank you all – especially Jean Fullerton
and Alison May – best writing buddies ever!

Thanks as always to the team at Choc Lit for
taking such care of my story. Especially Karen M.,
Kim B., Vanessa O., Samantha E., Lizzie D.,

Ester V., Claire W., Isabelle, Gill L., Linda Sp.,
Jo O., Nicola G., Anja N., Sigi, Alma H., Ros P.,
Katie P., Julie R. and Jenny W. on the tasting panel,
who fell in love with Coorah Creek again.

And John – proof reader and tea maker, website designer
and possessor of a keen literary eye, a sympathetic
ear and at times a very damp shoulder. Thank you for
being my toughest critic and my biggest supporter.
I have no idea what I would do without you.

Chapter One

The huge yellow machine moved forward slowly on wheels that were twice the height of the men watching. Like some prehistoric monster, it growled softly as the powerful engine hauled more than two hundred tonnes of rock and dirt and precious ore out of the mine pit. The machine turned towards the railhead and the skeletal iron gantries silhouetted against the brilliant blue outback sky.

Inside the air-conditioned cab, the hands on the wheel seemed far too small to control such a gigantic and powerful machine. But they were steady, giving no indication of the driver's nervousness, or the importance of the next couple of minutes.

The watchers on the ground followed at a safe distance as the truck crossed those last few metres, and finally came to rest next to the railhead.

Inside the cab, the driver turned off the engine and waited with bated breath.

One of the watchers stepped closer to the vehicle, peered closely at the precise placement of the wheels in relation to the railhead, then stepped back and looked up at the cab. He raised one arm, his thumb pointed skywards and a ragged cheer broke out from the men around him.

From her place so far above them Tia Walsh couldn't hear the cheer, but she saw that thumbs up. She had done it!

An unfamiliar feeling swept through her. Pride at her accomplishment. It was such a very long time since she had felt pride in anything. It was an unlikely job she had chosen, driving a huge Caterpillar truck in an open cut mine, but that only made this moment all the sweeter. She had trained and now passed the test. She was something and somewhere she had never expected to be.

Somewhere no one would ever think to look for her.

Rising from her seat, she opened the cab door and quickly descended the metal steps, before jumping the last distance to the ground. Her steel-tipped safety boots raised a small puff of red dust as she landed.

'Well done, Walsh. That's it. You're one of us now. Welcome to the Goongalla Mine team.'

Mine manager Chris Powell held out his hand, as a small collection of drivers behind him gave another cheer. The drivers were all clad in protective clothing: hard hats and safety boots, Day-Glo yellow vests and heavy cotton long trousers. They were even wearing long-sleeved shirts despite the heat. Safety was paramount at the mine, and to a man they adhered to the rules.

To a woman, too. Tia was quite happy to wear all that safety gear. It couldn't disguise the fact that she was the only woman in the crowd, but it did help her to blend in.

She wished they weren't making such a fuss. The mine, they said, was a community as much as it was a job. Tia didn't really care. She didn't want to be part of a community. She'd been part of something like that once before, and never wanted to repeat the experience. She just wanted to do her job and be left alone. She hated being the centre of so much attention.

She shook the manager's offered hand. 'Thanks.'

Powell beamed and nodded, then stepped back as Tia's fellow drivers crowded around to shake her hand. Tia did her best to accept the congratulations with good grace, but she was beginning to feel trapped.

'So, everyone who is off shift, the first round at the Mineside is on me.' Blue, Tia's instructor, and the mine's senior driver, received his own cheer for that offer.

'Not for me, thanks,' Tia said quickly.

'What?' The other drivers were starting to move in the direction of the mine gates, but Blue held back. 'You've got to come. It's tradition when someone passes the test.'

'Thanks, but no thanks.'

'Tia ...'

She knew that tone, and immediately shook her head. She had been waiting for this and she was going to set the record straight right now. Hopefully Blue would pass it on to the rest of the men.

'As I said thanks, but no thanks.' They both knew she wasn't talking about beer.

Her instructor shrugged. 'Fair enough. No harm in asking.'

'See you tomorrow.'

They parted company, Blue heading towards the pub, and Tia towards the accommodation compound that she now called home.

Like most of the big outback mines, Goongalla Uranium had a large number of workers who were flown in to work a ten-day shift then flown out, back to their homes, for a week off. These FIFO workers lived in small portable tin huts, with just a bed and bathroom and a TV. The dongas sat in lines around a central mess building, where everyone ate, and spent hours playing pool or watching the footy on TV.

Although Tia wasn't a FIFO worker, she had been allowed to rent one of the two big trailer homes in the compound. They were set back from the dongas for a little extra privacy and had been used by the engineers during the mine's construction phase. It was a true mobile home, with a kitchen as well as the bathroom and TV. Tia had been here a week now, and hadn't cooked a meal in that kitchen. She was twenty-five years old and had never cooked a meal in any kitchen. It wasn't that she was a bad cook. She simply did not know how to cook. She'd never had the chance to learn.

She unlocked the door. That was another thing strange to her: a home with a door that she could lock and to which she held the only key.

The trailer showed very few signs that anyone lived there. It was clean and tidy, the bed at the back neatly made and a coffee cup upturned in the draining rack next to the sink. The only personal item was a red and black full-face motorcycle helmet sitting in a corner of the couch. Tia had learned long ago that anything left where it could be seen would probably not be there when she came back. Nothing as simple as a locked door was going to change such hard-learned habits.

She opened the small refrigerator. It held a dozen cans of Coke and some milk for her coffee. Nothing else. She pulled out a can of Coke, but hesitated before opening it. She had just taken a big step forward. Maybe she should celebrate. She was now licensed and trusted to drive a truck worth maybe a million dollars. That wasn't bad going for a homeless runaway. She could have a drink and maybe even treat herself to a pub meal. The food at the mess was hearty and filling, but the menu wasn't very varied. A change would be nice. She was still avoiding the Mineside pub and her workmates, but the town had one other pub.

She stripped off her work clothes and after a quick wash, slid into a pair of jeans and a simple white T-shirt. She ran a brush through her long hair and slipped it into a ponytail. Then she reached for the motorcycle helmet.

The Harley was parked outside, its elegant chrome tailpipes gleaming softly in the sunlight. A light layer of red dust had begun to settle over it, as it did over everything around the mine, but that couldn't hide its beauty. Tia had been told the bike was worth a lot of money. She didn't know how much. She hadn't paid for it. She checked the registration plates. The mud she had smeared over them to obscure the lettering was still there. Good. Anyone who wanted to check the bike would have to get pretty close to do it. And she wasn't letting anyone get that close. Not now. Not again. Not ever.

She slipped the helmet over her head and swung her leg over the bike. It was time to check out Coorah Creek.

Sergeant Max Delaney liked to walk the streets at sundown. He'd developed the habit as a young police constable, newly graduated from the Academy and assigned to Fortitude Valley in Brisbane. The Valley had been a run-down, crime-ridden black spot littered with illegal gambling dens and brothels, but when he was assigned there it was starting to develop into a hub of inner-city nightlife and entertainment. Max had loved watching the bright neon lights flare into life as the sun set. He'd loved the smell of the exotic spices from the restaurants in Chinatown. He'd loved that final flare of sunlight off the glass office towers of the inner-city business district, visible from the high spots on his beat. But, most of all, he'd loved the knowledge that he was making it safe for people to walk those streets.

The sun was setting as Max left his office and walked out into the streets that he now patrolled. From the west, a glow of molten gold spread over his new town. The light painted the wooden buildings in the main street with a soft glow that hid the faded paint and softened the corrugated iron roofs. Even the fine red dust that seemed to cover everything looked better in this light. On the other side of the road, the Coorah Creek Hotel – possibly the most prosperous establishment in the outback town – glowed with welcome. There were no people on the street and the only sound was the distant cry of a crow.

He had come a long, long way since the Academy and those early exciting years as an inner-city beat constable. Coorah Creek wasn't exactly a crime hotspot. The occasional drunk driver or pub brawl kept him busy on a Friday night. There were accidents on the long straight highways that ran east and north back towards civilisation. Like everywhere else, there was a bit of underage drinking and the odd bit of teenage shoplifting, although there was not much in the town's few shops to tempt them. Teenagers here were in little danger of falling headlong into a life of crime.

This wasn't how he had imagined his life at thirty-three. In his youth he'd seen himself as a detective, homicide maybe, or organised crime. Something exciting that would lead to commendations and possibly TV appearances. Back then he had even occasionally thought about having a family and a home in some nice leafy suburb, with good schools and neighbours to invite over for a backyard barbecue. He had never for one moment thought he'd end up in a tiny town in Queensland's far west, just a stone's throw from the desert.

Sometimes life didn't go the way you planned.

But still his life was far better than some.

Swinging a plastic shopping bag from his hand, he turned up a narrow dirt road that ran off at right angles to the highway. It wasn't much of a road, more a rutted laneway. There were only two houses in the lane. One was dark and deserted. The other had a light showing through a window. Both houses were old and run-down, but the home with the light had a flash of green around it. Someone tended that garden with a great deal of love. Early spring flowers were in full bloom. They would fade soon as the heat of high summer sapped the life out of the west country, but for their brief moment in time, the flowers were a bright splash of colour amid the long brown grass and the cracked, bare dirt.

Max walked past a group of rose bushes tipped with brilliant yellow and white blooms, climbed the wooden stairs and knocked on the door.

The woman who opened it had a toddler balanced on her hips. She was quite thin and looked tired. The sadness and lines on her face were those of a middle-aged woman, but Max knew Nikki was much younger than she looked. She was barely out of her teens, but life had made her old before her time.

'Oh, hello, Sergeant.' She lifted a hand to smooth the hair from her face.

'Hello, Nikki. How are you?'

'I'm doing all right,' Nikki said in a voice that suggested even she didn't believe it.

'Anna looks lovely,' Max said, gently stroking the toddler's hair. The little girl's clothes were faded and worn, but she was freshly bathed and her hair was combed. Nikki didn't have money to lavish on her child, but she made up for this by the strength of her love.

The young mother's face glowed. 'She's such a good girl,' she said.

Max nodded. He held out the shopping bag for Nikki to take. 'I thought she might like these.'

'Oh.' Nikki juggled her daughter a bit and opened the bag. She reached inside and withdrew a beautifully carved wooden horse, painted a golden brown with a creamy mane and tail.

'Horsey …' said Anna as she grabbed it with both hands.

Nikki reached back into the bag and this time withdrew a black and brown dog. With the horse clasped firmly in one hand, Anna reached for the dog.

'They're beautiful,' said Nikki in a very little voice. 'We can't accept—'

'Yes you can,' Max interrupted her. 'I carve these things in the evenings, just to keep my hands busy. My place is littered with them. You'd be doing me a favour taking them.'

They both knew that wasn't strictly true, but it was a way for Nikki to save face.

Anna settled the discussion by holding both toys close to her heart and laughing out loud.

'She loves them,' Nikki said. 'She doesn't get new toys very often. Steve's job doesn't … well, we're hoping he'll get moved into a new job soon.'

'That's good news,' Max said.

'Oh, where are my manners?' Nikki said. 'Would you like to come in for a cup of tea or something?'

Max was touched by the invitation. This family had barely enough for themselves, let alone to share. Nikki had still been at school when Anna was conceived. Her boyfriend Steve was a few months older and had just started working at the mine when his daughter entered the world. They were far too young to be parents. Steve did his best, but they struggled. Max wasn't the only person in town who helped them.

'Thank you, but no,' Max said. 'I'd better get back.'

She nodded. 'Thank you so much for the toys.'

'You are very welcome.' Max turned and walked away. As he did he could hear the little girl laughing. It was a wonderful sound.

He'd just turned back onto the main road when he heard a low rumble. He stopped walking and listened as the noise grew louder. He recognised it in an instant. Only one motorcycle made that sound. That was a Harley-Davidson. He'd heard some talk that there was a Harley in town. It belonged to a new worker at the Goongalla mine, a couple of kilometres south of the town. Max hadn't seen either the bike or its rider. That was about to change.

The Harley rumbled into view on the road from the mine. The rider was wearing leathers and a full-face helmet. Max felt his policeman's instinct twitch a little. The bike roared past and pulled into a space outside the Coorah Creek Hotel. The rider dismounted and walked up the stairs. From this distance Max couldn't see much about him. He hadn't even removed his helmet. That set off alarm bells. He'd spent enough time dealing with biker gangs back in the city to know that this could mean trouble for his sleepy little town.

Max crossed the road, walking with more speed and purpose.

The Harley was quite something. A classic American muscle machine. It had a custom paint job – black and red flames covering the petrol tank. The polished chrome of the raised handlebars gleamed in the light of the late afternoon sun. The big headlight would send a brilliant shaft of light down the outback roads at night, no doubt encouraging the rider to ride the big machine hard and fast. The powerful engine was astonishingly clean. The Harley owner clearly loved his hog and spent a lot of time working on it. Except for one thing. Max frowned as he tried to read the bike's reggo. The plates were covered with dried mud. He could even see the marks where someone had used their fingers to press the wet mud over the plate, making it impossible to read. There was only one reason why someone would do that.

Max glanced towards the pub. As Coorah Creek's police chief and the only law enforcement officer for three hundred kilometres in any direction, he should check out the guy who rode this bike. Most of the mineworkers drank at the town's only other pub, the Mineside. They didn't mix too much with the townsfolk. It wasn't a strict rule, but it seemed to work. The Mineside was a little rougher. The men could relax there without the need to mind their language. The Coorah Creek Hotel was more for the long-term residents of the town. And for families. The Harley owner either didn't know that or else he didn't care.

Max resisted the urge to run his fingers along the shining paintwork of the hog. As a rule, Harley owners didn't like people touching their machines. Max didn't want to start anything with this guy, not yet at least. He walked up the stairs into the pub.

The fans above the long wooden bar were not turning. By Queensland standards it was positively cool for this time of year, but spring wouldn't last long. It was getting hotter every day. There were a handful of people in the bar, but Max knew them all. He nodded to acknowledge their hellos, and stepped up to the bar.

'Well, hello, Max. Nice evening, isn't it? Not too warm for this time of the year. The long-term weather forecast says we're in for a really hot summer. They say that as if it's something special. Or some kind of surprise. But I ask you, when did we ever have anything but a really hot summer. OJ?' Trish Warren, the owner of the pub and its chief barmaid, was in her mid-sixties. A short, grey-haired woman with shrewd eyes and a mind to match, she knew he never drank beer when he was in uniform.

'Thanks, Trish.'

Max cast a quick glance through the doorway from the public bar to the lounge. It was empty. Turning back to the bar, he noticed a half-finished beer slowly dripping condensation onto the highly polished wood of Trish's bar. A leather biker's jacket hung over a nearby bar stool. A black and red full-face helmet sat on top of it.

Trish placed a glass of juice in front of Max, following his glance to the beer.

'I see what's going on here. You're looking for the Harley rider?'

Max shrugged.

Trish grinned. Max knew that grin. It usually meant Trish was up to something. She nodded her head in the general direction of the toilets at the back of the pub.

Max picked up his juice. He would wait. He braced himself for a verbal downpour from Trish. The publican was a good woman. Some said she was the heart of this small town. But she talked like no one Max Delaney had ever met. He had no idea how her husband Syd had lived with it all these years.

But Trish said nothing. With a smirk twitching the corners of her mouth, she went back to polishing glasses.

Max's instincts went on an even higher alert. When Trish wasn't talking, something was up.

He caught movement from the corner of his eye. He slowly turned to look at the figure walking towards him from the direction of the toilets.

The Harley owner was wearing blue jeans and a white T-shirt, but looked nothing like any biker Max had ever seen. His first thought was how did someone so small and frail manage a big bike like the Harley? She was tiny. She would barely reach Max's chin. And she was thin. He could see the shape of the bones on her shoulders. Her breasts were small but shapely under the tight white fabric of her top. Her hair was a dark mahogany colour, caught into a ponytail that hung halfway down her back. It was slightly ruffled, no doubt from wearing a motorcycle helmet. Max just knew her eyes would be green. They couldn't be any other colour. Not if there was any justice in this world.

She should have been beautiful, but she was a little too

thin and something about the way she walked robbed her of her beauty. She kept her head down, her shoulders hunched as if she was trying not to be noticed. She knew he was watching her, and glanced in his direction. Her eyes were indeed green, and reminded him of a wild animal, poised to fight or to run. But there was something else in those eyes. Something that suggested she was stronger than she looked. Something that suggested she could be dangerous.

She slid back onto her stool and reached for her glass. Her fingers were long and thin and devoid of either rings or polish on the nails. They looked as fragile as a bird's wing. She raised the beer and took a long drink.

As she moved, the low curved neck of her T-shirt flexed and Max caught a hint of colour above her right breast. She had a tattoo. He couldn't see it clearly and had no idea what the image might be. Max wasn't a fan of tattoos, but that hint of colour was nothing if not sexy.

Max turned his eyes back to his own glass and let out the breath he had unconsciously been holding. From the moment he'd seen the Harley, he'd been afraid it meant trouble in his town. He was right. This girl was trouble, but not the sort of trouble he'd expected.

Tia kept her gaze on her beer glass as she turned it slowly in her hands.

The problem with the Harley was that it attracted all sorts of attention. She'd stayed in the mine compound since her arrival two weeks ago to avoid notice. Just her luck. Her first visit to the town and she runs into a cop. She took another drink, knowing this would be her first and last beer. Ordering a second would simply guarantee that the cop would be breathalysing her the minute she swung her leg over the bike. That would be a joke. She seldom drank much, and certainly wasn't stupid enough to step onto the Harley when she was drunk. Nor was she stupid enough to give a cop any chance to pull her over. She knew enough about cops to stay well away from them.

'Can I get you another beer or something to eat? The food here is pretty good,' the grey-haired barmaid asked.

Tia shook her head. She had planned to grab a burger, but she wasn't going to stay here with the cop. She'd get something to eat later, back at the mine mess. She drained the last of her beer and stood up. Keeping her eyes firmly fixed on the bar in front of her, she slung her jacket over her shoulder and picked up her helmet. As she turned towards the door, she couldn't resist casting a quick sideways glance at the cop. He was making no attempt to hide the fact that he was staring at her. Her defences rose. Tia had no illusions about her looks. Men found her attractive. On more than one occasion she had been forced to use her looks to get herself out of trouble. But things were different now. She wasn't that same girl any more. She didn't like to be stared at. And certainly not by a cop. She had good reason not to like cops.

She walked out of the bar. Standing beside her bike, she shrugged into the leather jacket. Her helmet still in her hands, she slung one leg over the Harley and looked back at the pub. The cop was standing in the doorway, watching her. He was tall and fit. A few years older than her. During the quick look they had shared in the bar, she'd decided he was quite handsome, with tanned skin and dark eyes. He wasn't one of the fat pigs she had met in the past, but he was still a cop. And cops were the enemy.

Tia pulled the helmet over her head, feeling an unexpected relief when she knew he could no longer see her face. She slipped on her leather gloves and hit the Harley's starter. The engine roared into life. She felt the bike vibrating beneath her, like some animal waiting to be let loose.

She couldn't resist. She gunned the engine and spun the bike, sliding the rear wheels and sending a small shower of loose gravel flying in the general direction of the pub. Then she roared off down the street, a hair's breadth over the limit. In her mirrors she saw the cop still standing in the doorway of the pub, watching her taillight fade into the darkness.

She smiled as the hog carried her back towards the mine.

Chapter Two

Sarah Travers wished she was coming home under different circumstances. It wasn't going to be a happy homecoming. Maybe that's why she hadn't told her parents she was arriving on this afternoon's train. She had left her bags at the station and decided to walk into town. She wanted to take the time to remind herself of everything she had left behind more than three years ago.

The huge arc of blue sky was somehow different here to the huge arc of blue sky on the coast. It seemed a brighter blue. Maybe that was because it rained so seldom. The few trees that survived this far west were more grey than green. In recent years, the Creek had acquired a better water supply and there were some patches of green lawn in places. But still red and brown remained the predominant colours.

She kicked a rock with the toe of her brown leather boots and watched it bounce along the red dust at the side of the road. She had forgotten about the dust. It got everywhere! No matter how much a person cleaned or how often they washed their car, that red dust ruled supreme. She paused for a second to bend over and touch the dirt. When she looked at her hand, her fingertips were stained red.

Sarah gazed with new eyes at her old school. She hadn't spent a lot of time there. The mine had come to the town when she was fourteen years old. The school had followed not long after. Before the mine and the arrival of the internet, it was school-of-the-air for her, learning her lessons at home via shortwave radio, because a simple storekeeper couldn't afford to send his daughter to boarding school. Not that she wanted to go. As a child she'd had an unshakeable belief that the Creek would always be her home.

She walked past the row of dilapidated old wooden homes that used to be the aboriginal housing, before the mine bought the land and the people moved on to better homes or, in some cases, back to their traditional lands. The paint had faded away and the bare timber was bleached white by the sun. The corrugated iron roofs were red with rust, and the windows were either boarded up or open to the elements. They'd been deserted for years, but no one had seen fit to pull them down. Although, as she looked closely, she could see places where some of the timber had been removed. She wondered if that was entirely legal. And if it wasn't, did anyone care? The houses were a lot shabbier than she remembered. In fact, the whole town seemed somehow smaller now.

It was about two kilometres from the railway station to the intersection at the centre of town. Sarah wasn't a tall girl and her short steps were not hurried. If anything she was dragging her steps because of what faced her. But at last she saw the landmark pub that sat on the northern side of the road she was following. The Coorah Creek Hotel was one of the town's original buildings. It was surprisingly elegant for such a small town. Two storeys, with a wide veranda top and bottom. The wrought iron on the top storey was rare and beautiful and the whole building had an aura of being well cared for. It had been there when the mine came, and Sarah guessed it would be there long after the mine closed – as one day it surely must.

As she drew closer to the corner, she could see past the pub to the town's main street, and the few shops that serviced the town. Beyond the street, the land rose slightly to give a view of the newer houses that stretched to the north. The people who lived in those houses had been brought in by the mine. They worked there, or supported those who worked there. There were far more houses than she remembered. That part of the town, at least, had grown in her absence.

Three years wasn't really such a long time, and she had come home. Twice, although both visits had been short. She'd meant to come more often, but somehow she was always too busy. She did feel a little bit guilty that she hadn't been back last Christmas. She'd had a chance to spend the holidays in Sydney with a friend and then to watch the New Year fireworks on the bridge. That was too good an opportunity to miss. It didn't matter if she missed one holiday. Coorah Creek was always going to be here waiting for her. Exactly the same as it had always been.

She stopped walking to look at the building on the other side of the road. Her parents' store was the only general store in town. It had expanded with the town to provide essentials not just for the outlying properties, but also for the new residents. It wasn't exactly a Target or Woolworths, but it served the town well. Like the pub, it looked well cared for and prosperous. It was painted the same pale yellow that it had always been. The same wide awning shaded the big glass windows and front door of the building. The iron roof rose to a low peak, and was partly shaded by a huge gum tree that grew near the corner. From this angle, she couldn't see the house behind the store. But in her mind's eye she could see it. She assumed it too had barely changed. Tears pricked her eyes and she fought back feelings of guilt. She really hadn't planned to be away for so long, but neither had she planned to be back here today. Bad news had a way of changing plans.

Sarah's steps quickened. She was eager to see her mother

and father. Especially her father.

She stepped into the shade under the awning outside the shop windows, and hesitated for a heartbeat. Just long enough to ensure her emotions were under control. Then she stepped inside.

Gina Travers was serving someone at the front counter. She hadn't changed. She was, like Sarah, quite small and thin. There was more grey in her hair than Sarah remembered, but the look on her face when she saw her daughter was exactly what Sarah expected.

'Sarah!' Gina dropped what she was doing and bustled out from behind the counter. She wrapped her arms around Sarah in a breathtakingly tight hug.

Sarah hugged her back, surprised to find she was almost about to cry.

'Sorry it took so long, Mum,' she said, her voice muffled against her mother's shoulder. 'But it's good to be back now.'

'And it's good to have you back, honey.' Her mother's voice cracked with emotion.

Behind them, the customer, a middle-aged woman Sarah didn't know, cleared her throat.

'Oh, I'm sorry.' Gina wiped a hand over her suspiciously bright eyes. 'It's my daughter just arrived home after being away at college.'

The woman smiled absently.

'I'd better get on,' Gina said to Sarah. 'Why don't you go out back and see your dad. He's in the lounge.'

'Okay.'

Sarah turned to go.

'Honey,' her mother's voice stopped her. 'Your dad …' The soft whisper trailed off to nothing.

Sarah nodded. She knew what to expect. She was prepared for this.

She opened the door almost hidden between two rows of shelves at the back of the shop and walked through the big storeroom, packed to the ceiling with brown cardboard boxes of everything from canned spaghetti to shoe laces and ice cube trays. Another door led out of the store itself, along a short covered walkway to the big timber house that Sarah still thought of as her home, despite the fact that she no longer really lived there. The kitchen door was, as always, unlocked. Sarah breathed in deeply as she entered and stood in the kitchen, surrounded by the sights and smells of her childhood. The place was exactly the same: the bright colour of the cabinets her father had painted, the sun streaming through the window onto the immaculately clean table, and the wonderful smell of home-cooked biscuits.

Sarah moved swiftly across the kitchen, through the open doorway into the lounge. She stopped when she saw her father. She thought she was prepared, but she wasn't. Not for this. There was no way she could have been. Tears poured unchecked down her face.

Her father was asleep in a big reclining armchair. The chair was new, but the man in it looked old. Too old. Illness had stripped her father of his weight and his strength and his youth. His face was thin, and his hair had turned completely grey. His short-sleeved cotton shirt hung loosely on him and the hands lying so still on the armchair looked almost skeletal. For the first time in Sarah's memory her father was not wearing his watch. He'd always run his days by the big silver watch that seemed permanently affixed to his left wrist. That watch told him when to open the store and when to close it. When his small daughter should be at her lessons. When the transport would arrive with supplies to restock his shelves. That bare wrist almost broke her heart.

She now understood why he'd missed her graduation last month. When her mother had come to the ceremony alone, Sarah had been both surprised and hurt. She'd always imagined both parents would be there. After all, they were the ones who had encouraged her to go to college in the first place. He mother had made excuses for Ken's absence, saying he couldn't get away from the shop. There was also mention of the flu. Gina had taken a million photographs to show him, but Sarah had sensed there was something wrong. That suspicion had prompted her to cut short a post-graduation holiday and come home instead. She was so glad she had.

A small sound near her feet dragged Sarah's shocked eyes away from her father. A big ginger cat was rubbing himself enthusiastically against her legs.

'Hi, Meggs,' she whispered as she bent to pat him, her heart crying out against the unfairness that had seen the cat change not one whit, while her father had become an old man. Old and frail.

How sick was he?

In a heartbeat her grief was swamped by anger. She spun on her heel and walked back into the store. Her mother was still finishing up with her customer. Sarah waited impatiently until the front door had closed behind the woman, before turning on her mother.

'What is it? Cancer?'

Her mother nodded. 'Lymphoma.'

'You didn't tell me that. You just said he was sick. Why didn't you tell me it was cancer?'

'Honey, he asked me not to.'

'But if I'd known I would have come home earlier.'

'Don't you see? We didn't want you to. We wanted you to finish your exams first, with nothing to distract you.'

'He's my father!' Sarah had to fight to keep from

shouting. 'Nothing is more important to me than that. I would happily have walked away from college.'

'Yes. I know you would.' Gina Travers took a deep breath and crossed her arms. 'That's why I didn't tell you. You had to finish—'

'But—'

'For HIS sake!' Gina overrode her daughter's objections. 'He has worked hard all his life to give you a better chance than he had. Than we had. There was no way I was going to let you disappoint him by walking away before you graduated.'

'That's not fair. How could you not tell me that he's dying?'

'Don't say that!' Gina's face contorted with anger and her words were like a slap in the face for Sarah. 'Don't say that. Ever. Not to me. And not to him. He's not dying. I won't let him.'

Sarah was shocked by the outburst; she had so seldom seen her mother angry. Gina was shaking slightly and Sarah realised that her anger was stirred by fear. She stepped forward and wrapped her arms around her mother.

'I'm sorry, Mum. I won't say it again. I promise.'

Gina leaned against her daughter for a few seconds. 'Thank you,' she murmured softly. Then with an obvious effort of great will, she pulled herself upright and took a deep breath. 'It's good that you are here. Your father has to go to Toowoomba for chemotherapy every month. He gets very tired, so it will be better if I can go with him.'

'You drive all that way?'

'No. Chris, the mine manager, lets your dad go on the FIFO plane. It's very kind of him.'

Sarah felt a moment of guilt. Other people had been more help to her parents than she had. Well, that was about to change. She looked closely at her mother, seeing for the first time the lines on her face, the shadows under her eyes. She had lost weight too. Gina had always been a slender woman. Now, like her husband, she looked frail.

'Now that I'm here, Mum, do you want to take a break? I can look after the shop for you.'

Gina smiled and shook her head. 'You've just arrived. Take some time for yourself. Spend some time with your father. There'll be plenty of other days for you to mind the shop for me.'

Reluctantly, Sarah agreed. But she didn't want to go back into the house. She needed a few minutes to herself to absorb all the terrible things she had learned. She left the shop by the rear door, turned left and walked to the water tank that sat behind the shop. In the wet season the huge tank collected enough water from the large shop roof to keep the family supplied throughout the dry months. The town had a proper water supply now, but the old-timers like the Travers family still used their rainwater tanks for drinking water. It had its own special taste that Sarah had never found anywhere else.

As a kid, Sarah had liked to climb the water tank and on to the roof of the shop. In one corner the shade from the tall gum tree made the iron roof cool enough to sit on. She'd spent long hours up there, staring up and down the long highway that passed through the Creek, waiting for her knight in shining armour to come along and rescue her. She smiled a small fond smile. Her younger self had even found a knight in the form of a handsome young truck driver who delivered supplies to the store on a weekly run. She'd changed since then. Three years in the city had expanded her horizons. The girl who had always believed her future was here in the Creek now had thoughts of travelling and exploring the world. Maybe even finding a real knight out there somewhere.

If ever she could use a knight, she thought, this was the time.

All the possibilities of her future were on hold now. She was needed here. And here she would stay.

Sarah turned and walked back into the house to sit by her father and wait for him to wake.

Chapter Three

'So, whadda you say? Can I buy you a beer?'

'No, thanks.' Tia kept walking.

'But why not? What harm can it do? It's just a drink. Between friends. Workmates, even.'

'And that's what you'll tell your wife when you go home next week?'

There was a smattering of laughter from the nearby men. The one walking next to her had the grace to look slightly abashed.

'If not him, how about me? I'm not married,' his companion offered.

'No. Sorry.'

Didn't these guys ever get sick of asking? It was annoying.

'Tia has the good sense to recognise a bunch of losers when she sees them,' Blue stepped in, with a mock punch at Tia's admirers. 'Come on, the first one is on me.'

There was a rumble of approval from the group. Blue caught Tia's eye and she smiled her thanks.

'Don't worry, any day now these thickheads will get the message,' Blue said to her as he led his team away.

Tia hoped so. All these attempts to get her on a date were getting a bit annoying, although some small part of her that she kept hidden deep behind her rough exterior might be a little bit flattered. But accepting any of the offers was out of the question.

'Have one for me,' she said as she left them at the gates. Her refusal was as much for their sakes as it was for hers. They had no idea of what she had been and who she really was. If they knew the baggage she carried they'd avoid her like the plague, which would be the best thing for everyone.

It was far too soon. She still didn't know if she was truly free of her past. Getting close to her was dangerous for everyone.

She walked slowly back to the residential compound. Dusk was falling, but that had little effect on the energy-sapping heat. Inside her trailer, she splashed some water over her face and grabbed the black and red motorcycle helmet that was sitting on her table.

The Harley was parked next to her trailer. The FIFO workers didn't have cars – they used mine vehicles when necessary. The hog had created as much of a stir as Tia herself the day she arrived, but the men had quickly learned the bike was as out of their reach as she was.

She ran a hand over the black and red flames painted on the tank, feeling the thin layer of gritty dust that seemed to settle there within seconds of her cleaning the machine. She shrugged. There was nothing she could do about the dust. And it wasn't as if she loved the bike. She didn't. She loved what the hog represented. She'd spent too much time as a pillion passenger on this bike, forced to hold on for dear life to a man she hated as he broke every rule in the book. And not only the road rules. She was done with that now. Even though she might have preferred a car, riding the bike was a constant reminder that she was a new person now. In the front seat. In control. She never ever wanted to forget how she had turned her life around. It hadn't been easy. It still wasn't. But she was working on it.

She slung her leg over the Harley and straightened it off its stand. She pulled her gloves on before pressing the starter on the handlebars. The engine roared instantly into life. She slipped the helmet over her head and twisted the throttle to set the big bike into motion.

Tia paused where the mine road met the highway. North was the town. There were people there. Probably good people with whom she could be friends. But she wasn't ready for that. That cop was in the town too. She needed to avoid him in case he got curious about her. Or the Harley. The last thing she needed was him sticking his nose into her life. Instead, she turned the bike south, away from the town. She hadn't explored the Birdsville Road yet. It couldn't hurt to know where that road led. In case she had to run again.

There was something to be said for outback roads. They were long and straight and mostly empty. A girl on a motorcycle could really let her hair down. Tia opened the throttle. The big engine roared like the monster it was, as the bike gathered speed. The noise was almost loud enough to drown out her thoughts and her memories. The rushing wind was almost enough to make her forget the dark stuffy rooms and the stifling smell of lost souls. The feel of the powerful machine was almost enough for her to forget the feel of cruel hands reaching for her in the darkness, and the sound of harsh laughter. The rush of adrenaline was almost enough to make her forget the rush from the weed and the speed.

Almost, but not quite.

She twisted the throttle again, forcing the Harley to even greater speeds, right down the dotted white line in the centre of the road. Ahead of her, a truck suddenly appeared through the heat haze. A road train pulled by a huge blue and white Mercedes prime mover. Their combined speed was enough to make it appear that she was driving headlong into a wall and she was about to die in a terrible scream of twisted and torn metal.

At what seemed the last second, she twisted the handlebar a fraction and raced past the huge truck on into the slowly gathering dusk.

* * *

'Shit!' Pete Rankin exclaimed at the blur disappearing in his rear-view mirrors. That biker was a nut job. He'd pushed that far too close for comfort. Didn't he realise that road trains couldn't stop or turn as quickly as a bike? Or a standard truck for that matter. He was driving nearly eighty tonnes at ninety kilometres an hour. If he'd hit the bike, there would have been nothing left of bike or rider but a thin smear along the bitumen.

Pete shook his head. He was a professional driver. He knew the road and how to treat it with respect. He really hated amateurs. The people who thought the roads were a playground. He'd seen far too many accidents in the last ten years and seen too many people hurt or killed by the amateurs.

He sighed and flexed his fingers on the steering wheel. He'd been driving steadily for several hours and would need to take a break soon. He looked forward to a chance to stretch his legs and relax his concentration. Maybe talk to someone. A lot of drivers had dogs. They wanted another living creature to share the long hours on the road. But he didn't. It didn't seem much of a life for a dog. But more than that, he enjoyed the solitude. He would occasionally turn on the radio, or listen to some music on his iPod, but mostly he drove accompanied by nothing more than the noise of the big powerful engine and the hum of eighteen tyres on the road surface.

Pete liked to read. When he pulled over to sleep, there was always time to read a chapter, lying in the bed at the rear of the cab. He read almost anything and everything. He read fiction and non-fiction. He liked crime novels and books about nature. But most of all, he liked to read biographies. The stories of people who had done great things. Travelled and invented. People who made discoveries. He admired people like that because he would never be one of them.

Not that it mattered; he was content with his life. He liked the solitude that allowed time for his mind to do the travelling for him, the feel of the steering wheel under his hands and the long straight line of bitumen.

At least, that had been enough.

He grimaced. Here it was again; that restlessness that had been pulling at him for weeks now. He blamed the wedding.

A few weeks ago one of his fellow drivers had married his long-term girlfriend at a tiny wooden church on the outskirts of Mount Isa. All the drivers from the depot were there to celebrate. Pete had taken his girlfriend Linda to that wedding. For almost a year Linda had been a barmaid at the pub next to the transport depot. It was the drivers' favourite watering hole and they all knew and liked her. Some had even made a pass at her, but she'd made it clear right from the start that Pete was her favourite. They dated, in a casual way, and it had seemed the right thing to take her with him to the wedding.

The wedding was small but nice. The bride and groom looked very happy together and Pete was happy for them. He was a big believer in marriage. His parents had set him a wonderful example in their relationship, and he had always thought that one day he would like to settle down and maybe have some kids of his own. But not yet. He wasn't ready for a house and a picket fence, kids and a dog. He liked his freedom. That's why the relationship with Linda worked so well. When he was in town, they were together, but not once had she ever tried to tie him down. Nor had he hinted at any sort of commitment. He'd made it clear to her right from the start that he wasn't that sort of a man. They didn't have that sort of a relationship.

But since the wedding, Linda had changed. Maybe marriage was contagious, and she had caught it. She was dropping hints. Talking about houses and families and not wanting to be a barmaid all her life. There was nothing wrong with that ... but he couldn't see himself in the picture she painted. He liked Linda. Cared about her. But he didn't love her. Not the sort of love that led to marriage.

Pete ran a hand through his close-cropped brown hair. It was this birthday thing. He knew it was. He was going to turn thirty in a few days, and it seemed everything was changing. He had no idea why. Thirty wasn't old.

A sign flashed past and he began slowing down. In a couple of minutes he was driving through Coorah Creek. It was a nice town. Small but friendly. He'd been delivering supplies to the shop since he was a trainee driver and in recent years he'd taken some really big loads to the mine, stopping occasionally for a meal at the pub.

He saw a figure emerge from the town's one big general store. A girl with long blonde hair. She was wearing shorts that showed off a pair of very nice legs. She waited on the footpath as the truck went past. Pete looked in his mirrors as she crossed the road behind him. She was really attractive, the sort of girl he'd like to meet.

And there it was.

If he loved Linda enough to consider marriage then he wouldn't be checking out a blonde in his rear-view mirror.

It was time to break if off. Linda deserved the chance to find someone who was right for her and could give her the things she dreamed of. Because he couldn't do that. Last week, Linda had decided to throw him a birthday party. He wasn't all that keen, but she was enthusiastic so he had agreed. It was set for this Friday at the pub. All his driver mates would be there. He wouldn't break it off with her before then. That would be too cruel after she'd gone to so much trouble for him.

But as soon as possible after that, he'd break it to her as gently as he could.

He felt as if a weight was lifted from his shoulders. That was the right thing to do. As he drove past the northern edge of the town for the last stage of the run back to base, he turned on some music and the evening light began to fade into darkness.

Chapter Four

The little girl was running as she came through the door of the shop and collided with Tia.

'Hey.' Tia reached down to grab the girl by the shoulders. She crouched down in front of her. The little girl was clutching a carved wooden toy of some description. 'Where are you off too?'

A second later a young woman came hurrying out of the store, her eyes wide with anxiety. She saw Tia and the little girl, and immediately swung the youngster up into her arms.

'Anna, you mustn't do that,' the young woman said. 'You must never run away like that. You might get lost.'

'Sorry, Mummy.' The little girl looked crestfallen.

The young mother turned to Tia. 'Thank you for stopping her. I only turned my back for an instant and she was gone.'

'I want Sergeant Max.' The little girl waved the toy she was holding. 'More animals. I wanna make a farm.'

'Sergeant Delaney has more important things to do than make you more toys,' her mother said. 'Come on we have to go home and make dinner for your daddy.' With another tentative smile at Tia, the woman carried her child away.

That was interesting. The cop made toys for children. In her experience cops destroyed more than they made. Shrugging the thought aside, Tia entered the shop.

'Can I help you?' the girl behind the counter asked.

Tia's first instinct was to say no. She'd been to the store before and knew where to find the essentials she needed. But she bit the word back. The girl had done her no harm. She'd simply offered to help. It wasn't her fault that she was so young and pretty, with her long blonde ponytail and sweet summer dress. It wasn't her fault that she looked so innocent, or that she had a freshness about her that Tia had lost a long time ago. She felt a twinge of envy, but crushed it quickly. There was no point in envy or regret. She was who she was. Her life was what it was. She had started turning it around the day she left Brisbane. And she'd done all right. She had a job, and a place of her own to live. A place that had a kitchen and a door she could lock. That was the first step. She needed to feel a lot more secure before she took another. It would be so easy to fall, and falling would bring too much pain.

'Shampoo,' she said. 'And I don't suppose you carry kitchen stuff, do you?'

'Shampoo is over there to your left,' the girl said. 'And we do have some crockery and cookware, if that's what you're looking for.'

'Yes. Just the basics to stock my kitchen.'

'Sure. By the way,'—the girl smiled—'I'm Sarah. Sarah Travers. My parents own this place. You're new in town, aren't you?'

Tia nodded abruptly and went in search of the shampoo. The girl was simply being friendly. But Tia wasn't looking for friends. And certainly not a young girl like that. A girl like that wouldn't last a week in Tia's world. Tia glanced at her again. Thinking she was unobserved, the smile on the girl's face had faltered a little. She looked thoughtful and kind of sad. Perhaps worried would be a better word. Tia suddenly realised that just because Sarah had everything that Tia didn't, her life was not necessarily a bed of roses. Perhaps the two of them were not quite such a world apart.

Tia wandered around the store, selecting some items she needed. The store was fairly large, but nothing like the supermarkets she had been used to in town. This wasn't a supermarket – it was well … a shop that sold everything. From shampoo to casserole dishes. There were huge bags of dry dog food, Akubra hats and what looked like plumbing supplies. Well, she thought, maybe it was a *super* market after all.

She grimaced at her own bad joke and returned to the main counter where her purchases were accumulating into quite a large pile. And she wasn't finished yet. Surely she didn't need all this stuff! She'd lived for years without a Pyrex casserole dish. Why on earth did she need one now? Because now she had a kitchen and she wanted to cook. Her trailer wasn't everybody's idea of a home, but she'd spent much of her life in places far worse. It couldn't be wrong to want to try her hand at cooking. Or to want nice towels when she showered.

She had lived for so long with next to nothing; just what she could borrow or sometimes steal. There was little point in having nice things when you lived in a squat. Someone would steal it the first time you turned your back. But now she had money. A job and a place of her own. It couldn't be wrong to want these things … but it felt strange.

She was as out of place in this world as the girl behind the counter would be in hers.

Sarah was tapping numbers into a calculator as she bagged Tia's supplies. That brought a smile to Tia's face. The few times she'd had money to shop in a 'proper' supermarket, it had been all bar code scanners and card readers. This small town store had no such technology. She kind of liked that. It made her feel a little more relaxed. A little safer.

'That'll be a hundred and thirty dollars,' Sarah said.

It sounded like a lot of money to Tia. She slipped her hand into the pocket of her leather jacket. Her fingers closed around a wad of notes there. She'd had her first pay day at the mine. The money was paid into her bank account, but she had instantly removed it. She preferred to carry cash. In case she had to run. ATM records made it too easy to find a person, so she had spent her day off riding all the way to Mount Isa to withdraw her money in cash at the bank. That was a waste of a day off, but it had seemed the right thing to do. She would be harder to trace if her bank activity suggested she lived in a town several hundred kilometres away. Maybe when she was more settled here, she would use the bank and the cash machines in Coorah Creek, but she wasn't ready for that yet.

'Are you going to be able to carry all that on your bike?' Sarah asked.

Tia looked at the bags and suddenly realised Sarah had a point. There were panniers on the Harley, but they'd never hold all that.

'Umm … I guess I'll need to make a couple of trips. If you could hold it all here for me.'

'Don't worry. You're staying at the mine, aren't you? I can drop it off for you after work. I've got some stuff for a few other people as well.'

'You deliver?' Tia couldn't keep the surprise out of her voice.

'It's that sort of town.' Sarah smiled in what Tia imagined was a welcoming and encouraging manner. 'We are happy to drop stuff off when people need us to.'

That sounded an awful lot like home delivery to Tia, but she wasn't going to argue. She handed over her cash.

'There's a cream trailer home on the left as you drive in,' she said as she put her change back in her pocket. 'Set a bit back from the others. That's me.'

'I'll find you,' Sarah said. 'I'll just look for your bike.'

Tia nodded and turned to go. She took a couple of steps, and then hesitated. She was here to start over. That's what she should do. This girl seemed friendly enough. Harmless. It might be time to relax. Find a friend. Just one. Then maybe she would spend fewer nights riding the roads alone. Sarah had no connection with the past. There was no threat here.

But there was. Unconsciously, Tia lifted her hand to rub the place on the right side of her chest where her tattoo was hidden under her shirt. The threat was Tia herself. And those who would still be hunting her. She walked out the door.

The store was particularly quiet that afternoon. Sarah had been left in charge. Her father was asleep. He'd returned from his latest treatment looking even more frail, telling Sarah there was nothing to worry about. The side effects were expected. The chemotherapy was almost as tough on him as it was on his disease. But, he reassured her, it would cure him, he was certain. Sarah desperately wanted to believe him.

She was also terribly worried about her mother. Gina's hair, which, a few years ago, had been the same golden-brown as her daughter's, was now a dull grey. Her face was lined with worry, making her look so much older than her years. She had been working in the shop with Sarah that morning, but Sarah could tell she was both exhausted and distracted by worry. At lunchtime, Sarah had banished her mother to the house, where she was hopefully resting.

To keep herself occupied on such a slow day, Sarah was organising the shelves and dusting. Since her father had fallen ill, things had been let go a bit. Ken Travers would never have allowed so much as a single dust mote to accumulate in the store of which he was so proud. As a child Sarah had often sat on a wooden crate and talked with him as he'd sorted and stacked, dusted and put tiny white price labels on each item. It had been a special treat for her to use the label machine. Her father would set the correct price, and she would then work her way along the row of canned fruit or bottles of jam, carefully placing the labels just so in the middle of each lid.

Sarah took a can off a shelf, and looked at the fine film of dust on the top. She should have come home much sooner. If her parents had only told her how sick her father really was. Going to college had always been more her parents dream than hers. She wished now that she hadn't agreed. She'd certainly enjoyed her time in the city. She'd met people and gone to parties. She'd even taken a few holidays with her friends. But her college degree really didn't matter to her. She was unlikely ever to use it. One didn't really need a degree in business to run a store in a tiny town on the edge of nowhere. Still, her parents had worked hard to afford to send her to college, and she would not deny them the pleasure and pride of knowing she'd achieved something they had never been able to even attempt. She had spent those years away from home because it was right for her to know a little more about the world before she did the one thing she had always known she would do – settle back in Coorah Creek.

She used a cloth to remove the dust from the can before setting it back in place. Tears pricked the back of her eyes and she angrily rubbed them away. She wasn't going to cry. Her parents had given her so much. It was her turn to give back. Her turn to be the strong one. She set back to work.

The results soon began to show. The store began to take on the familiar air of prosperity and care. Sarah wiped her hands on a rag, feeling satisfied with her afternoon's work, but still restless. Leaving the connecting door open in case a customer came in, she turned her attention to the storeroom.

The first thing she noticed was that the boxes were neatly stacked, in a logical order. That had always been her father's way, but she doubted he'd done this. He wasn't really strong enough to be hauling boxes about and nor was her mother. Perhaps the delivery man had stacked them. She took a closer look at the boxes. Yes. That must be it. The boxes were neat, but not arranged quite to the same order her father had always used. She turned in a slow circle, noting as she did some half empty boxes, and shelf space that was not being used. The storeroom, like the shop, was suffering from lack of attention. Well, she could fix that.

Sarah started sorting the contents of some half empty boxes, setting aside new stock to go on the shelves, and stacking the rest for later use. As she did, she noticed a small cardboard box pushed to the back of a high shelf. The sides of the box were battered and stained and very dusty. That box had not moved in a long time. Sarah stood on a wooden crate and reached to retrieve it. She smiled as she realised it was the box that had once contained her first pair of heeled shoes: some sandals she had been given for her twelfth birthday.

Deeply curious, she sat on the crate and placed the shoebox on her lap. Trying not to create a dust cloud, she opened it. Inside she found the sort of accumulated nearly-useful things most people put into small boxes and then forget. There was a key ring with a couple of keys, although Sarah had no idea what they might open. There were a couple of old pens, which would obviously no longer work. A pile of rubber bands had more or less melted together and lay on top of an envelope that was old and brittle and yellow and empty.

Sarah reached into the box and retrieved the keys. She'd show them to her father before she threw them away. Nothing else in the box looked like it was worth salvaging. She shuffled the contents around a little, and the corner of an old photo appeared underneath the envelope. She removed it and turned it to catch the light streaming through the storeroom window.

The colours had faded over the years, and the edges of the paper were curling, but the photograph clearly showed a girl of about ten sitting behind the wheel of a big prime mover. Her small hands gripped the big steering wheel tightly, but her feet were far too short to reach the pedals. She was grinning widely as she strained to see through the windscreen. Sitting beside her, his arm protectively around her shoulders was a handsome young man. His hair was long and dark and slightly wavy. He was smiling in a slightly bemused way.

Memories of that day came flooding back, bringing a smile to her face. She'd had a terrible crush on that driver. Pete, his name was. It was a moment of such excitement to be lifted up by him and placed gently in the driver's seat of his truck. How far up she had felt. How very grown up. And how wonderful it had felt to have Pete's arm around her. To have his approval. Her father had ducked back into the house and grabbed his cheap little camera to capture the moment. They had kept the photograph on a corkboard at the back of the shop for a while, before it got lost among the receipts and orders and notes. Strange that it had ended up here.

It would have been different for Pete, of course. To him it had no doubt been a little act of kindness to a lonely girl in an isolated store at a tiny truck stop on his road. She doubted that he would remember it now. She had forgotten all about it, until she saw the photo. Briefly she wondered where Pete was. Was he still driving this same route? Maybe he was the one who had stacked the boxes for her parents? If so, it just went to show that he was – if not a knight in shining armour – a good Samaritan at the very least. He was probably married now with a house full of kids. As for her; she had an education and a degree that could take her away from here. If she wanted to go. And right now, she didn't. She couldn't. She wouldn't leave her father. If she did, she might never …

She caught herself. No. She'd promised her mother she wouldn't say it. She wouldn't even think the words.

There were no knights in shining armour, but a positive attitude could make all the difference to her father's treatment. At least, that's what people said. She hoped they were right.

Chapter Five

Max was seated at the long wooden bar, a beer in front of him. He had changed into civvies before coming to the pub. That was unusual on a week day. Both the civvies and the beer. Trish raised an eyebrow when she saw him, but she didn't say anything. That was unusual for any day.

Max wasn't the only person in the bar. There were a couple of regulars sitting down at the other end of the expanse of polished timber. He had exchanged friendly greetings with them when he entered, but he sat alone as he usually did. He wanted to avoid the awkwardness of drinking with someone on one night, and perhaps arresting them for drink driving the next. He was part of the town, yet not part of it, and he was happy to keep it that way.

He heard steps on the wooden veranda. He glanced up, trying not to notice the anticipation he felt and then trying to hide his disappointment when Ed Collins, owner of the town's service station, walked in. They exchanged a greeting then Ed settled himself further down the bar. Ed had become a more frequent visitor to the pub since his reconciliation with his son last Christmas. Ed had a new laptop with him and was soon making use of the pub's much vaunted Wi-Fi. Max knew he was planning a trip to England to visit his son Steve and his fiancée. Max knew a lot about most people in the town. Perhaps not quite as much as Trish Warren and her gossip grapevine, but more than most. After all, that was his job. He told himself he was just here at the pub to keep up his casual contact with the town. He really wasn't waiting for anyone in particular.

And if he wasn't, he was therefore not at all disappointed

when the next person to walk in through the pub's front doors was one of the teachers from the school.

Max ordered a second beer. It would be his last for the evening. A few minutes later, Trish delivered a burger to one of the other patrons. It smelled good. Max suddenly realised he was hungry. For a few seconds he contemplated ordering a burger for himself, but stopped. In a moment of honesty he admitted to himself that he had really come to the pub in the hope of seeing a redhead in motorcycle leathers. To stay here still hoping she would appear was a bit sad. He stood up and left the last of his beer.

He paused on the top step long enough to glance up and down the road. He listened but heard nothing but normal night sounds. With a sigh he set off home.

It wasn't a long walk. He crossed the Mount Isa road and entered the tiny town square that fronted the road. The town hall, Coorah Creek's only brick building, was at the back of the square. The post office and police station formed the other two sides. Town square was perhaps too grand a name for the tiny patch of grass, bordered by a flower bed. But, thanks to the mine manager, Chris Powell, it was green and the flowers added a touch of colour. Not for long though. Come the soaring heat of mid-summer, not even the automatic watering system installed by mine engineers would save the square from the blistering midday sun.

Max walked along the side of the station to the house behind it. Once in his home, he headed for the kitchen. He was a reasonable cook, but cooking for one wasn't much fun. Once a week he'd make a big pot of something which would keep him fed for several days. At the moment it was spaghetti with a meat sauce. It wasn't grand enough to be called bolognese, but it was tasty none the less. He spooned a helping into a dish and set it in the microwave. While it heated, he ripped the top off a can of Coke.

He carried his dinner through the kitchen door into the garage he'd turned into a workshop. He perched on a chair and ate, all the time studying the pile of old timber in front of him. It had come from one of the old houses by the railway station. Those houses were now owned by the mine, and he'd done a deal with Chris to take whatever timber he wanted. The boards were weathered by years of outback sun; any paint they had once known was long gone. There was something about this old wood that spoke to him. This was part of a house. It had echoed to the sounds of families. Of mothers and children. It was wrong to simply let it rot.

By the time he'd finished his spaghetti, he had a picture in his mind. He knew what the timber wanted to be.

There was a sketchbook on the bench, but he didn't bother making a plan. He could see the image so strongly in his head he didn't need one. He drank the last of his Coke and picked up a plank. He weighed it in his hand for a few seconds, feeling its weight and its strength. Then he set it into a vice and picked up a plane. He slid the tool along the side of the wood, feeling the first layer of weathered timber flake away to reveal a darker, richer colour underneath. He was quickly engrossed in his task. He worked until the small hours, bringing that piece of wood back to life. Just as he went to bed, around one o'clock, the Harley roared through town in the direction of the mine.

He couldn't begin to guess where the girl had been or why. In fact, he knew nothing at all about her and that wasn't good enough. He wanted to know more. He would even be happy to hear some gossip about her from Trish. Not that he listened to gossip, of course. But Trish always seemed to know everything about everyone. She knew what was happening in the town. Sometimes before it happened. And she was seldom wrong. But despite several visits to the pub this week, he'd learned nothing at all from Trish. In fact, Trish had been remarkably silent on the subject of the Creek's newest resident. That was unlike her. If he had a suspicious mind, he would think Trish was up to something.

His interest in the girl was work, he told himself as he settled himself for sleep. It was his job to check out any newcomers in town. Especially newcomers who might cause a problem. And if anyone was likely to cause a problem it was a good-looking redheaded girl on a Harley in a town full of single miners. Or, even worse, the FIFO workers who had left their wives behind.

Max had never planned to come to Coorah Creek. His honesty had brought him here. Well, that and a youthful tendency to speak without thinking. He winced as he remembered his words and the look on the commander's face the night Max had arrested a powerful man who had been driving home late at night, weaving all over the road. Max hadn't needed a breathalyser test to know the man was drunk. It would have been easy to let him go with a warning. Easy, but not honest. Three days after charging the man, Max had been reassigned to Coorah Creek, a promising career brought to a pretty abrupt halt.

He had no regrets. He'd done the right thing, although perhaps gone about it in the wrong way. And he had come to love Coorah Creek and its residents. He appreciated their community spirit. He loved the colours of the sunset. He loved the smell of the first drops of rain as the wet season arrived. He was happy dropping by the pub occasionally for a beer. If this was punishment, he was happy to accept it. There was plenty of time to reboot his career in the future, if he wanted to.

But if he prided himself on his honesty in his work, he was going to have to be honest with himself too. His desire to find out a bit more about the red-haired girl wasn't entirely work. There was a personal angle as well. He hadn't been able to get her out of his head. She was a beautiful girl … woman. Coorah Creek seldom saw the likes of her. But it was her haunted air that kept him awake at night. That and her late night rides on a very noisy motorcycle.

He had to know more about her.

Next morning, Max drove to the mine.

Chris Powell greeted him as he entered the office. 'What brings you out here? I hope one of my boys hasn't been causing trouble?'

Max shook his head. 'Not this time,' he said. 'Actually, it's a woman I've come to ask you about.'

Chris raised an eyebrow and indicated that they should go through to his office, away from the interested ears of the general office staff.

'I guess you mean Tia,' Chris said as he closed the office door.

Tia. Until now Max hadn't even known her name. It suited her. He wondered what, if anything, it might be short for.

'Yes. What do you know about her?'

'Not a lot. Tia Walsh. She's only just got her licence to drive the Cat 793. But she's good. She's got a trailer in the accommodation compound. Keeps very much to herself, I think. If you want I can get her personnel record.'

Max was about to say yes, but caught himself. This wasn't right. The girl … Tia … had done nothing wrong. He had no right to use his job to check up on her. No right at all. It would be an invasion of her privacy. Much as he wanted to say yes, he shook his head.

'No. It's fine.'

'If there's something I should know …'

'Absolutely nothing.' Max felt a pang of guilt. The last

thing he should be doing was giving Tia's boss any reason to doubt her. 'Nothing at all.'

Chris raised a questioning eyebrow which Max tried desperately to ignore. That and the knowing smirk that accompanied it.

'I'm off,' he said, making for the door. 'See you around, Chris.'

Walking back to his car, Max looked across the gravel car park towards the giant hole in the ground that was the source of the rare ore that had brought prosperity to the town. Some distance away from the office building, huge gantries clustered around the railhead, conveyer belts reaching into the sky like giant skeletons. A train was loading, and the mineral ore crashed down into the open ore wagons, sending a cloud of dust into the air. As he watched, another of the massive earth moving trucks appeared rumbling slowly up the path from the open cut working. It was huge. Every time he saw one Max was fascinated by the size of them. They towered over the mere men who worked the mine. The diggers that loaded the ore into the tray backs were even larger. He knew the enclosed cabs were air-conditioned and noise protected. The best possible hydraulics aided the drivers who guided the giants up and down the face of the cut. But still Max marvelled at the sheer size of these earth-eating giants.

And he marvelled at the thought that a slender slip of a girl named Tia Walsh drove one. Perhaps that very one. Sunlight glinted off the glass cab. Max squinted. He could see a dark shape inside, but he was unable to tell who it was.

He slid behind the wheel of his car, and backed out of the car park. At the gate, instead of driving forward towards the town, he turned right. The mine accommodation compound was a few hundred metres away. He drove slowly, the police car kicking up a cloud of dust that followed him. He reached the open entrance to the compound and pulled up, his motor still running. He could simply go inside. He was the town's policeman. No one would query what he was doing. He would no doubt find the Harley parked beside her trailer. It would be a simple matter to take down her reggo and then enter it into the police system. He'd be sure to find out something about her that way.

He gently tapped his open palm against the steering wheel. Then shook his head, his decision made. This wasn't right. Using his job to check out a woman for no reason other than because he found her attractive. That was wrong.

He slipped the car back into gear, dropped a U-turn and headed back to town.

From inside her trailer, Tia watched the car disappear behind a cloud of red dust. She waited for a few minutes as the dust settled slowly back to earth. The cop was checking up on her, she just knew it. How much did he know? Had there been some sort of a bulletin from the east coast? Perhaps something to do with the hog? She shouldn't have kept it. But when she walked away from Andrew Kelly, she had wanted to hurt him just as much as he'd hurt her. So she'd taken the things that mattered most to him. The hog was one of those things. Had he reported it stolen? She doubted that. He wouldn't admit it, but he was even more threatened by the police than she was.

The cloud of dust outside was gone and the road was empty. Tia heard voices and movement from the other side of the camp. A handful of men walked into her line of vision heading for the mine. It was time for the start of the next shift. She was due to start work with them. She glanced at her watch.

She could leave now. Jump aboard the Harley and head

46

through that gate, away from this town to some other place and try again for a new start. She turned away from the window. Her leathers hung behind the door. Her helmet sat in its customary place on the end of the table. She had all her wages in cash. The wages were pretty good. She had enough money to get a long way from here. Maybe she should head south into New South Wales, then cut across to Western Australia. Kelly would never find her there. It would be so easy to get on the bike and go. She reached out to retrieve her helmet, and as she did, her eyes fell on the glass casserole dish drying next to her sink. Last night she had used her new casserole dish to cook up a tuna pasta bake. The recipe had been on the tuna can in the store, and she'd purchased all the ingredients on the spot.

It was the first meal she had ever cooked in an oven. By most people's standards the tuna bake had probably been a pretty poor attempt at a home-cooked meal, but to Tia it had tasted wonderful, partly because of the satisfaction of using ingredients bought with money she had earned. Not only that, she knew the name of the girl who had delivered those ingredients. Sarah. She had felt able to open the door to her when she knocked. And, most importantly, the meal had been eaten at her own table ... well, the mine's table, but hers for now. It was just like being a normal person.

Nothing she had eaten had ever tasted that good.

Tia stood stock still in the middle of her little home and made a decision.

She wouldn't run. Not yet. She would make sure she was ready to go, but she'd wait and see what the cop did.

She nodded to herself. That seemed like the best thing to do. She grabbed her work gloves from the bench beside the door and stuck them in the back pocket of her jeans as she walked out the door, enjoying the feeling of locking the door behind her.

Chapter Six

'Gettin' old mate, gettin' old!' The hearty slap on his back caused some of the beer in Pete's glass to slosh over onto his hand. He put the beer on the table and shook off the liquid before clasping the hand of the newcomer.

'Glad you could make it, Mick.'

'Wouldn't miss this for the world. Let me buy you a beer.' Mick set off towards the bar without noticing either the glass Pete had just set down, or the other full glass queued next to it.

Pete let him go. He didn't know whether he would be drinking much beer that night, but it wouldn't be wasted. With six of his driving mates already here, and a couple more expected in later tonight, there would be plenty of people willing to drink whatever was going.

'Happy birthday, mate.' Mick was back, holding his beer high.

'Cheers, Mick.' Pete raised his own glass, but barely took a sip of the cold amber liquid.

Behind them the clatter of a ball and a chorus of rousing cheers indicated that the most recent pool challenge was over.

'Want a game?' Mick asked.

Pete shook his head. Mick deposited his beer on the table and picked up a cue. Pete left him to it. He left his beer on the table and walked towards the back of the pub. Instead of going into the Gents, he quickly slipped outside into the darkness.

The Overflow Pub sat on the Barclay Highway on the outskirts of Mount Isa, just a short walk from the trucking depot where Pete and the other drivers were based. Thus it was their regular watering hole. It was a little like the men who frequented it, a bit rough around the edges, but basically all right. And tonight it was the venue for Pete's thirtieth birthday party.

Thirty! Pete shook his head. How the hell did that happen? He didn't feel much different to the day he was handed his MR licence – his passport to driving medium-sized trucks and the first step towards the combination licence he now held as a road train driver. He was a better driver now, of course, after the many years on the road. Older, too, of course. But thirty? He couldn't be thirty!

Where had the years gone?

There was a wooden table and chairs behind the pub for the smokers to use, but they were empty at the moment. Pete leaned back against the table and looked up at the sky. He could see the stars, but not enough of them. Many were lost in the refracted light of the houses and cars and street lights. It was one of the things he didn't like about living in a town even this big. He liked the vast open skies at night, with so many stars a man would need a lifetime to count them all.

'Hey, birthday boy. What are you doing out here all alone?'

The scent of perfume cut through the night air as Linda approached.

'Just getting a breath of fresh air, Linda,' Pete replied.

'Do you mind if I join you?' It was a rhetorical question. Linda had already taken up position next to him, leaning against the same table, her leg gently touching his.

'I hope you're enjoying the party,' Linda said.

'Yeah. You've done a great job. Thank you.'

'No worries. Anything for you. You know that.' Her voice dripped with meaning.

They sat in silence for a few moments. Linda was pretty, with shoulder-length brown hair and a trim figure. She looked terrific in a tight T-shirt and even tighter jeans. She was funny too, and kind. All the drivers liked her, but none of them had ever made a move on her. Because she was Pete's girl.

Pete felt pretty bad about deceiving her tonight. It seemed cruel to pretend all was well between them, when he'd already decided to call it quits. But surely it would be even more cruel to end it now, when she'd gone to all this trouble to set up the party? Let her have tonight. He was heading out on a run to Birdsville tomorrow, stopping off at the mine near Coorah Creek. He'd be gone a couple of days. When he got back, he'd tell her.

He didn't think she'd be too upset. At least, he hoped she wouldn't be. In Pete's mind the relationship had never been more than casual. He thought she felt the same way and no doubt spent time with other men when he was away. That thought didn't bother him at all. He made no claims upon her – nor she on him.

'I have a present for you,' Linda said softly.

'You didn't have to. I mean, all the work you put into the party. That was enough.'

'That was nothing,' she said. She was looking at him intently now. He could see the emotion on her face. She looked uncertain. That was rare for Linda. She normally exuded confidence. It was part of her appeal.

He didn't say anything, he waited for her to go on.

'We're going to have a baby.'

Pete froze. The world around him did to. He struggled to understand what he'd just heard.

'A baby?'

'Yes. I'm pregnant. Isn't that wonderful!' Her voice held a slight tone of desperation.

'But we … always used … How?' Pete fought to get the words out.

'Just one of those things. It really doesn't matter now. We're going to have a baby. I love you, Pete. And I'm so happy.'

She stopped speaking, obviously expecting him to reply in a similar way. He struggled to find some words.

'How far? I mean … when …' he stammered.

'I've only just found out. I'm only a few weeks along. Please don't tell anyone. Not yet. I want to wait.'

Linda stopped speaking and stared into his eyes. Hers began to well with tears. 'Oh, Pete, tell me you're happy about this. That you and I …' She started to step away from him. 'You're not going to dump me, are you? You can't.'

The fear in her voice snapped him back. He reached for her and pulled her tight against his chest. Not because he wanted to hold her, but he had to get away from the accusing look on her face.

'Of course I won't,' he said. 'I'm shocked by the news, that's all. I'm here for you. And for the baby. I always will be.'

'I love you, Pete.' Her voice was muffled against his chest.

He knew the answer she was expecting, but he'd never said those words before. Not to Linda. Not to anyone. He couldn't do it now because it would be a lie.

'Have you seen a doctor?' he asked instead. 'Had a check-up. Made sure … that everything is all right.'

'I did this week,' she said. 'He says everything is fine. He says I'm healthy and so is our baby.'

Pete wondered just how much they could tell about the child this early. His mind went back to the last time he and Linda had been together. She hadn't looked any different. Even now she still looked as slim as ever. But, he

51

suddenly realised, she hadn't been drinking tonight. Linda had always liked a couple of glasses of wine at a party. Or something stronger. But tonight he'd seen her drinking orange juice.

She really was pregnant.

Linda took a step away from him and her eyes searched his face.

'I'm happy about this, Pete,' she said slowly. 'I've always wanted to be a mother. And you'll be a great dad. You will be there, won't you, Pete?'

'Of course I will,' he said. 'And the baby ...' he couldn't bring himself to say our baby '... couldn't have a better mother.'

Linda brushed a tear from her eye and kissed him. He kissed her back, although at that moment it was the last thing in the world he wanted to do.

'It's a shame we can't tell everyone yet,' Linda said. 'But we should wait for the end of the first trimester. That's what everybody says, anyway. Just in case.'

It was a whole new language, and a little bit more than he could cope with right now.

At that moment a yell from the direction of the pub told them they had been missed.

'We'd better go inside,' Linda said, tugging gently on his hand.

'You go,' he said. 'I think I need to take a couple of minutes.'

Her face fell.

'It's all right,' he hastened to assure her. 'This has just been such a surprise. I want to digest it properly before I go back in. I don't want to accidentally let the secret out.' He forced a smile onto his face.

Linda looked uncertain. 'All right,' she said. 'But don't be too long. People will think there's something wrong.'

Something wrong? Pete watched her walk away. That wasn't exactly the right term for it. But in the space of a few minutes his whole world had been turned on its head.

A baby?

He had always been careful in his sexual encounters. In fact, there was always a condom in his wallet. Condoms weren't guaranteed, of course, but he couldn't remember one breaking.

But he was going to be a father. Put like that, he felt a small quiver of pleasure. A father. That had a nice ring to it. He'd always assumed that some day ... Well, some day was here. Linda might not be the woman he would have chosen, but he liked her. She would be a good mother. They could make a good life together.

There was no way he was going to abandon his child.

The pocket of his jeans began to vibrate, and he fished out his phone.

'Hi, Mum,' he said.

'Happy birthday, darling. How did you know it was me?'

'Caller ID.' Pete's mother wasn't known for her technical skills.

'Isn't that clever. Anyway, where are you, Peter?'

'Back at the Isa. I'm having a few drinks to celebrate.'

'That's nice. It's a shame you couldn't have come here. Thirty is, after all, an important milestone.'

'Thanks, Mum, but it's busy at the moment. I think I may be doing a run down your way soon. If I do, I'll drop by.'

'That'd be lovely. Will you stay the night? We could have a small gathering for your birthday. Invite some friends. Maybe the Hoopers from down the road.'

She was matchmaking, again. That was an irony. For a moment he was tempted to tell her about Linda. And the baby. But he'd given his word. And besides, his mother would be on the next train west to come and visit. He definitely wasn't ready for that.

'Mum!' Pete scolded gently. 'I've told you before to stop matchmaking. I am not going to get involved with Joanie Hooper. Anyway, she's not interested in me.'

'You say that—'

'I do, Mum.'

'But she's such a lovely girl,' his mother persisted. 'And let's face it, son, you're thirty now. It's high time you settled down and started a family.'

The irony of that almost made him laugh out loud.

'All right. I know. I promise I'll stop nagging if you'll promise me just to stay in one place long enough to meet some nice girl some time. And soon. I do want grandchildren, you know.'

That was going to happen sooner than she expected. He said goodbye and slipped the phone back in his pocket.

His mother meant well. She had been happily married to his father for thirty-five years. They lived in a medium-sized brick home on the outskirts of Toowoomba, where his father ran a car sales yard. They were good together, complementing each other's strengths and weaknesses and still very much in love. On his last visit he had walked in on them kissing in the kitchen. It hadn't just been a peck on the cheek. And they were best friends too. If he was ever to marry, that's the sort of marriage he wanted.

But he wasn't ready for a life away from the road. Tied down to one place. Going to the same place of work day after day. Staring at the same four walls while he tapped away at a computer or shuffled paperwork. That wasn't for him.

It hadn't been for him. It was beginning to look like he'd have to get used to that sort of life … and far sooner than he had ever expected.

Chapter Seven

Max sat at his desk, staring at his computer, oblivious to the words on the screen. Unusually for him, he was still in uniform and still at his desk as the clock ticked over to eight o'clock. Outside, dusk was turning into night. There was no reason to be working this late. No emergency was claiming his time. There wasn't even outstanding paperwork to do. He was at his desk because from there he could clearly hear the sounds of traffic on the road. Not that there was much traffic. So far he'd heard a single truck and two cars. He hadn't heard what he was listening for ... a motorcycle.

Tia Walsh was a mystery to him. She hadn't appeared again at Trish's pub and Trish had offered no gossip about her on his visits. Nor had she been seen at the Mineside, the pub where the mine workers mostly drank. He'd been there to check too. According to Sarah Travers, Tia had bought supplies which had been delivered to the mine compound. Of course, that told him nothing except it seemed she was planning to stay a while, judging from the purchases Sarah had mentioned.

That was as far as his investigation had taken him, which was probably a good thing. He was already feeling a little uncomfortable. He really couldn't argue that his interest in Tia was professional. She'd done nothing to provoke official enquiries. At least not since she'd arrived in his town. He knew his preoccupation with her was purely personal, aroused by a mane of dark auburn hair, a pair of brilliant green eyes and a set of motorcycle leathers that did more than just hint at a lovely body beneath. He looked at the screen in front of him. He could enter her name into the police system and see what it had to offer. He clenched his fingers into fists. No. He couldn't do that. Tia had a right to her privacy.

Then he heard it. The throaty rumble of the Harley passing through the town on the road leading north. As she had done several times this past week, Tia was taking her bike onto the highway for a late night ride. Of course, she had every right to do that too. What she didn't have the right to do was break the speed limit, and Max was pretty sure those late night rides were not defined by anything as mundane as the speed limit.

Before he could think it through and before he could tell himself this wasn't right, Max grabbed his hat from the hook on the wall and headed for his car. He slid behind the wheel and started the engine. A tiny voice at the back of his head was whispering that this was not the kind of policeman he was, but he ignored it and turned onto the road, heading north.

There was no sign of a tail light ahead. Max kept his speed down as he passed through town. He wasn't that obsessed with catching the Harley. But as soon as he was on the highway heading north, he pushed his foot down. The police vehicle was a big four-wheel drive Land Cruiser. He couldn't hope to catch the hog if Tia really opened it up. But ...

Max put his foot to the floor.

At last he saw the glimmer of red light up ahead. He glanced down at his speedo and whistled under his breath. Now he did have an 'official' reason to pull her over. But even as he reached out to activate his police lights and siren, he knew it was highly unlikely he'd actually book her. He rarely booked anyone for speeding on these roads, where traffic was thin on the ground. Drink driving was another matter. Drunks on the road were a danger to themselves and everyone else. But he didn't expect Tia to be drunk. He might have only seen her once, but everything about her had told him she was both smart and wary. She would take risks; but not stupid or unnecessary ones.

The harsh wail of the police siren split the stillness of the night. Immediately, Max saw the Harley's brake light flash. He eased off the accelerator and followed the bike as it pulled over to the side of the road. He reached for his hat as he got out of the car because this was official business, but he left his ticket book behind. A girl on a Harley pushing the limit a bit was hardly a major crime. He would give her a stern warning though. Outback roads had dangers that city folk didn't understand.

The bike stuttered into silence. The night suddenly seemed eerily quiet. The road was empty except for the police car and the motorcycle caught in its headlights. Max's footsteps on the grey bitumen sounded very loud.

The girl on the bike turned her head towards him, but made no move to remove her full-face helmet. In the reflected light of his headlight, Max couldn't see her eyes. And he very much wanted to.

'Good evening, miss,' he said in his most official voice. 'Would you please remove your helmet?'

Without a word, she reached for the strap. She leaned forward as she pulled the helmet over her head, then placed it on the fuel tank in front of her before she turned to look at him again with those flashing eyes, so bright that even in this light he could see a glimmer of emerald. Her hair was caught back in a ponytail that vanished under her leather jacket.

'Miss, are you aware that you were speeding?'

Her eyes remained intensely fixed on his face, but she merely lifted a shoulder in a suggestion of a shrug.

'Could I see your licence, please?' Max said.

Without a word she began to slowly unzip her jacket. There was nothing sexual about the way she did it, but to Max it was the most erotic thing he'd seen in a very long time. His eyes were glued to her fingers as she slowly slid the zipper down and pulled the jacket open. She was wearing something white and tight fitting underneath. She reached into an inner pocket of the jacket. Her fingers felt around the pocket for a moment, then they emerged empty. She looked into his face and shrugged. She wasn't carrying a licence.

For the first time this evening his professional self took over from the part of him that was having trouble dragging his eyes off the woman in front of him.

'You're Tia Walsh, aren't you? You work at the mine.'

Her strong eyes met his and held his gaze as she nodded slightly.

'You need to present your licence to me at the Coorah Creek station within forty-eight hours.'

He paused, waiting for her to speak, but she didn't.

'If you don't you may suffer a penalty fine which could be one hundred and fifty dollars. Do you understand?'

Still she didn't speak. Max felt a childish urge to yell something, just to make her react. But he fought it down.

'If you do produce your licence, I won't take any action about the speeding … this time,' he said in his sternest voice.

Still she said nothing.

'You can go now. Don't make me come looking for you.'

Her lips moved then, sliding into the merest hint of a grin. Max almost blushed. That grin seemed to say that she knew very well he'd been looking for her on more than one occasion already.

She reached for her helmet.

'One more thing,' Max said, before she could pull it over

her head. 'There are a lot of roos on the roads out here. At that sort of speed you'd have trouble avoiding one. Slow down for you own sake. All right?'

The cheeky smile got a little bit broader. She slipped the helmet over her head and touched the starter. The engine roared into life. With a great deal of skill, she steered the bike into a very tight turn with Max at the centre, and headed back the way she had come.

Max watched her go, his jaw tightly set.

She hadn't said one word during the entire encounter. Nor had she spoken during their previous encounter at the pub. More than anything in the world, he wanted to hear her voice.

It didn't take long for his headlights to appear in her rear-view mirrors. Keeping herself carefully just under the speed limit, Tia rode back towards town, her mind racing.

Tonight's meeting hadn't been an accident. The cop had planned it. He'd been checking up on her since that day he'd first laid eyes on her. A couple of her workmates had mentioned he'd been at the pub looking for her. Chris Powell's secretary had also mentioned a visit and the day before yesterday, Tia had changed her mind about doing some shopping when she'd spotted a police uniform through the glass window of the general store.

Why was he stalking her?

She sort of expected it. He was a cop, after all. One of the pigs. He wasn't the first one to follow her and she doubted he would be the last. But despite the badge, he didn't feel as threatening as some of the other police who had crossed her path. There was a kindness to his face that she would have liked had it not been attached to the uniform.

She slowed even further as the lights of the town drew

close. By the time she passed the town sign she was within the speed limit. She thought about stopping at the pub. What would the cop do, she wondered. Would he wait outside in the hope of busting her for drink driving? Would he follow her inside? Would he ...

No. She gripped the handlebars more firmly and powered past the pub back towards the mine. She had already attracted far too much of his attention. And there was also the matter of producing her licence tomorrow. There was risk in that, if he looked too closely. If he checked her records or did a search on the Harley's reggo. Just because he seemed nicer than most of the cops in her experience, she couldn't afford to let down her guard. Not even out here, in a place so far removed from the rest of the world that it might as well be on another planet.

There were a few lights on in the dongas when she arrived back at the mine compound. And the mess was bright and noisy and crowded, as it always was. Tia rode past it, as she always did, and returned to her trailer.

Once the door was safely locked behind her, and the curtains pulled tight, Tia removed her leathers. From her fridge she took a can of beer. Pulling the ring top, she put it on the table, and dropped to her knees. From the back of a storage cupboard, under the bench seat, she pulled out a small vinyl rucksack.

She dropped it onto the table and slid onto the bench seat along the trailer wall. She glanced around to double check that no one could walk in on her, or see what she was doing.

She unzipped the bag and emptied the contents onto the table.

The gun landed on the wooden surface with a dull thump. It was enclosed in a plastic bag. Tia assumed it was still loaded. She had never checked. She hadn't touched it since the moment she'd picked it up and sealed it to preserve the evidence on it. She'd been around enough cops to know that was how it was done. She laid her hand on the cold plastic, feeling the hard shape inside and remembering what it represented and how she had come by it.

Tia didn't consider herself a criminal. Sure, she'd stolen a few things from time to time. You had to if you were fifteen and living on the streets. But she'd never mugged anyone. Never sold drugs. Never sold her body. Well, not for money. There were times she had used her body to help her survive. And, as far as she was concerned, there was nothing wrong with that. She would do it again if she had to; although she hoped it would never come to that again.

She had stolen the gun from her boyfriend on the day she fled her old life never to return. She wasn't really sure why she had taken it. She told herself it was to stop it being used again. Her one little contribution to crime control. Sometimes she thought it was for her own protection. She would never use it herself, but if Ned ever found her, she could trade the gun for her freedom. For her life, maybe.

As she looked at it her mind turned to the cop who pulled her over tonight. Sergeant Delaney. While he'd been checking her out she'd asked some questions of her own. He was an honest cop. That's what everyone said. If he found that rucksack and the contents …

She should get rid of the stuff. It would be easy enough way out here. All she had to do was head off into the bush somewhere and dump it. But it was her safety blanket, and she wasn't ready to let it go yet.

Tia pushed the gun aside and found a small sandwich bag. Inside were her driver's licence and a credit card that she never used. The rucksack also held some paperwork – letters and a very old, and slightly tatty, Christmas card. It was red and had once been covered with golden sparkles;

the sort of card you might give to a young teenage girl. And there was a small velvet box. She immediately tossed that back into the rucksack without opening it. She knew only too well what it contained.

She'd show her driver's licence to Delaney before the forty-eight hours were up. He'd no doubt check on it, but that was okay. It was real and legal and valid. With luck he'd stop there and wouldn't look any further. She put everything back in the rucksack and shoved it back into its hiding place. It occurred to her that the cop might already have taken a note of the Harley's reggo, if he'd been able to read it under the layer of mud. If so, there was nothing she could do about it. She'd face that problem when and if she had to.

Chapter Eight

A sign flashed past. Pete was coming into Coorah Creek. He'd been doing this run for a long time, and the Creek was one of his favourite places. But today, his mind was too far away to appreciate the town.

He was going to be a father.

He'd had a few days now to get used to the idea. He'd even gone with Linda to a doctor's appointment. He'd listened carefully to everything the doctor said about what was ahead of them, but he was still struggling to put himself in the picture the doctor's words had painted.

Linda was bubbling over with plans; talking about buying things for the baby and setting up a nursery. There hadn't been any mention of marriage, but he knew Linda was thinking about that too. Marriage and setting up a home together. All the things she had dreamed about since she was a little girl. All the things a family could want. All the things he didn't want. At least, not now. And not with Linda.

He was feeling trapped. He didn't want to feel that way, but he did. He liked to think he was a good man with a proper sense of right and wrong. He'd do the right thing by Linda and the baby, but he wasn't entirely sure exactly what the right thing was. Support, both emotional and financial was definitely right. Although their relationship had never been that serious, he didn't question that the baby was his. Linda wouldn't lie about something like that. However, he had to wonder if it was right to marry and set up a home if his heart wasn't in it? He liked Linda a lot. But love? No. He wasn't in love with her. Had it not been for the baby, he would have ended their relationship by now.

Pete ran his fingers through his hair. If there was an answer to these questions and all the others that were running around his mind, he had no idea where to find them.

He drove slowly through the town and out the other side, heading for the mine.

By the time he turned in at the mine gates, Pete had driven all thoughts of Linda and the baby from his mind. At least, that's what he told himself. He turned his rig and began backing up to the loading dock at the big storage shed. He'd done this a hundred times before, placing the rear doors of the trailer against the raised loading bay, so the pallets and drums could easily be rolled out.

'Hey, Pete,' a voice called from just outside his window. 'You're gonna miss it, buddy. More right hand down.'

Feeling a surge of embarrassment, Pete pulled forward a few metres and tried again, this time keeping his head squarely in the game.

In a couple of minutes, the rear of his rig was pressed hard against the wooden rail at the edge of the loading bay. The mine workers had been through this procedure as many times as Pete. They had the back open and were already starting to unload. Pete stood back and left them to it. There were drums of grease and oil for the huge mine machines and spare parts, the use of which he couldn't even begin to guess. An operation this big took a lot of support.

One of the huge mine trucks drove slowly past, to pull up beside the refuelling bullet. The door opened and, to Pete's surprise, a woman got out. He'd never seen a woman driver at the mine before. And she was quite some woman. She was slender and shapely despite her heavy-duty work wear and bright protective vest. Her hair was caught up in a clip at the back of her neck, with just a few wavy tendrils escaping. Pete could imagine that when she let it loose, it would cascade down her back like a red wave.

'Don't even bother, mate.'

One of the mine workers had seen the direction of his gaze.

'She keeps herself to herself that one. Most of the blokes have tried, but she's not interested.'

Pete shrugged and said nothing. He couldn't be interested in someone like that now. He was going to have to stop thinking about other women altogether. His relationship with Linda didn't stand any chance at all if he kept on thinking or acting like a single man still searching for "The One". He was only now beginning to realise that marrying Linda meant he was giving up on falling in love and having the same sort of relationship his parents had. He didn't want to do that. But he was going to have to. He owed it to Linda and their baby to try to build a strong, happy family.

When he left the mine, he turned north, back towards Coorah Creek. He had some boxes for the store and some kegs for the pub. He figured he might grab a meal at the pub before heading north back to base.

The main street was almost deserted as Pete drove slowly through. As always, there were a few cars parked outside the pub. Pete swerved off the road and parked his truck along the newly built kerb outside the store. He killed the engine and jumped to the ground. As he approached the door, he remembered that the storekeeper, Ken Travers, hadn't been looking well the last few times he'd been here. Of late, his wife Gina had been the one to meet Pete and supervise the unloading of the boxes of supplies. They had a young daughter too, a blonde girl. He hadn't seen her for a while and assumed she was away at school. Or maybe she would have started college by now. It was such a shame to see something like illness strike a nice family like that.

Still, all a person could do was take whatever life threw at them and do the best they could with it. He was beginning to understand that now.

Pete walked into the store, and almost collided with a ladder set against the shelves just inside the door. He caught himself and placed a hand on the ladder, to steady it, in case there was someone up there.

There certainly was. That someone was high enough up that ladder to leave Pete staring at her bare legs, for there was no doubt that the owner of those legs was female. Very female. The legs were not very long, but they were very shapely. They curved down to a pair of the prettiest bare feet he'd ever seen. The toenails of those feet were painted bright red.

He couldn't help himself; he let his eyes run slowly up those legs again to a pair of cut-off jeans shorts, filled out in the nicest possible way. The girl on the ladder was reaching for something on the highest shelf, and her top had ridden up to expose a few centimetres of skin on her lower back. Soft, silky skin. Not tanned like a lot of women were. Pete saw enough brown out the window of his truck when he was driving. This skin was creamy white and so smooth. It was like a drink of water in the desert. He wanted to run his fingers over that skin. Press his lips to it and taste it.

Pete didn't believe in love at first sight. But lust! That was a different matter and right now he was feeling decidedly lustful.

He dragged his eyes away from that silky skin and forced his gaze upwards. He needed to see the face of this woman who in just a few seconds had set his heart – and other parts of him – on fire.

She had twisted her body to look down at him. He took a moment to appreciate the curve of her breasts, and then looked past the blonde plait hanging over one shoulder to her face.

A pair of amber eyes, flecked with gold, widened as they looked down at him.

God! All his lustful thoughts vanished in an instant as a wave of shame swept over him. He jumped back from the ladder as if hit by an electric shock. It was the child, Sarah. Slowly she climbed down the ladder and turned to face him.

'Hello ... Pete.' She'd called him Uncle Pete once, but no more, it seemed.

'Umm. Hi, Sarah.'

A welcoming smile lit her face, and Pete felt the earth shift ever so slightly on its axis.

Sarah could hardly believe she was looking at Pete, the truck driver her younger self had hero-worshipped. He was older now, of course, but he was very handsome. She had obviously had good taste when she was a child. Sarah felt her heart lift a little as she looked at him. She hadn't seen him in more than four years. A lot had changed in four years. She should have grown out of that childhood crush on a man who was far too old for her. She had dated quite a few men since she'd last seen Pete, but apparently that didn't matter. She felt that same old feeling starting to return. Maybe it was just because she was feeling particularly vulnerable at the moment. Maybe she was looking too fondly at the past, because the future seemed very bleak, but it appeared from the lifting of her heart that he was still her knight in shining armour.

For a few long seconds they simply stared at each other. Pete was the first to drop his gaze. If she didn't know better, she would have suspected he was blushing under his tan.

She could see new lines around his eyes and on his forehead that hadn't been there when she left for college. The outback was hard on faces. But in her knight's case, the lines merely added to his good looks. His eyes were still the dark chocolate she remembered. His hair was cropped very short. It looked spiky but she knew that it wouldn't be. She would have loved to reach up and run her hand over the top of his head to check. But she couldn't do it. For starters, she wasn't a child any more, and for some strange reason her hands were shaking.

'It's good to see you again,' she said, noting that the words came out almost without trembling.

'I didn't know you were back. Um. How are you?'

'I'm fine thanks,' she said. 'And you. You look … well.'

'Umm. Yes.' Pete turned his head to look around the empty store. Almost as if he was seeking help. 'Are your parents here? I have a delivery to unload.'

Some of the joy went out of the moment.

'No. Mum had to take Dad to Toowoomba for treatment. He's gone on the mine plane with the FIFO workers.'

She saw the immediate understanding and sympathy on his face. 'I'm really sorry your dad's crook,' he said.

'Thanks.'

They were standing there, not certain what to say next, when the door swung open, almost hitting Pete. Sarah looked at her customer. It was Trish from the pub. The sharp blue eyes looked from Sarah to Pete and back again. Sarah had a feeling the older woman had a better idea of what was going on than either she or Pete did.

'I saw the truck,' Trish said briskly. 'We have some beer kegs coming. I just wanted to check you have them on board.'

'Yes, I do. I'll be over with them as soon as I've dropped off the boxes for here,' Pete said swiftly. He glanced at his watch. Sarah knew it was coming up for six o'clock. She would be closing the store soon.

'I'd better start unloading now.' Pete turned and left, not quite at a run, but pretty smartly. Sarah couldn't help but wonder if it was her or Trish Warren he was so eager to escape from.

Trish watched him go and then turned to Sarah. Her eyes were sparkling. 'He is such a lovely man, isn't he? So handsome too.' A look of speculation crossed her face.

Sarah sighed. This she had not missed while she was away.

'We are all so pleased to have you home, dear,' Trish continued.

The look on Trish's face told Sarah exactly who she meant by 'we'. Sarah looked through the glass window to the road train parked outside. Pete was busy unloading the supplies her father had ordered. She watched him heft the heavy boxes of canned goods as if they were filled with feathers.

The door opened and a customer came in. Followed quickly by another. Sarah had to turn to serving, but she kept one eye on Pete as he carried several loads through to her storeroom. She was still busy when he finished and vanished with just a lift of his hand to her. Through the window she could see him beginning to unload kegs of beer from the second trailer. She guessed he would stay and have a meal at the pub before setting out on a night run back to the Isa. For a few seconds she toyed with the idea of going over to the pub herself when she had closed the store. But the plane from Toowoomba was due to land any moment. Her parents would be home soon. Her mother would be tired and her father probably ill from his treatment. They needed her. She had come home to help them, not renew an old flame.

When she finally ushered out the last customer, she locked the door and headed back towards the house. Pete would be back on his next run in a week. That was what he did. Some things didn't change ... and she was pretty sure she didn't want them to.

Chapter Nine

The police station was locked. Tia stood in the lengthening shadows staring at the building. She was too late and she was now technically in trouble. She was supposed to have shown her licence to the cop before close of business today. But she'd spent too long wondering whether to run or to stay and now the door was closed against her.

That probably didn't leave her much choice. The cop was sure to start checking into her background now. She couldn't be sure there were no outstanding warrants for her arrest. And if Delaney charged her for even a small offence, it would start something she had no control over. Something that could only end in trouble for her. It might even bring trouble to this little town, and she wouldn't want that.

Common sense told her she had to run, but something was stopping her.

She had picked Coorah Creek almost at random because it was a long way from anywhere, and because the mine had jobs going for which they were offering all the training she'd need. There probably weren't that many people who would be happy to live way out here. But for Tia's purpose, it had seemed the perfect place to hide. The mere fact that it was such an unexpected and unlikely place for her had, in fact, made it exactly the right place. But she was starting to feel differently. It was funny how cooking a meal and talking to a girl in a shop could start changing things. Turning a hiding place into ... not quite a home yet ... but maybe one day.

She had made a mistake missing this deadline. She had to find that cop, show him her licence. But she had to do more than that. Everything about her behaviour until now would have just made him even more suspicious. She had to start acting like a normal human being and not some criminal on the run. She had to start doing that tonight, or her own paranoia might ruin this chance to start over again. If she lost this chance, she might never get another. She glanced at her watch. Seven o'clock. Maybe it wasn't too late yet.

Taking a deep breath, she walked up the stairs to the door of the station. There was a notice attached to the door with a phone number for emergencies if the station was unattended. She wasn't sure that was quite the right thing to do. This wasn't exactly an emergency. She glanced about and saw that the police car was sitting in a carport next to the station. That implied the cop had walked home, not driven. She went back down the stairs and walked to the corner of the station where she saw a concrete path running around the back of the building. Tentatively she followed it. As she turned the corner, she saw the house. It was like a million other outback homes. A sprawling wooden structure, it was about a metre above the ground, the wooden stumps leaving room for air and snakes to pass underneath. The stumps were, of course, topped with tin protectors. There would be no termites getting into this home. It was painted green but, like every other building in town, the paint was fading rapidly under the harsh sun. It was a big house. Big enough for a family.

That stopped her in her tracks. It hadn't occurred to her that the cop would have a family. For some reason, she hated that idea. She didn't want to explore why she wanted him to be single.

There was a light on at the back of the house. Trying not to feel like a criminal, she walked around the building and climbed the stairs to the back door. She peered through the window into the lighted kitchen. It was very tidy with no signs of a meal being prepared. And it was devoid of life. She knocked without hope of an answer, and then turned away.

It was then she noticed the big corrugated iron shed at the far side of the yard. It had a roller door at one end, presumably so it could be used as a garage. The lights were on and the door was open, but from this angle she couldn't see inside. But a cop wouldn't go out and leave a shed door open like that, would he?

Before she could change her mind, Tia began walking towards the shed. As she did, she heard the music and recognised it instantly. Really? She smiled. Suddenly the cop seemed less threatening. Almost human, in fact. This she had to see. She didn't exactly sneak up to the doorway, but she didn't go out of her way to announce her presence.

The cop had shed his uniform and was wearing a pair of faded jeans and a T-shirt; both of which look like they were overdue an encounter with a washing machine. His back was to her as he bent over a wood lathe that was sending showers of sawdust into the air. His sweat had made the shirt cling to his body in a way that showed off his shoulders in a most appealing fashion. The big safety goggles he was wearing didn't exactly add to the image but nor were they enough to detract from it.

From an iPod dock sitting on a bench, the Beatles asked her to 'Let It Be', but she just couldn't. The song was fading. At that moment, the lathe spun to a stop and the shed was suddenly quiet.

Tia coughed. Loudly.

If she was hoping to startle him, she was sadly disappointed. He lifted his head and turned. As he did, he slowly pulled the goggles off his head. He moved to the bench to dispose of his goggles and render John, Paul,

72

George and Ringo silent before they had truly begun to ask for 'Help'.

'You're a Beatles fan?' Tia asked, not even trying to hide her amusement. 'Hardly what I expected for a police sergeant.'

'When I'm in civvies, I'm not the sergeant. I'm Max Delaney and, yes, I'm a Beatles fan. Isn't everybody?' His mouth twitched into a hint of a smile.

Tia was disarmed. She didn't know what to say. Instead she reached into the back pocket of her jeans and drew out the small rectangle of plastic.

'I guess I'm too late to show this to the sergeant as required?' she asked.

Max reached out a hand to take it. 'In your case, I will make an exception.'

Tia looked away while he studied her licence. She didn't want her face to betray her uncertainty. Instead, she looked at the contents of the shed. After a few moments, she began to really see what she was looking at.

Furniture. Handmade furniture. A beautifully built squatters chair, stained a lovely dark brown, sat next to a table with the grain of the wood seeming almost liquid in the evening sunlight streaming through the open doors. A bench held hand-carved toys to delight any child. There was a mirror with an elaborate carved wooden frame. Ah. So that was how he'd known she was behind him. Tia picked up a beautiful wooden bowl, with elegant curved sides that served to highlight and accentuate a flaw in the wood. It was quite lovely.

Still holding the bowl, she turned back towards Max. He wasn't looking at her licence. He was looking at her.

'Did you make this?' she asked.

He nodded.

'It's just … beautiful.'

'Thank you.'

Tia cast her eyes around the shed, and noticed the piles of timber. Most of it was old and weathered, with the remains of paint peeling away. Other larger pieces had old nails protruding from them, and evidence of joins.

'You make this ...' Tia indicated the furniture and the toys '... from that?'

'I do.'

'Where do you get it?'

'Almost anywhere there's old timber or old houses. Some of it comes from the disused houses near the railway station.'

'Oh, Sergeant,' Tia raised a teasing eyebrow, 'You're not stealing this timber are you?'

He smiled. Tia's heart did a little skip. He looked so good when he smiled. And she couldn't remember the last time someone had smiled at her like that. With friendship and humour and a degree of admiration.

'Well, ma'am, I'm an honest cop, but you know how things are,' he said in a thick accent, directing the humour at himself. 'Actually,' he continued in his normal voice, 'the houses belong to the mine. I did a deal with Chris Powell – your boss. He lets me take all the timber I need in exchange for keeping a bit of an eye on the place. Which I would be doing anyway, so I think I got a bargain.'

'It's amazing that something this beautiful should come from something that has been abandoned and left to rot.'

'Just because something has been abandoned, there's no reason to write it off as rubbish,' Max said as he gently took the bowl from her hands. His long fingers caressed the curved surface. 'I believe in second chances. Sometimes, hidden underneath the roughness and ugliness of the surface, there's great beauty and strength waiting to be set free.'

Tia felt a lump in her throat. He could almost be talking about her. With great reverence, Max placed the bowl back on the workbench. When he turned to her, his eyes and hers met and a silence settled over them both. Those few words had formed a connection between them. They both knew it.

'I was about to grab some dinner,' Max said at last. 'There's a huge bowl of home-made chicken curry in my fridge. I'd be very happy to share it with you.'

Tia stepped back.

'Umm. No. I mean ... Thanks, but no.' She didn't want to go inside his home. That was getting too close. Far too close.

'Then I had better give you this.' He held out her licence and she took it, trying not to look like she was grabbing it. 'If you're living here now, you need to change the address on that.'

'I know. Thanks.'

She turned and took a couple of swift steps towards the door before she caught herself. She was doing it again. Running away. She wasn't ready to get too close to the cop ... to Max. Not the sort of closeness that involved the two of them eating at the big kitchen table, with the Beatles no doubt playing in the background, but that didn't mean there were no other possibilities.

She turned slowly back to face him. 'Actually. I haven't eaten. I was thinking of getting a burger across the road at the pub ...'

She let the sentence hang in mid-air and was rewarded by a broad smile.

'That sounds good. They do a good steak there, as well. I need to wash up first though.'

'I'll see you there.' This time when she turned to go, Tia was not running away.

* * *

Trish had her eyes on Max the moment he walked through the door. He'd expected the smirk on her face as he slid onto a bar stool next to Tia. He'd been in Coorah Creek nearly five years and, in all that time, he'd never had dinner with a woman in the pub. Not like this. Not a date, if that was what this was. But on this occasion he didn't care what Trish thought; or what she told the town. They could read anything they liked into this. All he was looking for was a chance to have dinner with this woman who had occupied his thoughts far too much since the day he had first laid eyes on her. Then maybe he'd find a way to put her into a proper place in his mind and move on.

Or maybe not. He glanced sideways at her and once again caught the hint of colour under her shirt. That tattoo! He really wanted to get a good look at it. He wondered what it might show and where it might lead.

A beer glass sat in front of Tia, dripping moisture slowly down to the bar mat beneath it. A second glass sat in front of the stool Max now occupied. Neither had been touched. Max reached for his drink. Tia took hers and held his eyes for a long moment. Her eyes were the brilliant green of emeralds and he felt as if he could lose himself in them. Slowly she raised her glass and tipped it gently towards him in salute. He followed suit and they both drank.

He knew he had to speak first. Their encounter on the road had taught him that. Tia wasn't the chatty sort. But when she did speak … oh boy! Her voice had been exactly as he expected. Low and controlled and sexy. It was exactly right for her and he knew that he was going to spend many hours awake, remembering the way she had called him Sergeant. Now he wanted to hear her speak his name.

He searched for a safe topic of conversation, suddenly feeling a bit awkward, like a teenager on his first date. He knew nothing about her and he wanted to know it all.

'So,' he said when the glasses were back on the bar, 'that's some bike you have. Tell me about it.'

It wasn't the right thing to say. He saw it in an instant. A veil came down over those lovely green eyes.

'I figured by now you would have run the reggo,' she said warily.

Max shook his head. 'I had no reason to. And remember,' he indicated his jeans and short-sleeved shirt, 'I'm out of uniform. I'm just interested in the bike. You don't see many like that out here. In fact, it's the first hog I've ever seen. What year is it?'

He saw her hesitate as she reached for the answer.

'I've only had it for about a year, I don't know much about its history,' she said in a tone that suggested she wasn't interested in taking that topic any further.

That was interesting. Harley owners were usually keen to talk about their precious bikes. They could and would tell you in a heartbeat everything about the bike from the size of the engine to the air pressure in the tyres. He fought back the policeman's instinct that was telling him something wasn't quite right. Not tonight, he told himself. Tonight I am not a police officer. Tonight I am just Max Delaney having dinner with a woman I very much want to get to know better.

They sat in silence for a moment, each taking another long drink of beer as the tension between them thickened.

'So, can I get you some food?' Trish appeared in front of them like some sort of lifesaver. 'We've got my famous lamb casserole on tonight. The steaks are good too, as always. And there's home-made lasagne, Ellen's recipe.'

'Do you know Jack North?' Max asked Tia. 'He does a bit of work at the mine. General maintenance. He looks after the airstrip and the plane and fills in here as barman sometimes. He's a good bloke and his wife Ellen is the best cook in Coorah Creek. She used to cook at the Mineside before they had their baby. Now she cooks here sometimes.'

Tia shook her head.

'Ellen and Jack are away east,' Trish continued. 'Taking their new baby to visit the grandparents, which is nice. They've got two older kids as well. They are Ellen's kids really but Jack treats them as his own. I do miss Ellen and the kids. I like being around babies. It makes me feel young. But even though I cooked the lasagne, it's still Ellen's recipe. And it's still very good.'

Max and Tia shared a subtle look. Trish was a talker; there was no doubt about that. Max was used to her, but for Tia it was still a novelty. She had yet to learn that the thing to do was simply let Trish talk. She usually didn't expect an answer. Except to the questions about food, of course.

'What do you want?' Max asked Tia. 'My shout.'

'I'll try the lamb casserole,' she said. 'But I pay my own way thanks.'

'I'll have the lamb too,' Max told Trish before turning to Tia. 'Didn't you just shout me a beer?'

'No, she didn't,' Trish jumped in. 'You owe me for the beer as well as your dinner.'

Max couldn't help but laugh. Beside him Tia laughed too. It was a lovely sound, like birds singing after a light summer shower. He guessed she didn't do it very often. When she stopped, he found himself searching for something to say or do that would make her laugh again.

'So, where did you learn how to make such beautiful things from old wood?' Tia asked.

'My dad started me off,' Max told her, happy to think she wanted to get to know him better. 'He was an old-fashioned cabinetmaker. He whittled too. He could turn a bit of wood into a bird or a horse or a kangaroo in no time at all. He gave me my first whittling knife when I was about twelve. My first effort was the strangest looking horse you've ever seen.' He smiled at the memory. 'I've been making things with wood ever since. I slowly got better. Most of my horses have four legs now, but my speciality is dinosaurs.'

He was rewarded with another laugh, and a smile that lit her eyes.

'Your house must be overflowing with little wooden birds and animals.'

'No. I give them away. Kids seem to like them.'

'And the furniture you make. It's really good.'

'Thanks. I give most of that away too.'

'Why?'

'I like working with my hands. Keeps me occupied in the evenings. And I get a lot of satisfaction from—'

'No. I mean why give it all away? You could get good money for handmade furniture like that. Especially back in the city. There must be rich people down there who would pay really good money for the sort of stuff you make.' Tia seemed genuinely puzzled.

Max shrugged. 'I get the wood for nothing. There are a lot of people around town who haven't got a lot of money, so I make stuff they can use. I like to help out. Besides, I'm not a wood carver or a carpenter. I'm a police officer. That's who I am.'

He watched the veil come down over her eyes as he spoke. He sensed her withdrawing as she picked up her glass and drank, not because she was thirsty so much as to break the communication between them. He'd seen that sort of behaviour before in police stations, interrogation rooms and cells when he'd been questioning suspects. His professional instincts were telling him there was a lot about Tia's background that he didn't know. And a lot

79

that probably wasn't good. The diverted eyes and the bike told him that. The tattoo, however sexy it might be, was another sign. If he didn't know better he'd think she was, or at least had been, a gang member. Or in trouble with the law. Maybe in a juvenile centre for a while. He glanced at her bare arms. There was no sign of needle marks, but he hadn't expected any. She wasn't behaving like a druggie; more like a runaway trying to hide her past.

He was a police officer. What or who was she?

Another thought he'd been ignoring pushed its way to the forefront of his mind. Her driver's licence had been in the name Felicity Walsh. Tia was pretty close, and the description matched. Just because she called herself Tia, that didn't mean anything. Maybe she didn't like the name Felicity. A lot of women wouldn't. He pushed the thought back to the far recesses of his mind. Much as he loved his work, there were times when he wished he could let it go, and simply be himself for a while.

Before he could think of another conversational tack to try, Trish arrived with two steaming plates of food. Tia started eating without a word. Max did too, while watching her out of the corner of his eye. She ate fast, as if determined to get the food down before it was taken from her. For his part, he didn't taste a single mouthful of Trish's most popular offering. His mind was too busy trying to solve the enigma of the woman sitting next to him.

They finished their meals in silence. Tia drank the last of her beer, then got to her feet.

'You could stay and have another,' Max said.

'No. I'm on overnights. I need to be back at work in a couple of hours. It's not a real good idea to drink before you get behind the wheel of a Cat 793.'

Picturing the massive mine trucks, Max had to agree.

'Some other time, then,' he said.

Tia shrugged and raised a hand to attract Trish's attention.

'What do I owe?' Tia asked when the older woman arrived.

Max wanted to tell her to forget it; that he would pay. However, he knew Tia well enough by now to know that would be a mistake. Instead, he remained silent while she paid her bill and headed for the door.

'Goodnight, Tia.'

'Goodnight ... Max.'

Max watched her go. She walked with a long, easy stride. Confident and strong. He was beginning to think that something softer lay beneath that tough girl exterior. He drank the last of his beer as outside the Harley roared into life and drove down the highway south towards the mine.

'Well?' Trish appeared in front of him again.

'Of course. Sorry. How much do I owe you?' Max pulled his wallet out of his back pocket. That wasn't what Trish was really after, but that was all she was going to get. Max was fond of Trish. Her encyclopaedic knowledge of everyone in the town and seemingly everything they did or thought had proved useful to him in his official role at times. But tonight wasn't one of those times.

He put the money on the bar and headed out into the night.

He stayed up late, working in his shed, replaying his conversation with Tia. Replaying every flash of her eyes and those rare but wonderful moments of her laughter. Hearing again the way she said his name. For once, he could not lose himself in the joy of working with his hands to turn something old and abandoned into something new and beautiful. His mind was elsewhere. When at last he went to bed, it was all he could do not to think of the lines

81

of her body under the motorcycle leathers, and that tattoo that peeped from beneath her top.

He was tired and still restless when dawn came. He got out of bed, donned his uniform and his professional demeanour and opened the station early. He was about to do something he had never done before – use his position for personal reasons.

He powered up his computer and logged in to the police department system.

He didn't give himself time to think. He typed in the name he had seen on that driver's licence last night. Felicity Walsh. He added the Brisbane suburb listed on the licence as her old address. The search found nothing. No traffic tickets or outstanding warrants for her. No criminal record of any kind. He was surprised to find himself breathing a sigh of relief. He hadn't realised how worried he was that the search might show something that would force him onto a path he did not want to take.

One more thing to check. He typed in the Harley's reggo.

The details flashed up on the screen – and his eyes widened. The Harley was not registered in Tia's name. It was in the name of Andrew Kelly. The reggo address was the same as the address on Tia's licence. The bike had not been reported stolen, in fact, the reggo had been paid just a few days before. Presumably by the owner; this Andrew Kelly. Why would he pay for reggo on the bike if it was stolen? Maybe there was some sort of relationship between Tia and this guy. He should check him out. See if he had a record.

Max frowned. Despite what his instincts were telling him, there was no crime he could see. And he was going to stop there. There was a mystery about Tia. But it was one Max would solve – as himself, not as Sergeant Delaney. He reached for the mouse to close the window before he could be tempted to look any further.

Chapter Ten

'Dad. Are you sure you're feeling up to this? I can handle it. Honestly.'

'Now, Sarah. Leave it be. I'm not dead yet, and until I am, I'll work.'

The words cut through Sarah like a knife, as did her father's anger. She took a half step back, biting her bottom lip to help maintain her calm.

'Oh, Sarah, honey, I'm sorry.' Ken's face softened. 'I didn't mean to snap at you. And I didn't mean to say ... well, I'm sorry.'

'It's okay, Dad.' Sarah stepped close to her father and wrapped her arms around him. Ken was thin and looking frail, and as she buried her head in his chest, she realised that he smelled different now. The cancer and the drugs he was taking to treat it had changed him. But he was still her dad and she loved him just as she had when she was a little girl, curled up in bed falling asleep to the sound of his voice reading her favourite stories. She loved him even more now she was an adult and knew enough about the world to understand what a good man he was. She loved him so much and she was so desperately afraid she was going to lose him.

His arms tightened around her and he placed a gentle kiss on the top of her head, just as he had always done when she was upset; ever since she was a small child.

'All right,' his voice was rough with emotion as he broke the embrace. 'Let's get to work. We need this storeroom tidied up by this afternoon. We've got a lot of new stock coming. I've decided to start carrying a small range of children's toys and things. I know you can get it all off the internet, but people sometimes leave it too late. So I thought, as the only general store in town, we should carry some kids' toys and small gifts. After all, people are always buying things for kids. And children get pocket money too. They need to be able to do something with it.'

Sarah's heart gave an unexpected little skip. 'When are you expecting the delivery?'

'This afternoon. Now, first thing we need to do is sort through the rest of the non-food items. I think they should all be kept in one section. The corner by the back door would be about right.'

Sarah nodded, her thoughts elsewhere. Right now, on the road north of the Creek, Pete was driving his big blue and white truck towards them. His strong hands would be on the wheel and he might be singing. He did that sometimes when he worked, although she doubted he was aware of it. She'd heard him singing softly as he unloaded boxes from his truck. He probably did it when he drove as well. He wasn't the world's greatest singer, but he had a pleasant voice. She'd happily listen to him any time, although that probably didn't have a lot to do with his voice. It was just because she liked being around him and was rather drawn to the idea of sitting beside him, listening to his songs as they travelled through the outback.

'Sarah? Did you hear? I said we may need to put up some new shelves in that corner to make the stock easier to get to.'

'Yeah. Sure, Dad. Have you got the necessary bits and pieces?'

If there were shelves to be built, she would be the one doing it. She had come home to take over those tasks that were now too much for her dad to handle. She braced herself to argue with him if he insisted on doing it himself. At the same time, she braced herself for the heartache if he stood back and handed control to her. That would be an acknowledgement of how ill he really was, and that was going to be just as hard to take.

'I do,' Ken said. 'There's a complete set of prefab shelving in the garage that will work fine here. I'll mind the store while you go and get them.'

Pete stretched his arms and flexed his fingers against the steering wheel. The road ahead seemed longer than it normally did and he was having trouble concentrating. That was not a good thing when you were driving a road train. He flicked his stereo on, seeking music he could sing along to. But turned it off again after a few minutes.

He was never going to drink that much beer again. Ever. He was a professional driver and seldom drank more than a single beer. But last night …

It had all started over dinner. Linda had pretty much moved in to live with him now. She'd cooked a nice dinner and there'd been plenty of beer in the fridge waiting for him. It was probably her idea of domestic bliss. After dinner, she'd kissed him long and hard. Her invitation and desire were clear, but he'd turned away. He'd had no desire for sex with Linda since she'd told him the news. She knew how he was feeling and he'd seen the hurt on her face. There had been something else there too. Fear, perhaps. She was afraid he would turn away from her and the child. He'd felt a little hurt by that. Surely she knew him well enough to know he would never desert a child. If she didn't, that said a lot about any future they might have together.

After that, he'd taken more beer from the fridge and gone outside to sit alone in the darkness and drink. He had drunk far too much of that beer and ended up falling asleep on a squatters chair on the veranda of his small rented house. When the first rays of the sun had hit him squarely in the face, he'd staggered inside to grab a couple more hours of sleep on the sofa before heading off to work before Linda woke. He was ashamed of his behaviour. It wasn't right and it wasn't the sort of person he was. It was time he got himself together and dealt with what life had thrown at him.

When he got back to the Isa tomorrow, he'd apologise to Linda. He was going to be a father. It was time to man up and do the right thing.

The Coorah Creek town sign flashed past, and instinctively he eased back on the accelerator, driving from habit as his mind continued its uncomfortable musings. When the truck rolled to a stop, he realised he'd pulled up in front of the Coorah Creek store. He had freight on board for Ken, but it was right at the front of the load. He was also carrying stuff for the mine. That would have to be unloaded first. There was no reason to stop at the store.

But he had.

For a minute he thought about starting the engine and simply driving on, but Ken – or Sarah – would have seen him pull up. To drive away without explanation would be rude. He reached for the door handle.

As he walked through the store's front door, Sarah was just emerging from the door at the back. Her head was turned to look back at someone behind her, and she was laughing. The sound danced through the air between them and he felt as if he was bathed in its glow.

Sarah turned her head and saw him. The laughter turned to a gentle, happy smile.

'Hi, Pete.'

How could two words sound better than the greatest symphony ever written?

'Hi, Sarah.'

She looked amazing. So bright and fresh and so terribly young. His heart skipped a beat, but then reality crashed home to him. She was young. Too young. He had no right to feel a surge of desire for this girl who had once called him uncle. And especially not when back in Mount Isa, Linda was carrying his child and looking to build a life with him. He had to stop himself before he let a passing attraction become more than that.

'I only stopped by to tell you I have a load on board for the mine. It has to come out first. I'll be back later.'

'Okay.' Her eyes twinkled as if she was in on some joke of which he was unaware.

'So, I mean, don't close up if I'm running late. This mine load might take a bit of time.'

'I'll be here, Pete,' she said. 'Waiting for you.'

There was something in the way she said it. It was an invitation far more appealing than Linda's kiss last night. But it was an invitation he could never accept.

'Ah, good. Then.' He turned to go.

He heard her move behind him. 'Pete,' she called.

He turned. She had opened a fridge and was holding a bottle of water.

'On the house,' Sarah said. 'You sound a bit dry.'

She tossed the water and he caught it.

'Thanks.'

He didn't open the water until he was back in the cab of the truck. He twisted the top and took a long deep swallow of the cool liquid. He'd drunk the whole bottle before he moved to touch his ignition. The huge truck moved slowly away from the kerb in the direction of the mine.

She was waiting for him when he got back to town a couple of hours later. The lights in the store were still on and as he pulled up he could see her through the window. She was moving things around on one of the shelves. He felt it again, that instant surge of longing. What would happen, he wondered, if he didn't drive away after unloading the supplies for the store? He could suggest they had dinner together at the pub. Just a burger and a beer. There was nothing wrong with that, was there?

There was, he suddenly realised because, for him at least, it wasn't just a burger and a beer. The little girl who had held a special place in his heart had grown up and something about her now called to him in a very different way and that was not right. For a start, she was too young. He honestly didn't know if she was over the legal drinking age. And then there was the situation he now faced. He couldn't drag someone as young and innocent as Sarah into the mess of his own making. It wouldn't be fair to her or to Linda.

Pete determined to unload as quickly as possible and get out of Coorah Creek before he did something he would later regret.

He opened the back of the truck, and hefted the first couple of boxes.

'Hello again, Pete,' Sarah said as she opened the door for him and took a careful look at the boxes he was carrying. 'Could you drop those first few over by those empty shelves, rather than in the storeroom, please?'

'Sure thing,' he said, determined to make this visit as short and as business-like as he could.

He set the boxes on the floor and quickly returned to the truck. The second and third loads he carried through to the storeroom, while Sarah opened those first boxes. His curiosity was aroused.

'What have you got there?' he asked, pausing beside her for a few moments between loads.

'Look!' Sarah said gaily as she turned towards him,

her hands full of brightly- coloured objects. 'Aren't they pretty?'

Pete's eyes widened with surprise. Sarah was holding out a bunch of toys to him – bright, soft babies' toys. The sort of toys an expectant parent would buy for a newborn baby. The sort of toys Linda was already looking at in shop windows and online.

'That's different,' he managed to say. 'I've never seen your dad carry that sort of thing before.'

'I know.' Sarah started placing the items onto the empty shelves, moving them around to make an attractive display. 'But he's decided the town's children will always need more toys, and they should buy them here, not from the internet. I hope it works out for him.'

Pete mumbled something appropriate and turned away for his next load of boxes. By the time he emerged from the stockroom the final time, Sarah was standing back, holding a big yellow teddy bear under her arm as she studied the results of her handiwork. She looked cute, standing there like that. This child who wasn't a child any more. She'd probably make a great mother some time. A great wife for some lucky man.

But not for him. The thought struck home like a hammer blow. Some other woman was having his child and that was an end to it.

'Yes. Very nice,' he stammered. 'I bet you'll have no trouble selling those. Well, I'm off. See you again next week.' He headed for the front door without really giving her time to reply.

He felt like a coward, but when it came to Sarah he was beginning to suspect running away was the best thing he could do. He had to run away from her because he couldn't run away from Linda or the child she carried.

Chapter Eleven

Max was taking his evening stroll a little earlier than normal. If anyone asked, he would say it was for no particular reason; he'd just finished his work early today. But he knew better. His feet had taken him past the pub, but there was no sign of a Harley parked outside. Crossing the road had brought him to the garage. Again, for no particular reason.

'Hi, Max.' The garage owner was outside locking up his petrol bowsers for the night.

'How's things?' Max asked.

'Not bad at all, thanks.'

'Have you heard from Scott and his nurse?'

The older man's face broke into a smile. Until very recently Ed had been estranged from his only son. But Scott had returned last Christmas and they had reconciled before Scott set out for a few years working in England. He'd taken the town's new nurse with him. She had also been the town's only nurse, but no one begrudged them their happiness. Coorah Creek was like that. The town's only doctor, Adam Gilmore, had simply begun looking for a new nurse. The problem with that, of course, was that nurses willing to work in the back of beyond were few and far between.

'They're great,' Ed said. 'Scott's job at the motor museum is really working out. He's restoring a 1952 Vincent Black Lightning motorcycle at the moment. I've never seen one of those. That's an added reason for me to make a trip over there to visit him.'

'Speaking of rare motorcycles,' Max grabbed at the chance he'd just been offered. 'I assume that, like everyone else, you've been admiring the Harley?'

'I have. And I hear tell a few people have been admiring the rider as well.'

Max shrugged noncommittally. He didn't want Ed to see that the words brought a flare of jealousy. In his position, he couldn't be the brunt of any gossip.

'Have you had a chance for a close-up … of the bike?'

'Sure,' said Ed. 'She needs petrol and I'm the only servo in town. Seems like a good kid.'

Max raised a mental eyebrow. He thought he'd asked about the bike. Was Ed becoming a male version of Trish Warren in the matchmaking stakes?

'Anyway, I'm off inside,' Ed said. 'I'm Skyping Scott and Katie in the UK soon. Then I'll be getting dinner at the pub. I'll buy you a beer if you're there.'

'Thanks.' Max turned south, in the direction of the mine, and kept walking.

The sun was still well above the horizon when he reached the gates to Coorah Creek's small hospital. The wooden building was set well back from the road, but he could see a couple of cars parked there, one of which he recognised. Ken Travers at the shop drove a green station wagon. He must be seeing Doctor Adam. Max shook his head. The Travers' family were good people having a pretty tough time of it right now. Sometimes life just wasn't fair.

He heard the Harley as he was turning to head back to town. It was approaching from behind him. He resisted the urge to turn around. As it came level with him, the bike slowed, and veered to the wrong side of the road. To Max's side of the road. It was less than a metre from him as it went past. The rider glanced over her shoulder. He couldn't see her face through the helmet, but he imagined her smile as she raised one arm in salute. Then she gunned the engine, swung back onto the right side of the road and powered away.

For a moment, the uniform took over. Such disrespect for the law usually led to trouble. And he was pretty sure the bike disappearing down the road was not exactly under the speed limit.

She was looking for trouble. Teasing him.

He stopped in mid-stride as the man supplanted the uniform. Wasn't teasing just another way of saying she was flirting with him? He thought about that for a very long minute, and gradually a smile touched his lips. By the time he had walked back to the garage, the bike was long gone, but Max was whistling.

He stopped whistling as a large expensive campervan pulled up outside the garage. No. Campervan was the wrong word. Campervan suggested something about the size of an old VW combi van. This was the size of a bus. What the Americans would call a recreational vehicle. The huge motorhome was painted gold and white and had tinted windows. The driver's side door opened and a man got out. He was dressed in immaculately ironed trousers and shirt. His feet were encased in what looked to Max like very expensive leather loafers. He clearly wasn't a local. As the man walked towards the locked bowsers, the door in the back of the motorhome opened. The woman who stepped down looked as expensive as the vehicle.

'Hello,' Max said in his sergeant's voice as he approached. 'Welcome to Coorah Creek.'

'Ah, hello.'

The man's accent was Australian, but Max would have bet a week's wages that this bloke had never been more than thirty or forty kilometres from the city before. He would have as little idea of the outback as any overseas visitor.

'Can I help you?'

'Well, yes. We need petrol. This beauty sure drinks a lot.'

Max assumed he meant the vehicle, not his wife.

'We're heading out to the Tyangi National Park to camp for a couple of weeks. We have a refrigerator and cooking and everything we need on board. We just need petrol and supplies.'

Max couldn't help but wonder if they had the knowledge and common sense they needed on board too. He thought probably not, but there was no law against that.

'The garage is closed for the night,' he said, dragging his errant thoughts back. 'The store too.' There was no way he was going to let them disturb the Travers' family. If Ken was at the hospital, they probably had more important things on their mind than catering for a rich city bloke who hadn't planned his trip properly. 'I suggest you spend the night here and stock up in the morning. It's a fair drive to Tyangi, and you'd be better off getting there in daylight.'

'Yes. I see. Well, that makes sense.'

And it would also give Max time to ring the park ranger, Dan Mitchell, and tell him these visitors might need his help. Dan would check them out and make sure they weren't doing anything too stupid or dangerous.

A childish scream made the blonde woman turn her attention back inside the motorhome.

'Stop it, Dustin, leave your little sister alone,' she admonished. 'So help me, I'm sick to death of the pair of you. If you don't start behaving ...'

'Where can we stay?' the driver asked quickly. 'It's been a long drive today and we are all pretty tired.'

Pretty cranky too, Max thought. At least the wife and kids are.

'There is a campsite down by the river,' he said. 'It's free and there's no one else there at the moment. At least, there wasn't yesterday.'

'Ah. Yes ...'

The man hesitated and cast a glance at the open door of the motorhome. His wife had vanished inside and from the raised tone of her voice, she was trying to bring the misbehaving children back under control. Max felt a brief wave of sympathy for the father.

'Of course, if you prefer, there are rooms at the pub. It's nothing flash, but it's clean and safe. The publican's wife cooks a good steak. They'd be happy to take the kids too.'

A look of relief washed across the man's face. 'Yes. That does sound better. There's not much point going to the trouble of setting up camp for just one night, is there? The pub, you say?'

Without a word, Max raised a hand and pointed across the street.

The man examined the building with a look that plainly said beggars couldn't be choosers. Max felt a little insulted, on behalf of Trish and Syd. They were good people and ran a good pub. The best anywhere. They deserved more respect than they were likely to get from this guy. But then, Max thought, Trish and Syd – Trish in particular – were perfectly capable of dealing with anyone. They didn't need Max to stand up for them. It might even be interesting to stop by the pub and watch what happened if these city folk so much as raised a questioning eyebrow around Trish.

'There's no room behind the pub to park something this big,' Max said. 'You can park just across the road from here. Pull up parallel to the kerb and you should be well off the road for the night. The vehicle will be safe there.'

'Yes, of course, officer. Thank you.'

Max kept on eye on the new arrivals as he walked back towards the police station. The driver took several attempts to get the huge vehicle parked properly. That set a few more alarm bells ringing inside his head.

Once inside his office, he called the ranger station to

94

alert Dan to the impending arrivals. Then he decided to head over to the pub.

The family had indeed moved in. In the lounge, two kids had their noses buried in a couple of beeping hand-held games, while their mother talked on her mobile phone. The father was in the bar, ordering drinks.

'Thanks for suggesting this.' The man shook Max's hand as if he was a long lost friend. 'My name is Evan Haywood. Can I buy you a beer?'

Max shook his head. 'What brings you all the way out here?'

'Family holiday. My wife says I work too hard so she thought it would do us all good to get away from everything.'

Max glanced through the doorway to the lounge, where the rest of the Haywoods were still engrossed in their electronic gadgets.

'I was wondering if there's much in the way of aboriginal art out here?' Haywood asked.

'This is a small town,' Max responded. 'There's no call for an art gallery here. There might be something in Mount Isa, but I really don't know.'

'Oh, I'm not looking for a gallery,' Haywood said. 'I'm an art dealer. I was thinking while I was here I could check out any local artists. Maybe with work to sell.'

'None that I know of,' Max said.

'Here's your drinks.' Syd placed a small tray with four glasses on the bar. 'My wife will be over in a moment to take your food order.'

Haywood frowned as he looked at the tray, before seeming to understand that he had to carry his own drinks to his table. He gingerly picked up the tray.

'I don't know. City folk,' Syd said under his breath to Max, raising an eyebrow as he turned to his next customer.

Max looked once more at the family sitting around the table. The parents were looking at the blackboard menu above the bar, but still it seemed, no one was talking. City folk, indeed.

Tia spotted the motorhome as she drove into town first thing in the morning after her night shift. She parked the bike outside the store and removed her helmet. She studied the vehicle for a long time, and let out a low slow whistle. She thought her trailer at the mine wasn't bad for a portable home – but that thing was like a palace. She wished she could see inside.

Before she could get off her bike, the front door of the store opened, and a family piled out. The father was carrying a huge box of purchases. The mother carried a couple of bags. There were two kids. A boy and a girl. Tia didn't know enough about kids to guess their ages, but the little girl was particularly cute, with her long blonde hair. She was clutching a big yellow teddy bear that still had the price tag hanging off its ear. She looked over at Tia and her bike, and the brown eyes widened. The little girl moved to the other side of her mother, and peered out at Tia from that place of safety. Tia felt a smile twitching the corners of her mouth as the family walked across the road to climb into the big motorhome.

'It's quite something, isn't it?' Sarah stepped out of the store.

'It sure is,' Tia replied.

'I wonder what it's like to drive,' Sarah said. 'A bit like a truck I should imagine.'

They watched in silence as the father emerged from the back of the home, and walked once around the vehicle, kicking the tyres with his expensive looking soft brown shoes.

'I wonder if he'd even recognise a problem if there was one,' Tia added.

'They're definitely city folk,' Sarah said. 'They wanted to buy a lot of things that we just don't have out here. As if we would carry fresh asparagus and Tasmanian Rain.'

'Tasmanian Rain? That's not what it sounds like, is it?'

'No. It's some sort of expensive bottled water. Twenty dollars for a tiny glass bottle. They had to manage with the ordinary stuff that comes in the big plastic bottles. Still, they did buy one of our new stuffed toys for that cute little girl.'

Across the road the engine of the motorhome roared into life and it started to move very slowly. It began to turn across the road, but there wasn't enough room. The driver had to go back and forth a few times before he was facing the direction he wanted to go.

'I hope he's better at camping than he is at driving that thing,' said a deep voice behind Tia.

Tia glanced to the side. Max was dressed in his uniform. He was watching the big motorhome with a professional eye.

'Do you know where they're headed?' Sarah asked.

'Tyangi,' Max replied. 'I've called ahead to let Dan know they're coming. He'll keep an eye on them.'

'Dan?' Tia asked.

'Dan Mitchell. The park ranger.'

As the motorhome moved out of view along the highway north, Max turned to Tia. 'Good morning.'

He was smiling and his brown eyes were alive with good humour. He was wearing his uniform, and for the first time in her life, Tia decided a uniform could look good on the right man. She felt a little flutter somewhere deep inside her as Max continued to look at her. Damn, but he was attractive. And she had been alone a long time.

Tia was suddenly very conscious of the fact that she had just come off night shift. She never went straight to bed after a shift. She needed an hour or two to relax first and had come into town to stock up on breakfast cereal and milk. She hadn't bothered with leathers today. She was still wearing her work clothes, standard-issue protective clothing complete with bright yellow safety stripe, long-sleeved shirt and long work pants.

The banging of the front door of the store made Tia jump. Sarah had gone back inside, leaving her alone with Max.

'Have you just come off shift?' Max asked, with a nod at her clothing.

'Yes. I was on overnight last night. I need some sleep, but I always like to take a bit of time to wind down first.'

'I'd invite you to join me for coffee,' Max said casually, 'but I guess that's the wrong thing for the end of a night shift.'

Tia felt a little surge of something that could easily have been pleasure. She quickly thrust it down. 'You're not wrong,' she said. 'I'd be bouncing off the walls instead of sleeping. And I get a bit cranky when I can't sleep.'

'Are you on shift tonight?' Max asked, his voice still casual.

She could lie. But she didn't want to. This new life was not going to be based on lies. And some small part deep inside of her was curious to see what Max would suggest.

'Actually, I've got a couple of days off now.'

'So do I, when I come off shift this afternoon. If I promise to leave my police hat at home, would you join me for that burger at the pub?'

She didn't hesitate or give herself time to think twice.

'Yes.'

Chapter Twelve

Sarah felt someone tugging at the leg of her jeans.

'Don't be impatient,' she said looking down. 'Just give me a minute.'

The response was a long plaintive wail.

'Yes. Meow! Dinner is on the way.' She finished opening the can of cat food and spooned some into a bowl. Taking care not to trip over the big ginger animal twined between her feet, she set the bowl down on a tray in the corner of the kitchen.

'There you go, Meggs.' She ran her hand along the cat's back, enjoying the softness of his fur. Meggs didn't respond. He was far too busy with his dinner.

Sarah put a plastic cover on the open can of cat food and put it back into the fridge. The big bowl of leftover chicken casserole on the top shelf caused her to pause. She'd cooked that for her parents last night for dinner, but neither had eaten much. And nor, for that matter, had she. Her father had been to Toowoomba for his last round of chemo. The side effects of the treatment were really taking their toll. He couldn't eat, and when Ken didn't eat, neither did Gina. Sarah was beginning to worry as much about her mother as she did about her father. Ken was seeing doctors and getting regular treatment. He was getting all the care he could. But her mother wasn't seeing any doctors. She was struggling to handle her worry and the workload, despite Sarah's help. She'd lost weight and looked so very frail.

There were times Sarah was afraid she was going to lose both of them

No! She took a deep breath and firm control of her emotions. She was not going to even contemplate losing either of them. She pulled the bowl of chicken out of the fridge. She could make some rice to go with it and this time, she'd make sure her parents ate something.

She was reaching for the rice, when the phone rang. Sarah quickly grabbed it, not wanting it to disturb her parents, who were resting in the lounge.

'Hello,' she said in a low voice.

'Ah, Sarah. So glad I got you. How are Ken and Gina after yesterday's long trip? Resting I hope. It's such a long way, even if it is by plane and I know Jess is a very good pilot and makes it as smooth a ride as she possibly can.'

'Hello, Trish.' Sarah recognised the rambling conversation as much as the voice.

'So, I was hoping you could help me. We have run out of burger rolls. We've been really busy these last couple of days and new supplies haven't come in yet. I just know you must have some in the freezer at the shop. We've got a few people in tonight and it seems every one of them is ordering a burger.'

'Trish … the shop's shut. I was about to start cooking dinner for Mum and Dad.'

'Oh, you are such a good daughter, helping out like that. I'm sure your mum and dad are really glad to have you home again. Although, of course, education is important and I know they are both very proud of you. This will only take a minute and then you can have a lovely evening with them.'

Sarah sighed. She knew Trish Warren well enough to know that there was no way out other than to open up the store and find the burger rolls she needed.

'All right,' she said, breaking into Trish's seemingly unending flow of words. 'I'll duck back into the shop and dig some rolls out of the freezer. Come straight over now and I'll give them to you.'

'Thank you, Sarah. You are so helpful. But I can't possibly come over there. The bar is too busy to leave right now. If you could just bring them over here for me. That would be lovely. Thanks, dear.'

Trish was gone before Sarah had time to argue.

Sarah stood and glared at the phone. Trish was a good woman and quite possibly the heart and soul – and conscience – of their small town, but there were times Sarah would gladly throttle her. She put the phone down and went through to the lounge. Her mother and father were sitting together in front of the TV, which was tuned to some cooking show that neither of them was watching. Her mother was asleep, her head cradled on her husband's shoulder. Ken looked up at Sarah in the doorway and smiled a sad, wistful smile that almost broke Sarah's heart.

She didn't want to wake her mother, or disturb this precious time her parents were sharing. With a series of arm movements and silently mouthed words, she indicated to her father that she was going to the pub. He nodded. Sarah decided that she would stay in the pub for a little while, to give them time together. But also she promised herself she would be home early enough to ensure that her parents ate a good dinner. They both needed their strength.

When she went into the store, she didn't bother putting the light on. Enough light streamed in through the big front windows for her to see what she was doing, and she knew from experience that turning on the light would simply attract more people who had forgotten something earlier in the day, and she'd have the shop open half the night. The rolls she needed were in one of the big freezers along one wall of the store, near the front door. As she walked down the aisle, she looked through those front windows. Pete's truck was parked on the side of the road just past the store.

She found herself smiling, not quite in the same way she

had as a child when she'd seen Pete's truck. She wasn't a child with a silly crush any more. Still, her heart lifted at the thought of seeing him.

Maybe Pete was the one who needed the burger roll. Or maybe Trish Warren was up to her old tricks – well-known matchmaker that she was. Sarah's hand stopped moving as she was about to slide the freezer door open. Was that such a bad idea? Pete was a great guy. Handsome too. They had known each other for years, and spending time with him was so easy. They already shared a bond and she liked him. She liked him a lot. The thought of letting that develop into something more made her heart skip a beat. Not that she was looking for a permanent relationship. There was too much in her life right now, and her future was still undecided. She was, however, a grown woman who could use a little bit of pleasant conversation, maybe even a bit of flirting, and a chance to escape the tough realities of life.

Not only that, Pete was just a friend and right now she could use all the friends she could get. Sarah dived into the freezer and grabbed a couple of bags of frozen rolls.

As she walked across the road, she was smiling again.

He saw her the moment she walked into the bar. He wasn't the only one. A man seated at the far end of the bar whistled softly under his breath. Pete could easily understand why. Sarah was wearing jeans that could well have been painted on, with some sort of little lacy top that didn't quite reach the top of her waistband, exposing a glimpse of the soft skin beneath. Her blonde hair was not caught in its usual long ponytail. It was loose and swayed as she walked, catching gold sparks from the overhead lights.

And for some reason she was carrying a couple of plastic bags filled with something frozen.

'Hey, Sarah, honey. Can I buy you a drink?'

Pete bristled at the sound of the voice. Who was that? And didn't he know Sarah was – okay not a child any more – but she was still under the legal drinking age. At least, he thought she was.

'Thanks for the offer,' Sarah responded as she breezed past, 'but Trish is waiting for these. If I don't get them through to the kitchen straight away … well, how many of you were planning on having burgers tonight?'

She let the question hang and most of Trish's customers chuckled.

Her eyes caught Pete's, and she nodded as she went past. His heart did something weird, and he turned back to the beer on the bar.

His heart was not behaving very well at the moment. Nor was his head. He was still struggling with the prospect of becoming a father, and possibly a husband. It was all too obvious that he wasn't ready, but it was equally obvious that it was coming, whether he was ready or not. Linda had been crying a lot during the past few days. He assumed it was something mysterious to do with pregnancy hormones. He'd tried to make her feel better by taking her shopping, a pastime she'd always enjoyed. That had helped, but all she was interested in these days was baby clothes and toys. He'd tried very hard to feel good about it, but he hadn't. The baby sections of Mount Isa's biggest department store had felt like an alien world. Far more alien, for example, than the Coorah Creek store and its new shelf of toys. Perhaps he should drop by the store and buy a present for the baby. But then Sarah and her family would know about Linda and the baby and that thought filled him with something close to dismay.

He was still gazing into his beer when a voice spoke close behind him.

'Hi, Pete.'

It was almost a caress. He lifted his eyes and turned towards the speaker. 'Hi, Sarah.'

She slid onto the stool beside him, as Trish's husband Syd approached from the other end of the bar.

'Thanks for bringing the rolls over, Sarah. What can I get you?'

'Just a beer. Thanks, Syd.'

Pete frowned. A beer?

'What are you frowning for Pete Rankin?'

He wasn't sure how to answer her. 'Umm ... aren't you ... I mean ...'

'What? Ah. I get it. You think I'm underage. Pete, the legal drinking age is eighteen. Just how young do you think I am?'

He opened his mouth, but couldn't speak. How old did he think she was? In his mind she was still a child. But there were those moments when he could feel the pull of a woman at his side. Moments like right now!

'Don't answer that, Pete,' Syd advised as he placed a foaming glass in front of Sarah. 'Whatever you say, it will be the wrong thing.'

'I'm twenty years old, Pete,' Sarah said loud enough for the whole room to hear. 'And don't forget, some of those were big city years.'

A rumble of laughter echoed around the room. Pete blinked and frowned. City years? What was she trying to say? Was she implying ... Pete tried hard not to blush.

Beside him, Sarah chuckled, a low throaty sound that, more than any words she could have said, told him that she really was no longer a child. Then she lifted her glass and drank her beer like any other adult would.

'How's your dad doing?' Pete asked, desperate to change the subject. She stiffened on the stool beside him, and he wished he'd chosen some other topic.

'The chemo is really taking it out of him,' she said in what was little more than a whisper, 'and the travelling back and forth is hard on both my parents. The last chemo treatment was this week. So now we just have to wait and see.'

'I hope it will all be okay,' he said, knowing it was wholly inadequate under the circumstances. What did you say to someone who was facing such a terrible thing? And facing it so bravely. He wondered if she ever cried about her father's illness. She probably did, but he would bet she did it in private, not to add to the tough burden her parents were already carrying.

'Thanks.' Sarah downed the rest of her beer.

They sat in total silence for a few heartbeats.

'Here's your burger, Pete.' Trish appeared holding a plate piled high with food. 'Sarah, can I get your something to eat? Maybe you'd like a burger too. Or, if you prefer, tonight's special is chicken Kiev.'

'No, thanks,' she said. 'I have something waiting at home.'

She looked down at Pete's plate and her face broke into a grin. Pete wondered what it was about his burger and fries that amused her. Not that he cared. He liked to see her smile. She probably didn't get to do that too often these days. She made no move to leave, and absently stole a couple of fries from Pete's plate while he downed what was definitely one of the better burgers he'd had for a long while. He wasn't sure how it was different from any other burger he'd eaten in the Coorah Creek Hotel. It just was.

'I like your new truck,' Sarah said. 'It's much bigger than the one you used to drive.'

'It is. Since the mine opened we get some pretty big loads to shift.'

'Can I have a look inside some time?'

'Sure.'

'I remember when I was small and you lifted me up to sit in the cab,' she said. 'I was so excited. I thought it was the best thing I had ever seen anywhere.'

'Of course, you hadn't had any big city years back then.' Pete made the joke to see her smile, and she did. At the same time, he wondered again at what those words meant, and just how much Sarah had grown and changed while she was away.

'No, I hadn't. You were like some knight in shining armour then. An adventurer. I used to sit on the roof of the store and look for the truck coming down the road.'

'I bet your parents weren't too pleased about you being on the roof.'

'They wouldn't have been, but they never found out ...' Her voice trailed off and he could almost feel the sadness settling back on her like a cape.

'I wish I could be that knight for you now,' he said softly. 'If there is anything at all I can do to make this easier for you, you know you only have to tell me.'

She nodded. 'Thanks.'

He finished his burger slowly, delaying the moment when he would have to get back in the cab of his rig and drive away. Sarah seemed content to sit beside him, sipping her beer just as slowly.

Chapter Thirteen

He was waiting for her, leaning against the door of the pub, obviously alerted to her imminent arrival by the sound of her motorcycle. Tia pulled up directly in front of him, and turned off the engine. The night seemed unusually quiet without the throb of the Harley's motor. Max didn't move. He was waiting for her to alight. From behind the safety of her full-face helmet, Tia took a long look at him. Without his uniform, he was simply a good-looking guy. A few years older than her and, no doubt, a whole heap wiser. In some ways. There were things she had learned the hard way that would most definitely surprise or possibly even shock the lawman.

But he was handsome, and nice. She liked the way he laughed, and she loved the fact that he did all that wonderful work with old wood. Too many people were happy to throw away old or damaged things, even damaged people. This copper was a good man. Fancy that, she thought, as she kicked the bike's stand into place and began to remove her helmet. She had a date with a good man. That must be a first.

'Hi.'

At that moment, she decided to stop thinking too hard. She would stop remembering he was a cop and stop thinking about other cops she had known in another time and place. Cops who were so very different to Max. She would forget where she had come from and what she had done. It was time she just let herself enjoy an evening without fear.

'Hi,' she said.

Their fingers brushed briefly as they walked into the pub side by side. It could almost have been an accidental touch. But it wasn't. Tia knew that and she suspected Max did too.

The bar was moderately busy. The first person Tia saw was Sarah from the store. She was sitting very close to a tall man who looked vaguely familiar to Tia, although she was certain he didn't work at the mine. Maybe she'd seen him around the town somewhere.

Sarah raised a hand in greeting and by unspoken accord, Tia and Max drifted towards the place where she was sitting.

'Hi, Pete,' Max said. 'Do you know Tia? She's a driver too. At the mine.'

That's where she'd seen him before; delivering equipment to the mine in the big blue and white Mercedes prime mover that was parked across the road. It looked a lot like he was Sarah's boyfriend. They looked good together. Kind of sweet.

Tia had a sudden thought. Were people looking at her and Max in the same way and thinking the same thing?

'Do you want to join us?' Sarah asked. 'Pete is just grabbing a cup of Trish's extra strong coffee before hitting the road back to the Isa.'

Her face was welcoming, but Tia thought she caught a hint of something in Sarah's voice that suggested she wouldn't be offended if Tia and Max sat elsewhere. It was a feeling Tia shared.

'Thanks, but we'll let you get on with it,' Max said. 'Be careful on the road, Pete. I've had reports of a lot of roos on the road north. More than we would normally see. They are probably on the move because of the dry weather. There's been a couple of near misses.'

'Thanks for the warning,' Pete said.

Tia and Max found a seat at the other end of the bar. Tia was secretly glad Max had taken this route, rather

108

than a table out the back. This seemed less personal somehow; less like a proper date. She could tell herself it was just two people having a beer. Of course, she might not believe it.

Trish Warren appeared in front of them, her eyes alight with speculation. 'Well, hello, Max. And Tia, isn't it? Nice to have you both here. If you're having dinner, I've got a lovely shepherd's pie. There's chicken Kiev too. It's new. No one has ordered it yet. You could be the first to try it. And the barramundi is good. Max, as you're not in uniform, I guess you'll be wanting a beer. And you?' She stopped speaking and looked at Tia.

Tia blinked a couple of times as she caught up with the flow of words. 'Beer for me too, please.'

Trish moved off towards the taps. Max caught Tia's eye and winked. She had to bite her lip to prevent herself from giggling.

The glass of cold beer materialised in front of her a few moments later.

'Now, have you decided what to have for dinner? You did see the full menu up on the chalkboard there, didn't you, dear? Oh, we don't have any burgers. Plenty of rolls, but no burgers to put inside them.'

'The barramundi sounds good,' Tia said quickly to interrupt before Trish could get fully in gear.

'Steak for me,' Max said. 'Rare.'

'Right.' Trish vanished again.

'She's a bit ...' Tia whispered.

'She is,' Max leaned forward to return the whisper, 'But she's good people. The best.'

He was very close to her. She could feel his breath on her skin. It made her tingle. She leaned back quickly and reached for her drink. Max did the same.

'So, how do you like working at the mine?'

'I like it. The hours are long, but the money is pretty good. And I like being in the open.'

'It would certainly beat spending all day in some tiny office staring at a computer.'

'But that's not what you do,' Tia said. 'I seem to remember you on the road late at night, harassing poor motorists.' She grinned to take the sting out of the words, and his smile showed he understood.

'You wouldn't believe the level of crime out here,' he responded. 'I've had cattle rustlers and horse thieves, that's not to mention the magpie attacks.'

'Magpie attacks?'

'In the nesting season, magpies get very territorial. There's a pair that always nest in that big gum tree near the store. They tend to swoop down on anyone who gets too close. They've never really hurt anyone. But it's a good idea to wear a hat around them at certain times of the year.'

'Hats stop them attacking?' Tia asked, not trying to hide her incredulity.

'They do.' Max grinned.

'Not always,' Trish added as she passed carrying a meal to someone at the end of the bar. 'And you, Max Delaney, need to do something about those birds. Nasty thieving things. That was my mother's favourite teaspoon it took.'

'What?' Tia asked as she watched Trish deliver the food.

'One of the magpies stole a silver teaspoon from Trish's window ledge last year,' Max said softly. 'At least, that's what she says. Personally, I think she just lost it.'

'I did no such thing.' Trish whisked past back to the kitchen, still muttering about 'thieving black and white fiends.'

Tia felt that giggle start to rise again, and this time she didn't stop it. Max joined her. Laughing softly, Tia looked into his face, noticing the fine laughter lines around his shining brown eyes. It felt good to be laughing at something as simple as a bird.

Slowly the smile on Max's face faded, and she caught something else in his eyes. A feeling that stirred a matching response somewhere deep inside her.

'Here we go.' Trish was back carrying two plates of food. 'You're lucky I haven't burned yours, Max, after that comment.' She tried to look stern as she placed the plates in front of them, but her grin gave her away.

Tia and Max didn't talk all that much as they ate. They didn't need to. It was probably the best meal Tia had eaten in years. Maybe ever. It wasn't just that the fish was good; it was the feeling of belonging that had slowly crept over her. It was her awareness of Max beside her, eating with great enjoyment, and still joking with the elderly barmaid. This was how ordinary people lived. People who had never known homelessness or abuse or despair. People who had never run for their lives, or watched a man fall to the floor with a bullet in his chest. For the first time in a very long time, she felt like everybody else. Not set apart by her past. It was a wonderful feeling.

They were finishing the last mouthfuls, when the phone at the end of the bar rang. Trish answered it, stiffening as she listened to the voice at the other end.

'Max. It's for you. Dan Mitchell.' Trish's voice was clipped and dry.

Without a word, Max left Tia's side and moved quickly along the bar to take the phone. A silence fell in the room. All eyes and ears were on Max as he listened intently to a voice on the other end of the line. Sarah and Pete, who had been on their feet ready to leave, waited. It was as if everyone recognised that the call meant trouble.

'How long?' Max asked the caller.

He listened for another few moments, his frown

deepening. Something was obviously wrong. Tia could see this first date was not going to end well.

'Right. Keep them at the campsite. It'll be dark by the time I get there. We don't want them wandering off too.'

He listened for a few seconds more. 'Good. See you soon as I can.'

Max dropped the phone back and turned to Tia. 'I am so sorry, I have to go.'

'What's happened?' She was asking on behalf of the whole bar.

'Remember that motorhome we saw this morning? Heading for Tyangi.'

She nodded.

'Their little girl is missing.'

The room fell still and silent. Max could feel every eye on him.

'Not that lovely little girl with the blonde hair,' Trish said. 'Oh, the poor thing.'

'They've only been out there a day,' someone muttered. 'How the hell did that happen in just one day. Weren't they watching her?'

'They didn't seem to pay much attention to the kids while they were here,' another voice added. 'He was too busy asking people about aboriginal art.'

'City folk,' Syd offered his harshest condemnation.

Secretly Max felt the same way, but he said nothing.

'Right then. I guess you'll need a search party.' Trish wiped her hands on a cloth as if getting ready to set out immediately.

'Can I help?' Tia's words caught him by surprise a little, but they shouldn't have. What else would she, or anyone, say?

'It'll be dark soon,' Max said to the room in general. 'Dan and I will search tonight. We don't want too many people out there in the dark. But if we haven't found her by daylight, I'm going to need everyone. There's a lot of ground to cover.'

There was a murmur of assent around the room.

'Tia,' Max said. 'Can you talk to Chris Powell and everyone at the mine? Anyone who is off shift can help tomorrow. And can you find out what the plane is doing? I could use a spotter up there at first light, if that's possible.'

'Sure.'

'I'll make some calls,' Trish said. 'Get some men on hand for tomorrow. Do you want horses as well?'

'Not immediately, but it would be good to have them on standby,' Max said. 'She can't have gone that far in a couple of hours. If we haven't got her by tomorrow evening, we'll bring in horses and trackers.'

'You're going to need water and food for the searchers,' Trish said. 'Leave that with me.'

'And me,' Sarah volunteered.

'Thanks.' The town was already doing what it did best – uniting to help. Max knew that he wasn't needed here any more. The good people of Coorah Creek would make sure he had the resources he needed. It was up to him to use them wisely.

'Thanks everyone,' Max said. 'I'm going out there now. But there's not much chance we'll find her tonight. If Dan hasn't been able to, no one will.' He turned to Trish. 'You said Jack and Ellen are away? When do they get back? I can always use another good man, and he knows the area.'

'Not for another couple of days,' Trish replied.

'Damn!' Max let the expletive escape softly.

'Can I help?' Pete asked. 'I've got a couple of pretty powerful torches in the truck. I don't know the area well, but I can handle myself in the bush.'

He could too, Max knew. Pete had stopped and helped

out at a nasty road accident a few months before. 'Good. Can you come out with me tonight?'

'I sure can. I'll let the depot know that I won't be back in the Isa for a while.'

'Do it now,' Max urged. 'Once we get out there, there's no mobile service. There's a phone at the ranger station, and Dan has a radio, but communications are going to be difficult.'

Max turned and gently touched Tia's hand. 'I'm sorry' he said in a voice for her ears alone. 'I didn't expect the evening would end like this.'

'Go,' she said gently. 'Just find that little girl.'

'I will.'

Chapter Fourteen

It was fully dark by the time Max pulled up in one of the Tyangi National Park camping areas. He immediately recognised the big motorhome parked to one side of the campground. There were lights on inside the vehicle, and outside lights shining onto a table and chairs set under a broad canvas awning. The ground below the awning was covered with what looked like AstroTurf. Beside him, Pete let out a long slow whistle.

'I know what you mean,' Max said. 'It is impressive. Unfortunately, from what I saw of the owner, he really hasn't got much of a clue. He can barely drive the thing. I've got no idea what he's doing all the way out here. He's obviously way out of his comfort zone.'

A big Land Rover painted in the livery of the National Parks Service was parked next to the motorhome. A tall figure emerged from the vehicle and headed their way.

'Hi, Dan.' Max shook the ranger's hand. 'This is Pete Rankin.'

'G'day.' Dan shook Pete's hand. 'Thanks for getting here so fast.'

'What can you tell me?' Max asked.

'The girl's name is Renee Haywood. She's six years old. She's here with her mum and dad and brother. The brother is seven. Apparently the kids were playing outside while the mother made dinner. When she called them, only the boy came. His name is Dustin. He said they were playing hide and seek and he couldn't find his sister.'

'And the father?'

'He says he was inside the van, working.'

115

Max raised an eyebrow. 'I thought they were here for a holiday.'

'I guess he doesn't take holidays.'

'Probably how he affords that thing,' Pete added.

'Yeah,' Dan agreed.

'How's the mother holding up?' Max asked.

'About how you'd expect,' said Dan. 'Mostly she's been blaming her husband. I've done a quick search of the immediate area, but no sign of the girl. She's been gone,' he looked at his watch, 'about four hours now.'

'Then we'd better get moving.' Max turned back to his car to collect the torches from the back seat. He also handed out water bottles.

On the bonnet of Max's car, Dan spread out a large detailed map of the park. In the harsh light of the torches, the search area looked big and rough. Between them, the two men decided the most likely areas for this first search. They would check all the marked walking trails that led from the campsite.

'That'll take us a couple of hours,' Dan said. 'But our best chance is if she has hidden close to one of the paths. Hopefully she'll see us or hear us. She's wearing blue shorts. Oh yes, she's carrying a yellow teddy bear. Or she was.'

Just then a man emerged from the motorhome. Max recognised him immediately from their conversation the day before. He hurried over to them, his face tense and strained.

'Have you found her?'

'Mr Haywood,' Max said. 'We are about to do another search.'

'Only the three of you?' Haywood's voice was almost a shout. 'That's not enough. We need a proper big search party.'

'Not tonight we don't,' Max said keeping a reasonable

tone to his voice. 'She probably hasn't gone very far. If we haven't found her by morning there will be more people coming to join the search. They'll be more useful in the daylight.' He didn't say what he was thinking, that it was unlikely they'd find the little girl in the dark.

'I'll come with you. Let me get a torch.'

Max held up a hand to stop him. 'You need to stay here.'

'No. I need to be out looking for my daughter!'

Max felt a surge of sympathy for the man. No doubt his rising anger was fuelled to some extent by guilt, but the last thing they needed right now was a townie blundering around in the dark. The very least he would do is spoil any tracks that might be out there. At worst, they'd have two missing people to search for.

'We know the area,' Max explained calmly, even though he wasn't sure that Pete had ever been to the park before. 'And we know how to handle this sort of terrain. You need to be here looking after your wife and son. And in case Renee finds her own way back. If she does, I want you to sound three blasts on the horn of the motorhome. Can you do that for me?'

'Do you think she might find her own way?' The desperate hope in the man's eyes was almost more than Max could bear.

'It's always possible.' Max thought it unlikely, but he wasn't going to say so. That family would need every bit of their strength and hope in the long dark hours ahead. 'Now, go back to the motorhome. Keep all the lights on. Have you any big outside spotlights? If you have, turn them on as well. Now we've got to get on with the search.'

Haywood hesitated, clearly torn between his desire to do something, and the common sense in Max's words. Finally he turned back towards the motorhome, his shoulders sagging. As he approached the vehicle, the door opened and his wife appeared.

'What are you doing?' she yelled, her voice harsh and ragged. 'Why aren't you out searching for her?'

Haywood said something too softly for Max to hear. Mrs Haywood stepped back inside the motorhome and after a moment's hesitation at the base of the stairs, her husband followed. The door slammed shut behind him.

'Okay. Let's go,' Max said to Dan and Pete. 'Keep those torches moving. If she's awake she might see the light. And keep calling her name.'

Pete and Dan nodded and set out along their allotted paths, their torches flashing through the trees. Max waited just long enough to be sure Haywood wasn't about to do something stupid like follow them, and then he too set out.

Within a few seconds, he had lost sight of the campground and he was alone in the darkness.

'Renee!' His voice cut through the night like a knife. He heard one of the others, Dan he thought, also calling the girl's name. But that noise quickly faded away and Max was surrounded by nothing but the night sounds of the bush.

He moved slowly, looking carefully around him. He shone his powerful torch into all the darkest places, and called the little girl's name until his throat was dry. The paths were clearly marked. Even in the darkness they would be easy to follow. But a little girl playing hide and seek wouldn't want to stick to the paths. She'd probably dashed off into the scrub without thinking. By now she would be frightened and lonely. She'd probably try to find her way back to the campsite, but with no path to guide her, could be moving further and further away.

The park didn't have many real predators, but it was still a dangerous place for a child. There were a lot of poisonous snakes. But the greatest danger would come from the sun. Dehydration and sunstroke were a threat, even though it was not yet high summer. A little girl alone out here without food or water would weaken very quickly and a weak child was vulnerable. There were dingoes, wild dogs and feral pigs in the park. They would be a real danger to her as her strength failed.

They had to find her – soon.

Two hours later he was back where they had all started. Pete and Dan were already there and one look at their faces told him everything he needed to know.

'There's not much more we can do tonight,' he said. 'Dan, why don't you head back to the ranger station? Call Trish Warren and let her know we need everyone tomorrow. First light. She won't be afraid to wake people up and get them out here.'

'Sure.'

'Is Quinn home?'

'She's just finished a shoot on the coast. Last I heard she was thinking of driving right through the night to get here in the morning.'

'Dan's partner is a photographer,' Max explained to Pete. 'I could use a good set of eyes in the spotter plane in the morning.'

'I'll call her when I get back to the station,' Dan said. 'She can stop at the Creek when she gets here.'

'Great. Jess should have the plane on standby for first light. Then, if we don't find Renee after a few sweeps from the air, I'll send Jess to pick up a tracker.'

'Sounds good.' Dan turned towards his vehicle.

'Bring back anything you think will be useful. We'll set up a command post here.' Max looked over at Pete. 'Are you with us, Pete? Or do you need to get back?'

'I'm here as long as you want me,' Pete said without hesitation.

'Thanks.'

With a nod, Dan set off back to his car. Max spread the park map out over the bonnet of the police vehicle, and began to plan the search.

'When we have more men and some daylight, we'll divide into grids like this,' he said to Pete, drawing lines on the map with his finger. 'I'll need someone back here to co-ordinate. And someone needs to stay with the family.'

As if on cue there was a sound from the nearby motorhome. The sound of a woman sobbing.

'This must be tough for them,' Pete said.

'Put yourself in their shoes. How would you feel?' Max said slowly. 'And there's always a measure of guilt. They feel it's their fault the little girl is missing.'

'Isn't it?' Pete's voice sounded harsh.

'Don't be too tough on them,' Max said. 'I don't have any kids, but in this job I've learned that being a parent is hard work. You let your guard down for even a second and they can just vanish. Like Renee did.'

There was no answer. Max glanced sideways at Pete. The younger man was frowning. His face set.

'Is there something wrong?' Max asked.

'No. It's nothing,' Pete said quickly. 'I'm going to do another loop around some of those paths. Just in case.'

'Okay. One of us needs to be awake all night, listening in case she's nearby and calls out. But we both need to get some sleep. So let's take it in turns to get a few hours rest. We're going to need all the energy we can muster in the morning.'

Pete didn't reply. Max watched his tall lean shape vanish into the darkness, and then turned back to studying the map.

She was alone in the darkness and she was terrified. She could hear noises. Somewhere out there were people who wanted to hurt her … or something worse. She had no home to go back to. If she was going to survive, she had to rely on her own wits. She was hungry and thirsty, but was too afraid to move. Then there was another sound close by. Too close. Over there, in the blackness of a doorway. A tall shape. A huge filthy hand in the darkness reaching for her as the sound of harsh rasping breath assaulted her ears.

With a short sharp scream, Tia sat upright, sleep falling away from her as she stared wild-eyed at her surroundings. Her heart was pounding as she tried to control her panicked breathing. She looked around her, taking in the bland walls of the trailer, the small kitchen with its fake wooden cupboards and the table with the motorcycle helmet sitting on it.

She swung her feet down to the floor and ran her hands through her hair. What a nightmare. It had taken her back to the dark days in the squats. She had run away from home when she was only fifteen. That was when her stepfather had started taking too much notice of her. She shivered as she remembered the way he had looked at her and that night he had walked into her room when she was in bed and her mother was at work. She'd fought him off that night, but knew he'd be back. Her mother would never have believed her, so she had run away and never gone back.

Of course, running away hadn't been a picnic either. She spent a long time living in squats and trying to feed herself by stealing. In those early days, when things were really bad, she'd been reduced to looking in the wheelie bins behind restaurants. She'd learned quickly that expensive restaurants threw away a lot of really good food. She'd also learned the hard way that if she was going to survive out there, she needed some sort of protection against the gangs that ruled the streets. Little had she known how that would turn out.

Tia got up and pulled back the curtains covering her window. The sky was still dark, just the smallest suggestion of dawn appearing on the horizon to the east. Somewhere out there was another small runaway. A little girl, lost and afraid, as she had been when she set out on her own. That little girl needed to be found. She needed to be protected and brought back to her family.

Tia headed for her tiny bathroom. There was no way she'd get back to sleep now. She packed anything she thought might prove useful into the panniers of the Harley. She hesitated for a moment, thinking about the gun hidden under the bench seat. A gunshot would be a sure-fire way of attracting the little girl's attention or of bringing help if Tia found her. But the gun was also something she wouldn't be able to explain to Max. Reluctantly she left it behind, consoling herself with the thought that Max would have a gun. And some of the other men would too. The searchers didn't need another gun. They needed more people. By the time the sun peeped over the horizon, she was well past the town and on her way to the Tyangi Crossing National Park.

She slowed down as she entered the park, suddenly aware that she didn't know where to go. She paused outside the ranger station. A man emerged. He was wearing a uniform, but this one didn't cause her any concern. He wasn't a cop.

'Dan Mitchell,' he introduced himself as he approached her. 'If you were planning to go hiking, I'm afraid the park is closed today.' He raised the sign he was holding in his left hand. 'I was about to post this.'

'I'm here to help with the search,' Tia said quickly. 'Unless you've found her?'

Dan shook his head. 'I think we're going to need all the help we can get today. It's going to be a hot one, and that little girl hasn't got any water.'

'Just tell me where I can be useful.'

Following Dan's directions, it took Tia about ten minutes to get to the campground. She instantly recognised the huge motorhome. And the police car parked nearby. By the time she'd parked her bike next to it, Max had appeared from the direction of the motorhome.

'Tell me how I can help,' she said by way of greeting.

He looked tired, she thought. But very determined. He exuded a strength and competence that must be a great comfort to the people who needed him.

'Do you know the park at all?'

'No,' Tia said. 'I'm a townie so I don't know how to handle the bush, but I do know how to organise things. I can help with food and water and keeping track of the search parties. Who has gone where, that sort of thing. I could even stay with the family, if you think that would help. Whatever you need me to do, just let me know and I'll do my best.'

He nodded slowly, his dark eyes softening for a moment. 'Thanks, Tia.'

He reached out and laid his hand on her shoulder for a second. It was just a fleeting touch, but it held a world of comfort and encouragement and thanks. She welcomed it as she had never welcomed a man's touch before.

Perhaps if it had been Max's hand reaching for her in the squalor of the squat on that dark night, her life might have been very, very different.

Chapter Fifteen

'There are a couple of large Esky water coolers in the storeroom. Fill those and take them too.'

'Thanks, Mum.' Sarah found the polystyrene coolers on the top shelf. She quickly filled them with water and added them to the growing pile near the front door of the store.

Her father emerged from the rear of the shop, carrying a couple of boxes of health food bars.

'These will help. The searchers will need to keep their strength up.'

Sarah nodded. 'Trish is organising food. Sandwiches for lunch and—'

She stopped. What happened after lunch depended upon how well the searchers fared. Maybe they would have found the little girl by lunchtime, or maybe they would still be searching into the evening and night. Sarah didn't want to even think about that possibility. One night in the bush was hard enough for a lost child. Two was almost unthinkable.

She opened the front door of the store just as two cars, both full of people, sped past in the direction of the park. The sun was only part way above the horizon, but the search teams were already gathering. She carried the first armload of supplies to the green station wagon parked at the kerb and was stowing them safely in the back, when she heard her father's voice.

'Hi, Doc.'

'Hello, Ken. Sarah.'

Adam Gilmore was carrying a large first aid kit. He handed it to Sarah to put in the car.

'I can't come out,' Adam said. 'I have a patient at the

hospital. An injured child and I can't leave him. Everything you might need is in there. I'll be close to the phone. You can get a message to me via radio to the Mount Isa police. Max and Dan know how.'

'Thanks. With luck, we won't need you,' Ken said, causing Sarah to freeze.

'Dad, you're not going out there.'

'Of course I am,' her father replied. 'They need all the help they can get.'

Sarah became aware of her mother standing in the doorway of the store. The big ginger cat was rubbing against her legs, demanding attention, but he was being ignored. Her mother's eyes were fixed on the small group by the car, and her face was white with fear.

'Dad. You're not up to this. You have to look after yourself.'

'There's a lost child,' Ken said in a firm voice. 'They are going to need all the help they can get looking for her. I'm coming!'

Sarah looked at the doctor. 'Please talk some sense into him, Adam.'

'She's right, Ken,' Adam said slowly. 'You've just finished chemo. You shouldn't be stomping around in the bush. You need to rest.'

'But I want to help!'

'It won't help if you collapse out there – then there'll be two people needing to be rescued.'

Sarah saw her father's shoulders sag at the harsh truth of it. Without a word, he turned and walked back, past his wife and into the shop. Gina threw a grateful look in Adam's direction.

'Take care out there,' she told Sarah as she turned to follow her husband into the building.

Sarah blinked back a tear. She hated the truth of it as

much as her father did. She felt a comforting hand on her shoulder.

'You were right,' Adam said quietly. 'He needs to take it easy.'

'Adam,' Sarah turned towards him. 'How is he? Really? What are his chances?'

The doctor held her gaze for a few seconds. 'Sarah, I'm going to be honest with you. His response to the chemo has been good, but it might not have been good enough. All we can do now is wait. He'll have some more tests soon and we'll have to wait and see what they show. If we're lucky, we've beaten it. If not … well, let's just say it's a good thing you came home.'

Sarah bit back the fear and the pain. 'Thanks for being honest with me.'

'Of course. Now, when you get out there, tell Max that Jess will be taking the plane up when it's full daylight. She'll have Rachel Quinn with her acting as spotter. A plane isn't as good as a chopper in these circumstances, but there isn't a chopper anywhere close. The plane is better than nothing. It's worth a try, at least.'

'I'll tell him.'

Across the road, the front door of the pub swung open to reveal Trish Warren. She waved at Sarah.

'Trish looks like she's ready to load the food for the searchers,' Sarah said.

'I won't hold you up,' Adam said.

Sarah started the car and swung it across the road, to where Syd was carrying boxes and Eskys down the stairs.

'It should all fit on the back seat,' Sarah said.

It was a tight fit, but eventually they had all the food and even more water on board. Water was the key to survival in the outback. Sarah didn't want to think about that little girl who was without it.

126

'Good luck,' Syd said as he opened the passenger door for his wife. 'I'll be standing by the phone. Tell Max he can route all calls through me and I'll make sure the messages get to wherever they need to go.'

'Don't worry,' Trish said, grasping his hand. 'We'll find her.'

Sarah watched the exchange between the pair, marvelling at the obvious affection between them even after what must have been several decades of marriage. When she was married, that's the sort of marriage she wanted. The sort of marriage her parents had. Then she remembered her mother's face. Her father's illness was taking a huge toll on the woman who had loved him for so many years. Sarah blinked back the tears again.

She hopped behind the wheel of the car, barely waiting until Trish was comfortably settled beside her before accelerating away from the town.

She sped past Pete's truck which was parked facing north, the direction he should have gone last night.

It looked like he was once again becoming a knight in shining armour for a little girl. She only hoped that Sir Knight would really come to the girl's rescue.

The little boy's eyes were huge and red ringed from crying. He sat on the steps of the motorhome, watching as the searchers began gathering. Pete's heart went out to him. He stepped away from the others for a few minutes, and walked over to crouch down beside the boy.

'You haven't found her yet, have you?' The boy's voice wavered.

'Not yet. But we haven't given up. Not by a long shot. We're just getting ready to start an even bigger search.'

'It's all my fault.' The little boy's voice broke and fresh tears ran down his face.

Pete resisted the urge to gather the crying boy in a hug. 'I'm Pete,' he said. 'You must be Dustin.'

The boy nodded, sniffing.

'Well, Dustin, tell me why you think it's your fault?'

'Mum and Dad were arguing. They were yelling at each other a lot so we went outside. Renee was really upset. She gets like that when Mum and Dad fight. I tried to distract her and said we should play hide and seek. She's not very good at it and the first time I found her really really fast. I told her she had to try harder.'

'Ah. And you think that's why she's lost?'

Dustin nodded, biting his lower lip in an effort not to cry.

'You know, Dustin. I don't see it quite like that.'

'You don't?' The tiny voice quivered a little.

'No. Let me guess ... Renee is always getting into trouble for wandering off, isn't she? She's inquisitive. Likes to explore and look at new things.'

The boy nodded.

'And I bet she doesn't play one game for very long before she wants to do something else.'

Another nod.

'Well, there you go. I bet she saw something. Maybe a pretty bird. Or even a kangaroo. And she forgot about playing hide and seek and went to look at it. That's how she got lost.'

The small tear-stained face that looked up at him was hopeful. 'Do you really think so?'

'I know one thing for a fact, Dustin. It wasn't your fault. Okay?'

This time the nod was a little more confident. 'Can I help to look for her?'

Pete felt as if his heart was about to explode. Was this what being a father was all about? He could see the new hope in the boy's eyes. Had he done that? And was it wrong to raise hopes that might yet be dashed? The boy's sister might never be found; or she might be … He didn't let his mind travel that road. He looked at Dustin who was bravely biting back his tears. Pete silently promised that he would be there for the boy as much as he could. If his parents were the kind who were too busy fighting to notice their kids, Pete would do whatever it took to make these next hours easier for Dustin. First he had to find Dustin something to do. Something that would make him feel like he was part of the rescue effort.

Sarah and Trish were at the other side of the campground. Someone had set up a trellis table in the shade of a small stand of gum trees. The two women were stacking boxes of food and water on the table and handing packages to the searchers who were getting ready to set out. Pete needed to start searching too. But there was something else he had to do first.

'Come with me.'

Dustin jumped down off the stairs. Pete felt a small hand slide into his and he squeezed it as he led the boy across the campsite.

Sarah saw him coming and smiled. That smile lifted the weariness of a long night from his shoulders.

'Dustin,' he said, 'this pretty lady is Sarah. Say hello to her.'

'Hello.'

'And this is Mrs Warren. She's nice too.'

Trish reached out to ruffle the boy's hair. 'And I'm a pretty good cook. I think I may well have some home-baked cookies in one of these boxes, if you'd like one.'

Dustin nodded.

'Dustin wants to help in the search for his sister,' Pete said.

'Oh, thank goodness.' Trish caught on immediately. 'I really do need help. There's all this food and water to hand out to people. I need to be certain that everyone has some – including you, young man. And your mum and dad.'

'They're still asleep,' Dustin offered. 'I think they were up all night hoping Renee would come home.'

Pete caught Sarah's eye and saw the sympathy there.

'I think we should let them sleep for a while longer,' Trish said. 'Now, do you think you can help me get some more food from the car?'

'Yes.'

'Let's go then.'

Trish and the boy moved off.

'That was a very nice thing to do,' Sarah said quietly. 'That poor boy. His parents must be out of their minds with worry.'

'I'd better get going now,' Pete said.

'I'll come with you.'

'You're not staying here with Trish?'

'No. I grew up around here. I know the country. I can be more use out there searching.'

Pete had to admit the sense of that. Sarah had obviously come ready to join the searchers. She was wearing jeans and strong hiking boots. Her hair was caught back in a ponytail, and an Akubra hat shaded her face. She may have spent those years in the city, but she still looked very much like she belonged in the outback.

'Let's go then.'

Dan was in the process of erecting a tent which would act as headquarters for the search. There were detailed maps of the park piled on a folding table. Max was handing them out to the teams of searchers, along with instructions regarding their specific search areas. At his side, Tia was noting down names and times in order to keep track of who was searching and where. Pete and Sarah waited their turn.

'I'd like the two of you to head this way.' Max ran his finger across the map. 'Pete, when you were out last night you must have seen the gully here.'

Pete nodded.

'It's not a path, but it is easy to follow. Easier than walking through the undergrowth or over the rocks. She might have gone that way. It leads some distance, to a billabong. I need you to check that out.'

'You don't think she ...' Sarah started to say.

'I don't think anything,' Max said. 'If you see any tracks, be careful not to disturb them. If we haven't found her by lunchtime, I'm going to call in a tracker.'

'Are you carrying plenty of water?' Tia asked.

Sarah nodded.

'If you find her, she'll be thirsty. Just give her small sips. Too much water too fast won't help her,' Max instructed.

'I know.' Sarah's voice broke a little. 'That poor little girl. Out there alone all night. She must be terrified.'

'We'll find her,' Tia said firmly. 'She'll be all right.'

Sarah nodded and took a deep breath.

'Right.' Pete turned to go.

'When you get back, make sure you check in with Tia again,' Max added. 'I don't want to lose anyone else out there.'

As Pete and Sarah crossed the campground, the door of the motorhome opened. Mrs Haywood appeared, her blonde hair mussed with sleep, her eyes wide with fear.

'Dustin!' she almost screamed.

'Mum.' Her son ran to her and she enveloped him in a crushing embrace.

'My heart just aches for those poor people,' Sarah said under her breath. 'I cannot imagine how hard this is for them.'

Mrs Haywood turned to lead Dustin back inside the motorhome. As he reached the top of the stairs, the boy turned and waved at Pete.

Pete waved back.

'One day you'll make a really good father,' Sarah said.

He almost told her then. Told her about Linda and the baby. About the future he really didn't want but couldn't avoid. He opened his mouth as if to speak, then stopped himself. This was not the right time or place for that conversation. His problems were nothing beside the fate of a lost little girl.

'Let's just hope that today I make a really good searcher,' he said as he led the way to the break in the trees where their path began.

Chapter Sixteen

The whole town had come to help. Or at least, that's how it seemed to Tia. She had taken up her station underneath a military-style tent erected to shade the search centre from the sun. There was a makeshift table covered with maps and a clipboard on which she was recording all the people in the search, when and where they were going. And even more importantly, when they came back.

In one corner of the tent, Max had set up a radio, with which he could communicate with the outside world. It wasn't quite as simple as it sounded. With no mobile phone service in this remote wilderness, Max would radio the police station in Mount Isa, who could then call the Coorah Creek Hotel on the phone and Syd would make sure any messages were delivered. Never before had she truly appreciated how useful mobile phones were.

Two more cars pulled into the camping area, which was now full of vehicles of every shape and size. She recognised Ed Collins from the garage. Three of her fellow mine workers got out of the second car. She glanced at her watch. They had probably just come off shift. Technically she should be going on shift now, but there was no way she was leaving this place until that little girl had been found … one way or the other.

The four men glanced about, obviously looking for direction.

'Over here,' she called. 'First I need you to check in.'

'Hi, Tia,' Blue, her former driving instructor, said as he approached. 'Any news?'

She shook her head. 'Thanks for coming out, Blue. It works like this. I sign you in. Max will give you an area to search. When you come back, the first thing you do is come here to me so I can mark that you are back. We don't need anyone else getting lost out there.'

'Got it!'

'See Trish before you go. Carry plenty of water. Make sure you keep some of it for the little girl, if you find her. Just have her sip the water slowly, okay. Not too much. It will make her sick. Trish will give you food too. Same rule.'

'Yes, ma'am.'

'Oh guys – the little girl – her name is Renee. Renee Haywood. She's probably got a yellow teddy bear with her.'

The men shared a solemn look before they stepped over to the map table. Tia heard Max's voice giving clear instructions about their search area and what to do if they found Renee. He also made sure they understood the need to be back by dark. The men listened carefully before setting off across the compound to get their supplies from Trish. A couple of minutes later, they vanished into the bush in the direction Max had sent them.

The campground was suddenly empty.

'You're pretty good at this.' Max appeared at her side and handed her a bottle of water.

'Thanks.' She opened the bottle and took a long drink. It was almost the middle of the day. Despite the shade of the big gum tree above them, it was getting hot. Hot and dry. Her thoughts went out to that little girl, lost somewhere in that vast wilderness, with no water and no one to help her. For the thousandth time, Tia looked over at the motorhome. The door was shut, the family hiding inside. Didn't those parents care at all about their little girl?

'Don't judge them too harshly,' Max said as if he had been reading her thoughts.

'How can they sit there in all that air-conditioned luxury? If it was my child, I wouldn't rest until I found her.'

'They have a boy to take care of. They can't leave him alone. And, quite frankly, they are both so shattered they would be more of a hindrance than a help out there. I'm glad they're staying put. I don't want to waste time and energy that is more needed elsewhere.'

Tia glanced up at Max's face. He looked tired. She knew he hadn't slept much last night, if at all. He'd been running this search since daybreak without taking a break.

'I don't know how or why someone like you ended up in this small town,' she said. 'But they are very lucky to have you.'

'I'm actually very glad to be here,' Max said. 'Just look at how many helpers we have. This is a good place, full of good people. Although it wasn't exactly the career path I had planned.'

'Really?' Tia feigned surprise. 'I thought being the only lawman in a town in the middle of nowhere was every young cop's dream.'

'I did something stupid,' Max said. There was no regret in his voice. If anything, she thought she heard just a hint of humour. As if he was laughing at his younger self.

'You can't leave it at that,' she said. 'Tell all, Sergeant.'

'It really was stupid,' Max said. 'It was back in Brisbane. I pulled over a drunk driver in a really fast car and booked him. I knew who he was, but I still booked him.'

'Who was it?'

'The Minister for Police.'

'Oops.' Tia felt her shoulders shaking. She didn't try to hold back the chuckle. 'I can see why that wouldn't help your career.'

'The next day the Commissioner suggested he could squash the ticket, but I would have none of it.'

'Squashing a ticket isn't exactly corruption.'

'Yes, it is.' The certainty in his voice was like a solid rock in the midst of a stormy sea. 'It may be a small step over the line, but it's still wrong. If I had it to do over again, I would do exactly the same thing.'

'You really are an honest cop, aren't you? I haven't met too many of those.'

He looked down at her, his brown eyes thoughtful. 'Yes. I really am. And so are a lot of others. But that's not how you see the police, is it? What happened to you to make you think so badly of us?'

Tia hesitated. Here in the strangely intimate setting of an army tent in the middle of nowhere, in the midst of a life or death hunt for a lost child, something had happened. Max had opened up to her in a way she suspected he never had to the townsfolk of Coorah Creek. He obviously felt a need to keep a small amount of distance between himself and the townspeople. Even those he counted as friends. That made sense, given the fact that one day he might have to arrest some of them, or at least book them for speeding. But for some reason, he wanted to get closer to her. That was perhaps the best compliment anyone had ever given her.

It was her turn now. She should open up to him and for the first time in her adult life, she actually wanted to talk about her past. Max was a kind and gentle man and he would understand. He wouldn't judge her. Maybe she could tell him everything – about the squats and the men, the crimes she had committed and the gun. Perhaps doing that would somehow set her free of her past.

As he stood there, waiting with infinite patience, she reminded herself that above all other things, Max was a cop. An honest cop. If he wouldn't forgive a drunk driver to save his own career, how could he ever forgive her? How could he forgive her involvement in the murder of one of his own?

'It's all right,' his voice was soft. 'You don't have to say anything right now. When you're ready to talk, I'm ready to listen.'

'And what if you hear things an honest cop can't ignore?'

'Then we'll deal with them. You and I. Together. There may have been bad things in your past, Tia, but you're not a bad person. That's all I need to know.'

Tears pricked her eyes. It was so tempting simply to let go and tell him everything. But she couldn't. If Max knew everything, he couldn't just ignore it. He'd have to act on what he knew. She'd probably go to prison, and the mere thought of that was enough to terrify her. But that's not what stopped her. Telling Max what was hidden in that rucksack in her trailer would set him on a dangerous course. He would have to act on the knowledge and if he did, he could get hurt ... or worse. She couldn't be responsible for that.

'Now, you two, I'm about to head back to town.' Trish suddenly appeared, breaking the moment, for which Tia was at once both profoundly sad and also very grateful.

'Those searchers are going to need some substantial food when they get back. Particularly if the search is going to go into the night and tomorrow. Syd has been getting the next load ready back at the pub. Max, could you just use your radio to let him know I'm on the way. He'll know what to do.'

'I will,' Max said.

'But you haven't got a car,' Tia said without thinking. 'You came with Sarah.'

'I'll take her car,' Trish said. 'There's plenty of room in that for the stuff I need to bring back.'

'Shouldn't you ask ...' Tia's voice trailed off at the look of puzzlement on Trish's face.

'Why would I bother her? She's busy searching. She

won't mind. That's how we are out here.' Trish paused and fixed Tia with her steely grey eyes. 'When you are part of this community – you're part of a family. We all pitch in and help each other. You should have learned that today.'

With a wave, Trish spun on her heel and headed for the row of parked cars.

'And I suppose everyone leaves their keys in the ignition too,' Tia said.

'I do tell them not to, but ...' Max smiled and shrugged.

It was so easy out here. Tia thought about the night she had stolen the Harley and headed west. Her hands had been shaking when she lifted the keys from the pocket of Andrew Kelly's leather jacket. It would have been so much easier if he'd left them in the ignition. But those keys weren't the only things she'd stolen that night. She thought about the rucksack hidden in her trailer and felt a shiver of fear, despite the heat of the day.

With Trish behind the wheel, Sarah's car pulled away, swerving to avoid a truck that was approaching.

'That will be Justin and Carrie with the horses,' Max said. 'That'll be a big help. I'll quickly call Syd while they unload. Then we should get them underway to take advantage of the rest of the daylight.'

Before he could move, a sound overhead caused both of them to look up. A light aircraft swooped fairly low over their location and began to bank into a tight circle.

'That's Jess and Quinn,' Max said. 'They might see something from the air. Keep a close ear on the radio. Jess will circle the search area a few times and if she doesn't see anything, she's going to head to Warrina Downs.'

'What's that?'

'It's a cattle property a couple of hours south-west of here. Big one. There's a large aboriginal community there. And the best tracker in Queensland.'

'Max,' Tia said softly. 'What are our chances of finding her … You know …?'

He reached out to grip her hand. 'We'll find her, Tia. I won't leave this park until we do. As for the other … I guess if you believe in God, now would be a good time to talk to him.'

There was a shout from the direction of the horse truck. Max held her hand for a few seconds longer, then squeezed it and turned away.

Chapter Seventeen

The sound of the low flying aircraft made Sarah look up. As she did, her boot landed on uneven ground. A shaft of pain shot up her ankle as her foot twisted and she fell.

'Oow!' The pain in her ankle was almost forgotten as something sharp and rough scraped along her side.

'Sarah. Are you all right?' Pete was on one knee beside her.

She nodded as she rolled into a sitting position, her hand grabbing at her side. 'I must have landed on something sharp,' she said.

'Let me see.'

With surprisingly gentle hands, Pete carefully lifted her shirt. She heard him suck in his breath.

'Go on,' she joked. 'Tell me the truth. I'm going to die, aren't I?'

'Not on my watch you're not.' Something told her he wasn't really joking.

Pete dropped his rucksack on the ground and looked around. 'Come and sit down,' he said as he indicated a large sandstone boulder. 'I want to have a better look at your side and at that ankle.'

'I'm fine,' she said but as she started to rise, Pete took her arm anyway, holding her firmly. She tentatively put the twisted ankle to the ground. It barely hurt at all. 'See,' she declared, walking almost without a limp to the indicated seat.

Sarah had to admit it was a relief to sit down. She and Pete had been walking for what seemed like hours. It was hot and she was sweating. Her throat was sore from calling Renee's name. And her heart was heavy because they had seen no sign of her.

Once more Pete knelt beside her and gently cradled her foot in his hands. Ever so carefully, he undid the laces of her boot and slid it off. Then he pulled down her thick hiking socks.

'Can you move it?' he asked, still holding the foot.

Sarah wriggled her toes, and then gently moved her foot in a circle.

Pete nodded. 'It's fine. You've just twisted it. You may have some swelling and a bit of a bruise there tomorrow, but you are definitely going to live.'

'That's a relief.'

Pete slipped her foot back into the boot and began lacing it tightly. 'The boots will give you all the support you need. Now, let's check your side.'

'That actually hurts more than the ankle does.'

'I'm not surprised.' Pete winced as he lifted her shirt. 'You've got a fair sort of a scratch there. You must have fallen onto a broken branch or something.'

Sarah twisted her body to try to see, but that actually made her side hurt even more.

'Stay still for a minute. Let me clean it.' In a few seconds, he had opened a water bottle. He pulled a handkerchief from his back pocket and liberally doused it with water. 'Don't worry. It's clean,' Pete said as he gently patted the scratch on her side. The damp cloth felt cool on such a hot day, but it came away lightly stained with her blood.

He poured some more water over the handkerchief and repeated the exercise. It hurt, just a little, but Sarah was amazed at how gentle he was. And also by the way the light brush of his fingers on her bare skin tingled.

'There you go,' Pete said, wringing the water from his hanky. He passed her the water bottle so she could take a drink.

'Do you want to go back?' he asked her.

'Absolutely not,' she said firmly. 'We should be very close to the billabong. I'm not going back without doing what we came here to do!'

'You are a very stubborn girl.'

'It runs in the family,' Sarah said, thinking about her father. He was stubborn too. Hopefully stubborn enough to beat the disease that was eating away at him.

Pete must have read her thoughts on her face. 'I was really sorry to hear about your dad,' he said. 'How's he doing?'

'He's finished his chemo,' she said. 'Now we just have to wait. It's hard.' Her voice broke.

Pete sat beside her on the rock, and his arms came about her shoulders. She leaned against him, taking comfort from the strength of him.

'He wanted to come today, you know,' Sarah continued. 'Luckily, Doctor Adam was there to back me up when I said he wasn't well enough.'

'It can be really hard for a man to admit he doesn't have the strength for something,' Pete said gently. 'Especially someone like your father. He's a good man. He wanted to do the right thing.'

'I know. But sometimes what looks like the right thing isn't really the right thing … if you know what I mean.'

Pete swallowed a lump in his throat and tightened the arm around her shoulders. He could tell himself he was holding her because she'd taken a nasty fall and was a bit shaky. He could tell himself he was holding her to comfort her because of her father. But, deep in his own heart, he knew he was holding her because it felt wonderful to hold her. So wonderful he wasn't entirely sure he could ever let her go. From the moment his fingers had touched her bare skin while tending her wound, he'd longed to touch her again.

And it was wrong.

Back in Mount Isa, Linda was carrying his child. And while he didn't love her, he would love the baby. He would care for them. It was the right thing to do. But, as Sarah said, the right thing wasn't always right. And in moments of complete honesty, he knew marrying Linda wasn't the right thing. Not for him, at least. And he wasn't altogether sure it was right for Linda and the child either. But he would do it, because he'd never be able to look at himself in the mirror again if he didn't.

He looked down at the top of Sarah's blonde head, where it lay on his shoulder. Her hair was messy and she was damp with sweat. Slowly she raised her head to look at him. Her eyes were wet with tears. Gently he reached one hand to wipe them away, and then he cupped her face and kissed her.

She tasted of salt and tears and sweat. She tasted of sadness and hope and joy. She tasted of youth and innocence and ... Sarah. His arms tightened and he pulled her even closer as her lips moved in answer to his. In all his life, he had never tasted anything so sweet.

When at last they broke the kiss, neither spoke for a very long time.

'We should keep going,' Pete finally said.

Sarah nodded. When they got to their feet, she twined her fingers through his. How could the simple act of holding hands seem so very important and meaningful?

Beside him, Sarah took a deep breath. 'Renee!' she called. 'Renee. Are you there? Can you hear us?'

They both listened. There was nothing but the sounds of the bush.

They started walking. Pete searched the undergrowth with his eyes, hoping for some sign of the missing girl. But every now and then, his eyes were drawn back to the woman at his side. Sometimes he found her looking at him, and they both smiled.

'You know, I had a terrible crush on you when I was small,' Sarah said when they stopped for a moment to rest.

'I kind of guessed that,' Pete said as he handed her a bottle of water. 'You were a cute kid.'

'And now,' she teased, her eyes sparkling as she tilted her head.

'Still cute. Definitely. But in a different way.' He leaned forward to kiss her again. He meant it to be a quick kiss, but instantly he felt the heat flare between the two of them, and many long moments passed before they could drag themselves away and resume their search.

They were now walking down a deep gorge. The bottom of the gorge was sandy beneath their feet. On either side of them, red sandstone cliffs rose into the blue searing sky. Even in the gorge, the sun was merciless.

'That poor little girl,' Sarah whispered. 'She must be so hot and thirsty. And frightened.'

'We won't give up.' Pete squeezed her hand. 'The whole town is here. We'll find Renee.'

'You know, I had forgotten just what Coorah Creek was like,' Sarah mused. 'The way everyone helps everyone else. That's not what it's like in the city.'

Pete felt his heart contract. Of course. The city. She had a life there. She'd want to go back some time. When her father was well … or …

'Do you miss the city?'

'I did for about the first week, but not now. I'm enjoying being home again.' The smile she gave him was almost enough to set him floating two inches above the sand. It wasn't right that he should feel such joy when somewhere out there in the bush, a small child was lost.

Just then, a noise caused them to halt in their tracks.

'Renee!' Sarah called again.

A call came in answer. A cooee from the top of the ridge above. They looked up and saw two people on horseback. For a moment hope flared in Pete's heart. Were the riders calling them back? Had Renee been found?

No. The riders raised an arm to indicate they were pushing on, further away from the campsite where the child's parents must be going crazy with worry. Pete and Sarah kept walking.

They saw no trace of the little girl in the gorge.

The red cliffs fell back as they approached the billabong, a surprisingly large body of water surrounded by grass and reeds that looked out of place in the harsh red, brown and orange landscape. The water was very still. Not even a breath of wind moved to create ripples on a mirror-flat surface that reflected the brilliant blue of the sky.

Pete's heart froze. If a small child had wandered into that water …

'What should we do?' Sarah turned to him, her eyes trusting and concerned.

'Let's split up,' Pete said. 'We need to circle the whole billabong. Look for anything in the mud on the edges that might be a footprint.'

Sarah nodded and set off, circling to the right. Pete turned in the other direction, walking swiftly, but keeping his eyes glued to the banks of the billabong. A couple of times he saw marks in the mud on the bank, but each time a closer look showed them to be animal tracks. Kangaroos obviously came here seeking the sweet green grass. There were other tracks too, that might have been dingoes. But he saw nothing to indicate Renee had come this way.

They had almost completed their circuit of the billabong, when Sarah suddenly darted forward towards the water's edge. Pete's heart leaped in his chest, he took two strides to run to her, when she stood again, waving him off. Whatever she'd seen, it was not what they were searching for. When he and Sarah met at the far side of the water, she was carrying a scrap of cloth, but it's weathered appearance showed it had lain by the billabong for quite a long time.

Renee had not come this way, and for that, in some ways, they were both grateful.

They kept calling and searching as they made their way back towards the campground, but with little hope of success. As they neared the campground, Pete allowed himself to hope that maybe one of the other searchers had succeeded where they had failed. But no. The campsite was fairly busy. It was almost dark and searchers were returning. All looked forlorn and dejected. In a spot by the big gum tree, someone had erected a second huge canvas tent. In her new shelter, Trish Warren was handing out food and water to the searchers before they collapsed, exhausted and dejected. Pete frowned as he spotted Max in animated conversation with a man clutching a camera. Max escorted him away from the big gold motorhome, and then turned away in apparent disgust.

Before Pete could do more than wonder what that was about, a fierce crash of thunder almost shook the ground beneath their feet. Pete looked up to see thick black storm clouds rolling above them. They'd been so intent in their search they hadn't even noticed the storm arrive. There was a bright flash of lightning, followed by another deafening crash of thunder as the first few huge droplets of water fell.

'That poor child will be terrified out there alone in this,' Sarah said.

The rain was getting heavier with every passing second. Already the ground was damp. A storm like this wouldn't last long, but the rain would be fierce.

'Maybe it will help. She needs water. This may save her.'

Sarah nodded, and they both raised their faces to the sky to let the water wash away the dust and dry despair of a long fruitless day of searching.

147

Chapter Eighteen

Tia watched as the man with the camera got back into his car, to protect his expensive equipment from the rain, which was now pouring down quite heavily. The rain didn't seem to bother Max at all. He remained where he was, the water soaking into his uniform as he stared after the man with the camera for a long time. He looked quite intimidating, Tia thought. The very picture of the severity of the law. Had she not known him a little, she might have felt uneasy. As it was, the man with the camera was causing her heart to thump wildly. It wasn't hard to guess what he was. Word of the search had obviously spread. She should have realised that the news people would get involved at some point. At least there were no television cameras. Not yet anyway. Unconsciously, she moved a little further into the tent, where her face would be well hidden.

'Any word?' Sarah and Pete ducked into the shelter, shaking the rain from their clothes as they did.

'No.'

She saw their shoulders sag.

'Do you need some dry clothes?' she asked, not that she had any to offer, but it seemed the right thing to say.

'We'll be fine,' Sarah said. 'In fact, it's quite refreshing in a way. We'll dry out soon enough.'

'Who was that?' Pete asked as Max joined them in the tent.

'John Hewitt. He's a reporter. A stringer. He'll sell this story to the papers in Mount Isa and Brisbane. He'll probably do some radio too, when he can. But he's got to leave here and drive most of the way back to the Creek if

148

he's going to do that. There are some advantages to having no mobile signal out here.' He gave a wry smile.

Tia flicked her eyes towards the car, and the man inside barely visible through the driving rain. She wondered just how many photos he had already taken. And of what.

'We don't have to worry too much about him,' Max said as casually as he could. 'If he gets too troublesome we can always get Jessica on to him.'

He looked around as if expecting people to react. Tia had no idea what he was talking about. Nor, it seemed, did the others.

'When Jess first arrived in the Creek,' Max explained, 'she was trying to get away from some bad publicity over her past. Drug agents found cocaine on her plane. She didn't know it was there. She had been tricked by some scumbag drug dealer. She turned him in and wasn't ever charged. In fact she was a witness against the guilty ones, but the press gave her a hard time. She came here to hide, I guess. That reporter spotted her and figured out who she was. He threatened to expose her. But in the end, she stood up for herself. She decided it was time to stop running and instead she gave him a piece of her mind. That was before Jess and Adam got married.'

He looked directly at Tia as he spoke. She could read the message in his eyes. It's all right to have a past, he was telling her. A past can be forgiven and overcome. But Max didn't see the yawning gap between Jess's story and Tia's. Jess had been innocent. Tia was not.

'Can't you get rid of him?' Tia asked. She tried to sound unconcerned, but failed.

'It's not that easy,' Max answered. 'If I try to send him away, he'll only get more persistent and stick his nose in even further where it's not wanted. However, I can keep him away from that family. They've got enough to deal with right now, without him. If anyone sees him getting too pushy, just let me know. And speaking of Jess, have we had any word?'

Tia nodded.

'Yes. She headed down to pick up the tracker as soon as she'd finished the sweeps over the search area. She landed there, but then a storm hit them too. It was much worse than this one. I get the feeling it was pretty fierce and for a while it looked like she was going to be stuck there overnight, but it's cleared now and she's on the way back to the Creek. She radioed through that she should land just before sunset. She'll bring the trackers out here at first light tomorrow.'

'Not tonight?' Sarah frowned.

'Grandpa Pindarri is as old as Methuselah,' said Max with a half-smile. 'He hates flying too, so I expect he'll be a bit shaky when he gets off the plane. It's too late now to do much good. It'll be dark soon and there's no moon. It'll be better tomorrow, when he's at least had some rest. And speaking of rest, we're going to need all hands in the morning. So you two should get some food and a few hours' sleep if you can. We'll be heading out again as soon as it's light.'

Nodding, Pete and Sarah moved off together.

'You've called in an aboriginal tracker?' Tia had to ask. 'I didn't think they existed as such any more.'

Max moved a little closer to her, giving her his full attention. Those brown eyes were compelling, and made her feel a little self-conscious.

'They do and they are very good.'

'I thought that was back in the old days. That it went out with – I don't know – modern technology.'

Max shook his head and grinned. 'There's not much technology way out here.'

He pulled a bottle of almost cold water from the Esky that sat on the ground nearby. He gave it to Tia and then helped himself to another.

'The last tracker officially attached to the police force retired in 2014,' Max said. 'There's nothing official about Grandpa Pindarri. He's lived around this area all his life and I swear he knows every rock and every blade of grass. If anyone can find Renee, it's him.'

'Won't the rain have made it hard? Washed away her footprints?'

'Grandpa doesn't need footprints. He can track like no one else I have ever seen. It's almost as if the earth and the trees and the wind tell him what he needs to know. It's almost mystical, watching him.'

That was surprising. She had thought Max was a pragmatist. It was nice to think he might be willing to believe in miracles, because Tia was beginning to think that was what it was going to take to find the lost child.

'She's been lost and alone for so long. Do you think ...?' Tia's voice trailed off.

'Don't give up.' Max stepped even closer to Tia. He put his hands on her shoulders and looked intently into her face. 'You hear me. Don't give up. Never.'

Was he talking about the search, or was he telling her not to give up on herself? Tia wasn't sure. His hands seemed to almost burn into her shoulders with the intensity of his feelings. His determination and his hope. She so much wanted to believe.

The rain had intensified; it was falling almost like a solid wall, blurring their view of the rest of the campground. Isolating them. Tia felt an overwhelming desire to take that final half step forward, so Max could put his arms around her. So she could lean into his chest and draw strength and comfort from him. And if he wanted to kiss her ...

A sudden burst of blinding light followed instantly by a crash of thunder caused them both to jump. Max let his hands fall and Tia felt almost bereft.

'Did you ever hear that song,' Max said. 'It's an old song called "Little Boy Lost". It was a hit back in the sixties. And no, I'm not that old, but I remember my parents playing it. Mum loved it.' He hummed a few bars.

'Don't give up the day job.' Tia had to smile.

'The point is that it tells a true story of a little boy who went missing in the mountains of New South Wales. He was only four or five years old. I read about it at the academy. It was the biggest search in Australia's history. Four days and three nights. They finally found him with the help of an aboriginal tracker. Found him alive. If they did it – so can we. We will find Renee. I won't stop until we do.'

Tia watched his face as he talked. She saw the passion there and determination. Max really cared. An honest cop who cared about people. Why hadn't she come face to face with someone like Max when she was a runaway and lost in the squats and squalor and the gangs on the wrong side of the tracks?

As quickly as it had arrived, the storm was passing. The rain had eased and the darkness was lifting into a dim twilight. Within minutes the campsite was steaming as the rainwater evaporated or sank into the parched earth.

'I'm going to get some searchers out, make use of this last bit of light,' Max said. 'If she was asleep, the storm would have woken her up. They won't get too far before we lose the light altogether. But we have to try.'

He set off across the campground to where weary searchers were struggling out of the cars they had sheltered in. The door of the motorhome opened, and a man emerged to join them. Tia saw the reporter snapping photographs – but from a distance. He was obviously taking Max's warning to heart. She was tempted to stay in her shelter. Stay hidden. No. She'd had enough of hiding. Instead, she followed Max, notebook in hand, ready to take down the names of the searchers.

Max woke in the pre-dawn darkness, to the sound of someone sobbing. He lay for a moment, listening and gathering his sleep-scattered thoughts. He was lying inside his search headquarters, his head resting on a rolled up jacket. The folding table with radio and clipboards and empty water bottles was almost within arm's reach. He lay still for a minute, knowing that when he did move, every bone in his body would hurt from sleeping on a hard earth floor.

Last night, the exhausted and disheartened searchers had stumbled back into camp just after full darkness had fallen. Once they had all checked in, it had been Max's duty to knock on the door of the motorhome and tell the Haywoods that the search was over for the day. It would resume in the morning. He had backed quietly out of the door, leaving the family alone with their fear and pain. He'd also made damn sure that reporter didn't disturb them.

The searchers had clustered around the food tent, where Sarah and Tia had dished out food and water and sympathy. Not one of them so much as suggested going home. Every single one had found a place to snatch a few hours rest. Exhausted as they were, they would all be ready to start again at first light.

These were good people. The very best.

Max slowly lifted his aching body into a sitting position and looked around. The first thing he saw was Tia.

She was asleep beside him. Close enough that he could simply reach out and brush that lovely red hair from her face. A few of the searchers had thought to bring blankets or sleeping bags with them. He'd made sure Tia got one. It had been well after midnight when she finally curled up and dropped almost instantly into a heavy sleep. Like the rest of them, she'd had a restless night. She had pushed the blanket aside and her clothes were rucked and rumpled. He could easily see the tattoo that disappeared so enticingly under the fabric of her top, but in the darkness, he couldn't quite make out what it was. She'd kicked off her boots and socks, and her bare feet twitched a little as she slept.

Max could have spent an hour there, just watching her sleep. Everything about her moved him. The sexy tattoo and those shapely feet. The luscious dark red hair, that even tangled and unkempt made his fingers ache to touch it. She was smart and funny. She cared about people too, even though she tried to hide it. And there was that vulnerability about her. She was running away from something. He didn't have to be a policeman to know that. When he got back to Coorah Creek, he could run some more checks through the police system. But he knew he wouldn't. Tia had to let go. More than anything, he wanted Tia to trust him enough to tell him what she was running from. Or maybe who she was running from. He couldn't help her until she was ready to help herself.

He heard the sobbing again and for one moment thought it was Tia. But she lay softly sleeping. Careful not to disturb her, Max got to his feet. Stepping out of the tent, he stretched to ease the aches from his body and looked around.

The little boy, Dustin, was sitting on the steps of the motorhome, sobbing as if his heart was breaking. Max felt a surge of sympathy. This must be so hard for him. He was about to head over to the child when he saw someone approaching from the direction of some parked cars. It was

Pete. Max watched the truck driver take a seat next to the boy and place his arms around those shaking shoulders. The boy turned his face into the man's chest, and cried for his sister.

Max looked up at the sky. Stars still shone in the inky blackness, but in the east there was maybe the faintest suggestion of light. Dawn wasn't far away. He needed to start planning. Despite what he'd said to Tia, if they didn't find Renee today ...

Max was beginning to feel desperate for a cup of coffee, when the sound of approaching engines began waking the sleeping searchers. One by one they struggled to their feet. Syd Warren emerged quickly from the first car and began carrying boxes to the food tent which his wife had run the day before. Within minutes, he had a gas fire burning and the rich smell of coffee began to waft across the campsite.

'Thanks,' Max said as Syd handed him the first steaming tin mug. 'Trish staying in town today?'

'Yep. She was pretty exhausted yesterday. We're neither of us as young as we used to be. She's got the phones though if you need her.'

'Thanks for coming out. You've got no idea how much I needed this.' Max raised the coffee mug. 'In fact, can I grab another one for Tia before you get swamped?'

The waking search teams were gathering around, drawn by the smell of coffee and the chance of food.

Max carried the two mugs back to his search HQ, where Tia was now on her feet, talking to her boss, Chris Powell.

'Hi, Chris,' Max said, handing a mug to Tia. She sent him a grateful look.

'I've got everyone who's not needed at the mine with me,' Chris said. 'I figured some fresh eyes might help. Jess is staying at the airstrip. The plane is refuelled and ready to go ... just in case.'

'Good,' said Max.

'I brought Grandpa Pindarri too. He's over there.'

Max looked across the campsite. An impossibly old aboriginal man was standing staring out into the bush. Two younger men were beside him.

'It looks like he's already started,' Max said. 'I'd better go talk to him and find out where he wants me to concentrate the search.'

'Max ...' Tia stepped to his side. She was watching the old man. 'Today, I want to go out there. I'm fresher than some of the others. I can help.'

Max nodded. 'Yes, you can. Sarah hurt her ankle yesterday. She doesn't want to make a fuss, but she was limping when she got back. I'll get her to take over the HQ and you can go with Pete. Maybe you'll bring us good luck.'

She smiled almost shyly and nodded. Max wished he could put his arms around her. He wanted to tell her that he understood how hard it was for her to let down her guard and let people get close to her. He wanted her to know how glad he was that she was becoming part of this community that he cared so much about. But he didn't have time. There was a child out there, and every wasted moment reduced their chances of finding her alive.

A young man detached himself from the group of searchers and came over to where Max stood.

'Sergeant Delaney. I just wanted to say thank you for the carvings that you gave to Anna. She loves them.'

'You're welcome, Steve,' Max said. 'And thank you for coming out today.'

'Of course. I had to. I can only imagine how I would feel if it was Anna out there. Just tell me how I can help.'

'Come with me.' Max put his arm on the younger man's shoulder. 'It's time we got the search teams out there.'

Chapter Nineteen

'How does he do it?' Tia watched fascinated as Grandpa Pindarri moved his gnarled and twisted hands through the wispy tops of the long dry grass.

'I have no idea,' Pete said. 'But apparently he's done this before and always found the person he was looking for.'

'It's all about observation.' One of the younger aboriginal men joined them. 'His father taught him. He taught my father. And me too. He's the best.'

'What's he see that we don't?' Tia asked. 'There can't be any footprints. They will have washed away in the rain last night.'

'Maybe. Maybe not. There will be some traces left. He sees the way the grass is bent. Or a rock recently overturned. A scuff mark is all he needs.'

'But there have been dozens of people out here searching,' Pete added. 'The ground must be covered with scuff marks.'

'A man makes a very different mark to a little girl.'

'Eh, Dave. Come 'ere.'

'Coming, Grandpa.' Dave gave Tia and Pete a nod and moved forward to offer his grandfather a hand as he climbed over some jagged rocks.

'This way,' the old man said. 'She went this way.'

There were about ten people following where the tracker led. Dave had warned them to stay back a bit. His grandfather didn't like a lot of noise when he tracked.

'He likes us to think he's listening to the earth and the wind,' Dave had said with a smile as they started out. 'Maybe he is. But maybe he just doesn't like too many people near him.'

Tia had smiled at the affection in Dave's voice.

Now, watching the old man at work, she almost believed the part about the earth and the wind. He would simply stop suddenly, for no obvious reason. He'd look slowly around him, his dark eyes appearing almost unfocused beneath a shock of curly snow-white hair. He might even bend over to touch the red earth. Or perhaps a tuft of wiry brown grass that to Tia looked no different from the rest of the grass around it. Then he would take a deep breath.

'That way.' There was never any doubt in his voice and the finger he pointed didn't ever waver.

She wondered how many years he had been tracking. He certainly looked as old as the weathered red rocks around him. His dark face was deeply lined and parched by the sun. His hands shook and he paused frequently to catch his breath. But something about him inspired confidence. Tia knew that if she was the one lost in the bush, this was the man she would want tracking her. And Max was the man she would want leading the search.

The old man belonged to the land. He was part of it and it was part of him. Max, on the other hand, belonged to the town and its people. He might not see it that way. But he was part of them, as they were of him.

How she envied that. It must feel very good to belong. To be a part of something. Maybe one day she would have that too.

'So, you ride that red Harley,' Pete offered as they made their way through the scrub, peering about them for any sign of Renee.

Tia felt her hackles rise, but fought down the feeling. It was a harmless question. She shouldn't let it get to her.

'Yep.'

'You almost drove it under my truck one night, you know.'

Tia paused and thought back. 'You drive the big white Merc.' It wasn't a question.

'Yep,' Pete echoed.

'Sorry.' She meant it too, and that surprised her. She had spent most of her life refusing to apologise for anything. Maybe the town was getting to her. Or maybe it was someone in the town …

In the distance they heard a sound. They both froze and listened carefully. The voice came again. It was someone calling the little girl's name.

'It feels strange not to be calling for her,' Pete said. 'Sarah spent all day yesterday calling her name. By the end of the day she could hardly talk.'

'I bet she's glad not to be out here today. She was hobbling earlier when she came into the radio tent.'

'Honestly, I think she'd rather be out here helping. That's the sort of person she is, but her foot just wasn't up to it.'

'Well, I'm glad to have the chance to do my bit,' Tia said.

They walked in silence for a few more minutes. The old man paused and turned in a circle. He bent and touched the earth. Then he stood and stretched his arms wide.

'She was here,' the old man said. 'Twice. She walks in circles. You.' He pointed to Tia and Pete. 'You go there.' He indicated the hint of a trail of to their left. 'Kangaroos made that trail. She might follow. Dave, you go too. You others. You come with me.'

Another of the old man's relatives stepped to his side, ready to assist him if he needed it. Dave caught Pete and Tia's eye, and nodded in the direction they were to go. He set out a little more briskly than his grandfather, but soon slowed down, peering carefully at the earth and the rocks and grass. As he tracked, he was very much a younger version of the man who had taught him.

Pete and Tia followed at a distance, looking into the

undergrowth and the shadows beside the rocks. Just in case.

'This waiting is going to kill me.'

There was no answer. Sarah was alone at the campsite. After sending all the search teams on their way, Max had taken only a few minutes to show Sarah how to use the radio, before he too had set out. He and the park ranger, Dan Mitchell, were going to check out some caves. They were at the very edge of what Max considered the reasonable search area, but, as he said, a small girl could run a very long way if she was scared enough.

The Haywood family were still here. Or at least the mother and son were inside the motorhome. The father had gone with Dan and Max, saying he had to do something. He couldn't stand another day of just waiting for news.

Sarah understood how he felt. She felt like that at times, wondering about her father. It was a month until his next set of tests. And even if those tests were clear, there'd be more ahead. It would be a year or two before they could feel relatively certain he had the disease beaten. Even then, would they ever be totally sure? Which left Sarah facing a difficult decision. Should she stay in Coorah Creek or go back to building a life away from her home town? She had a degree now. She could get a good job. She could travel to the far-flung places she had often read about. When she was a child, the road had called to her. She had watched Pete drive off into the distance, wishing she could go with him. Now she could go as far as she wanted. Brisbane. Sydney. Even New York or London. They were out there waiting for her. There were so many places to go and people to meet. It was what she had always wanted.

But did she still want it?

She looked around the empty campsite. It was empty

because almost the entire town of Coorah Creek was out there in the bush, sweating under the blazing sun. They were there to help a little girl who was a stranger to them. To help a family they had never met. It felt awesome to be part of such a community effort. She knew all these same people would be there for her father and mother too, if things got worse. How could Sarah leave?

And then there was Pete. All those childish feelings for Pete had come back – but this time they were different. They were a woman's feelings. She had never felt like this about anyone she'd dated in the city.

Why on earth would she go back to Brisbane, when it seemed everything she wanted and needed to be a part of was right here in Coorah Creek? She didn't have to make the decision now, but soon she would.

The door of the motorhome opened, and a small boy descended the steps, looking about him. From the corner of her eye, Sarah saw movement near the car park. It was that reporter. Quickly she walked over to the lad, using her body to shield him from the reporter's view.

'Is Pete here?' Dustin asked in a very small voice.

'No, honey, he's out helping to look for your sister.'

The boy nodded. His face almost broke Sarah's heart.

'Where's your mother?'

'She's asleep. I think she and Daddy were awake most of the night. They argued too. And I heard Mummy crying.'

Sarah put her arm around the boy's hunched shoulders and drew him closer for a quick hug. 'Parents argue sometimes. But it's not important. The important thing is that they love each other. And they love you and your sister. That's why your mummy was crying. Because she wants Renee to come home.'

'I want her to come home too.'

'I know you do.' Sarah thought quickly. 'I have to go sit over there,' she pointed to her tent, 'near the radio.'

'Can I come too?'

'Of course you can.' The news that came out of that radio might be good or it might be bad. But sitting alone and waiting would be worse for young Dustin. 'You could keep me company,' she said. 'And help me listen to the radio.'

'I can do that,' Dustin offered. 'Will Pete be calling in?'

'He might.'

The boy's face brightened. 'And if you want something to eat or drink, I know where it's all put over in the other tent. Syd showed me before he went back into town for more supplies. He said I was to make sure that no one went without food or water.'

'That's an important job,' Sarah said as they moved back into the shade of the tent and settled near the radio. 'I'm sure you'll do it well.'

The boy sat down. 'Will Pete be back soon?' he asked. 'He's just great. I feel better when Pete is here.'

Sarah ruffled the boy's hair. 'So do I, Dustin. So do I.'

Chapter Twenty

Max ran his fingers through his hair, and looked up at the sky. The sun was moving inexorably towards the west but there were still three or four hours of daylight left. Their search of the caves had been fruitless. He had expected as much, but they were running out of time, and he was not going to leave any place unchecked. Over by their vehicle, Dan was on the radio. He caught Max's eye and shook his head a fraction. No news.

No news was good news. Right?

Not at the end of the second full day of searching it wasn't.

He thought back to the case he'd studied at the academy. Four-year-old Steven Walls had survived for four days and three nights and been found eleven kilometres from where he went missing. Renee was six, but where Steven had been bush born and bred, she was a city kid. She didn't know what to eat or not eat in the bush. And Tyangi was a very different place to the mountains where Steven had gone missing. In the mountains, there had been creeks with clean water and shady places for the child to rest. There was no water here, and under the blazing sun in this part of the outback, water was everything.

He looked over to the mouth of the caves they had just searched. Renee's father was slumped against a red sandstone boulder. His head was in his hands, and his hunched shoulders were shaking. Max knew the man was crying. His despair hung over him like a cloud. In all his years as a policeman, Max had never felt able to help someone suffering such profound grief. They didn't teach that at the academy. He did his best, but was never sure he'd done it right.

Like this search. He'd done the best he could. The townsfolk had rallied around, as they always did. Jess was back in the air again today, with Rachel Quinn as spotter. The trackers he'd brought in were the very best. But there were too few of them. When they had found Steven Walls alive, it had taken more than four thousand people. And several aircraft. He didn't have those resources to call upon. But he was not about to give up. Not while there was even a glimmer of hope. If he had to search alone, he would do so until he found her.

Dan appeared beside him. 'I guess we should head back.'

'I guess so.'

They stood in silence for a few moments, watching the broken man by the cave mouth.

'The poor bugger,' Dan said.

That was something of an understatement.

'I'll get him.' Max walked slowly over to Mr Haywood.

At the sound of Max's footsteps, Haywood looked up. His eyes were ringed with red and tears streaked the sweat and dirt on his cheeks. The hope that flared in his eyes was quashed instantly when he saw the look on Max's face. His shoulders heaved and he buried his face in his hands again.

'She ... she's dead, isn't she?' His voice broke.

'Don't say that.' Max laid his hand on the distraught man's shoulder. 'Kids are stronger than we think. You're a father. You know that. Don't give up on Renee, Evan. I don't plan to, so you can't either.'

'It's my fault,' the distraught father sobbed. 'Hazel was always at me for spending too much time at work. She insisted we take a family holiday. She wanted to go to the beach, but I said we should come out here. It wasn't just for the holiday. I wanted to look at some aboriginal art. I thought that would be good for my business. I was working again. I wasn't paying attention when Renee ... And now she's lost and it's my fault.'

Privately, Max might have thought there was some truth in those words. But dishing out blame wasn't going to do anyone any good.

'No,' he said. 'It's not anyone's fault. What we need to do now is focus on finding her. All right?'

Haywood nodded.

'Good.' Max gave him a minute to pull himself together. He picked up a water bottle that was sitting at the man's feet and passed it to him.

'We're heading back to camp now.'

Haywood looked at the bottle in his hands. 'Oh God. She hasn't got any water out there. And it's so hot ...'

'Stop that!' Max said firmly. 'That's not going to help. Your wife and son are back at camp. They need you to be strong.'

Haywood took a long deep breath, then slowly stood up. 'You're right,' he said. 'Let's go.'

They walked back to the car. Evan got into the back seat and remained silent as they drove back to the main search site.

The camp was almost deserted when they returned. Max saw John Hewitt, the reporter, helping himself to water at the food tent. Sarah was standing by the radio. No sooner had Haywood stepped out of the car, than his son appeared at Sarah's side.

'Dad!' The boy raced across the campsite and flung himself into his father's arms. Haywood gathered Dustin into a massive bear hug, lifting him off the ground.

The click of Hewitt's camera made Max frown. He knew the man was just doing a job, but at times like this, it was a shitty job. If he could, Max would ban him from

165

the search site. But he really couldn't, and now wasn't the time to start a fight.

Haywood looked over his son's head at Max, his eyes full of gratitude and despair. Then he turned and carried the boy back towards the motorhome. As he approached, the door opened. Mrs Haywood ran down the stairs to fling her arms around her son and her husband. For a long minute they just stood there, any past problems pushed aside by their desperate need for comfort. Max had to wonder if maybe the family might end up stronger as a result of these few terrible days. But that would only happen if they found Renee ... alive.

Max joined Sarah in the shade of the tent, keeping a close eye on Hewitt to make sure he didn't bother the Haywoods.

'My heart aches for them,' Sarah said as the door of the motorhome closed behind the small family.

'I know,' Max said. He glanced up at the sky. 'There's still a fair stretch of daylight left. Let's not give up hope yet.'

Pete had long since given up any attempt to really see the track they were following. Dave just seemed to know where to go. He paused now, looking in two directions.

'See, she was here,' he said, pointing to the ground.

Pete and Tia both crowded forward. Pete looked down at the ground and saw nothing to indicate the girl had been there; just red dirt that had already lost all traces of moisture from yesterday's downpour. Thank goodness they weren't relying on Pete's eyes. He trusted Dave. The tracker knew what he was doing.

'How long?' he asked.

'Hard to say. Today. Definitely today. See here, the dirt is still wet where she kicked that rock.'

It didn't look wet to Pete, although it might have been just a fraction darker than the ground around it.

'Then she can't be too far away.' Pete glanced at Tia and saw her face reflecting his own hope.

'Now you call for her,' Dave instructed.

'Renee! Renee!' Tia called.

They held their breaths and waited, listening carefully. There was no reply.

'Maybe she's asleep. Tired. We'll keep going. You keep calling her name.' Dave cast his eye over the ground again and started walking.

Pete felt his energy return. They were close. He glanced at Tia and saw the same hope in her eyes. The sun was sinking in the west. They had some daylight left, but not too much. They had to find her. Soon. His instincts told him that the little girl might not survive another night out here alone.

'Do you think we should try to get more searchers to this area?' Tia asked.

The same thought was forming in Pete's mind. There were other search parties not too far away.

'Maybe,' he said.

Tia called Renee's name again. Still no answer.

Just ahead of them, Dave stopped in his tracks. He bent down to touch his fingers to the earth.

'She's close,' he said. 'We need more people.' Dave lifted his hands to his face and took a deep breath. 'Cooee!'

The harsh cry seemed to echo through the bush. Nearby, a big white bird flew startled from a tree.

'Cooee!' Dave called again, his voice rising to a high note that swept through the bush like the crack of a whip.

This time there was an answering call, faint but clear, from some distance away.

'That's Grandpa,' Dave said. 'I bet their track is coming

back towards us from the other side of that ridge there. They'll be with us soon.'

Tia suddenly froze.

'Wait. Listen!'

Pete listened carefully. 'I don't hear—'

Tia grabbed his arm and motioned him into silence.

'Renee,' she called, loud enough for her voice to carry, but not loud enough to frighten an already terrified child.

Then Pete heard it too. It sounded like someone sobbing.

'This way,' Tia said, moving to her left.

Pete followed, his heart thumping. Tia reached out to grab his hand and he held on to her as if he were afraid that she too would get lost.

'Renee!' Tia called again.

This time she was answered with what sounded like a child calling for her mother.

'Renee!'

Tia let go of Pete's hand and pushed her way through a patch of scrubby undergrowth. He was right behind her when she stopped dead in her tracks. Pete looked past her.

The little girl was huddled against a fallen tree. Her clothes were torn and her skin was burned a fierce red by the sun. Her face was dirty and scratched and streaked with tears and her brown eyes were wide open. In her hands she clutched a bedraggled yellow teddy bear.

'I want my mummy,' Renee cried.

Chapter Twenty-One

The little girl's cry went straight to Tia's heart. In three steps she had closed the distance between them. She dropped to her knees and gathered Renee up into her arms. The girl stiffened for a few moments then she dropped her teddy bear and wrapped her thin arms around Tia's neck and started to sob in earnest.

Tia lifted her gently and then sat down on the tree trunk. She cradled the child in her lap, rocking backwards and forwards.

'It's all right, Renee. You're safe now. We'll have you back with your mummy and daddy real soon, honey. I promise we will.'

The arms around her neck tightened, and the sobs continued. Tia thought her own heart would break. She remembered all the times when she had been alone and hurt and crying, and no one had come to her. Tears welled up in her eyes and slid silently down her cheeks.

'Shhh, it's all right,' she crooned, using the words she had longed to hear when she was a lost and frightened child. 'You're safe now.'

Something tapped Tia on the shoulder. She looked up to see Pete holding a bottle of water for her. Tears were on his cheeks too.

'Thanks.' She took it. Pete had already removed the lid. 'Here, Renee, I bet you're thirsty.'

Renee lifted her face from Tia's shirt and grabbed for the bottle with both hands.

'Careful,' Tia said. 'Sip it slowly, honey, or else you'll make yourself sick.'

Renee wasn't listening, so Tia gently took the bottle from her after a couple of mouthfuls.

'Slowly,' she said again.

Renee looked up at her with tear-filled brown eyes and nodded.

'Good,' Tia said gently. 'Now, honey, are you hurt?'

Renee nodded. 'I scratched myself. It hurt.'

Tia looked carefully at the scratches on the girl's face and arms. There were brown smears of dried blood, but none of them looked serious. Of more concern was the bright redness of her sunburned skin. Renee was going to suffer with that.

'I can see you did scratch yourself,' Tia told the little girl. 'But I think it's going to be all right. You are such a brave little girl. I bet your sunburn hurts too.'

With a solemn face, Renee nodded.

'We'll get you to see Doctor Adam soon. He's a nice man and a very good doctor. He'll make it all better. But in the meantime here, you should wear my hat.' Tia placed her hat over the little girl's head. It was far too large, but it would still help protect Renee from the sun.

Tia continued to carefully monitor how much Renee drank while all the time talking to her gently.

'That's enough for now, honey,' she said as she took the bottle again and handed it back to Pete. 'You can have some more in a little while.'

She suddenly realised there was noise all around her. She had been so concerned with the little girl, she hadn't noticed that Dave's 'cooee' had brought other searchers to their location. She could hear them talking and slapping Pete and Dave on the back, celebrating a longed-for but uncertain happy end to their search.

'I'm hungry,' Renee said. 'And I want my mummy and daddy.'

'I know, honey.'

Tia looked at Pete. He swung his pack off his back and dug inside for a sandwich.

'All right, Renee,' Tia said. 'We have a sandwich here. But you can't eat it all at once. Just a couple of small bites for now, okay? You can have some more when we get back to the camp.'

Renee nodded as she took the offered food.

Tia stood up, the child still in her arms. Any weariness she had been feeling had been driven away by the euphoria of the moment. Renee stared over her shoulder at the men and women clustered around them.

'Do you want me to take her?' Pete asked.

'No. I've got her,' Tia said.

'Can someone run on ahead and let them know,' Pete asked of the crowd around them. 'Tell her parents she's safe. Get Doctor Adam on the radio so we can find out what he wants us to do.'

'I can do that,' a voice said from the back of the crowd, followed immediately by the sound of someone running through the bush.

The group parted to let Tia carry Renee through. Pete walked at her side, carrying Renee's battered teddy bear. A few people reached out to touch the little girl, as if to reassure themselves that she really was alive and well.

As they passed Dave and Grandpa Pindarri, the old man gently patted Renee's head. It was almost a blessing.

'Thank you,' Tia said to the two trackers, and was answered with two very happy smiles.

They walked back, gathering more searchers as they went. At one point, Tia handed Renee to Pete, while she caught her breath. Her arms felt empty without the little girl and, as soon as she felt able, she took Renee back. For her part, the child was happy to bury her face in Tia's shoulder, although she occasionally lifted her head to stare wide-eyed at the people following behind them.

They were quite a crowd by the time they reached the campsite. When she emerged from among the trees, the first thing Tia saw was Renee's parents standing by the tent. The second thing she saw was Max standing with them. He heard the people approaching and turned. A huge smile lit his face as he saw Tia and her companions.

'Mummy!'

'Renee!'

The little girl wriggled in Tia's arms. Tia put her down and she ran towards her family. Her parents scooped her up and she was lost in a joyous reunion. The little girl almost disappeared in a family embrace that also included her big brother. Tia felt tears pricking her eyes. All around the campsite, people were cheering and applauding.

Max left the reunited family for a few moments and came to hug her.

'Thank you, from everyone,' he whispered in her ear.

'It wasn't me,' she said. 'Dave led us to her. I just ...'

'You just helped save a little girl's life,' Max said. 'We are all so proud of you.'

How good his arms felt around her. And his words of praise were the sweetest thing she had ever heard. Exhausted as she was, she suddenly felt about ten feet tall.

'Go get some food and water,' Max said as he, reluctantly it seemed, released her. 'And when all this is over, I am buying you dinner. No arguments.'

'I wasn't going to argue.'

The smile he gave her seemed full of meaning. Feeling as if her heart was going to burst, she slipped quietly away from the crowd and wandered over to the food tent where Syd Warren stood, sporting a smile so broad it looked as if his face would split in half.

'Drop by the pub some time soon,' he said. 'Dinner is on the house.'

She nodded as she picked up a bottle of water, twisted the top off and drank deeply. Then she looked around her with the feeling of deepest satisfaction. She had played her part in something amazing and in doing so, for the first time in a very long time, she felt like she belonged. Not only that, but this place to which she belonged was a good place.

Like many people in the campground, Sarah had tears in her eyes as she watched Renee reunited with her family. When two of the searchers had run into camp a few minutes ago with the news, a cheer had gone up that must have been heard for miles. The Haywood family had emerged from their motorhome, and the looks on their faces had been enough to lift even the most exhausted searcher's heart.

She'd radioed the news to Mount Isa police, who were now trying to set up a link with Doctor Adam. Their first concern had to be getting the little girl to him for a check-up. There was no way Jess's air ambulance could land here. They'd have to drive Renee back to Coorah Creek. Max had already decided they weren't going to leave until they had at least talked to Adam on the radio and had instructions on what to do. It was a long drive to the Creek, and they wanted the little girl to be as comfortable as possible.

A tall figure detached itself from the crowd and Pete walked over to join her in the tent where she was seated with her injured ankle bandaged and resting on another chair.

'So I guess you're her knight in shining armour now as well,' Sarah said. 'I always knew you were a hero.' She stood awkwardly on her toes and kissed him on the cheek.

'I just happened to be in the right place at the right time,'

Pete said, running his hand through his hair. 'I'm not a hero.'

'You are just a man who has spent two days and nights out here searching for a little lost girl. A little girl who is now safe. Don't tell me that's nothing.'

Pete's lips twitched, and slowly a smile spread over his face.

'We found her,' he said quietly. 'We found her!' This time it was a cry of satisfaction as he picked Sarah up and laughed joyfully as he spun her around. He lowered her carefully back to the ground and crushed her to him in a vigorous hug. 'She's going to be fine. That's just—'

Before Pete could finish the sentence, the radio beside them crackled into life.

Keeping one hand on Pete's arm for support, Sarah hopped over to the table and grabbed the handset.

'Adam. Is that you?'

'You've found her?'

'Yes.' Sarah couldn't keep the joy from her voice. 'Pete and Tia found her. She's back here now with her parents.'

'She's likely to be suffering from symptoms of exposure. Dehydration too. Be careful – don't let her drink too much.'

Pete reached out to take the radio microphone from Sarah's hand. 'Doc, it's Pete here. She's been sipping water, but only a small mouthful every few minutes, as you said.'

'Good. How does she look?'

'She's got a few cuts and scratches, but they don't look serious. She's really sunburnt but she's alert and talking to us. She said she was hungry so we let her eat half a vegemite sandwich.'

Sarah took half a step back and listened to Pete talk to the doctor. His answers were straight to the point and informative. He listened intently as Adam gave his instructions. There was such strength about Pete. Sarah knew that above all else he was a man you could depend on. Trust him to be there when he was needed. To do the right thing.

Sarah's emotions were already running high, with the joy and excitement of the last few minutes. But new feelings were swamping her now, and they were all to do with Pete. With the way he had kissed her. The way he looked at her now, his eyes shining with pleasure – not for himself but for others.

She knew it then. She had loved Pete Rankin since she was ten years old. And she still did. And he felt something for her too. She knew he did. A new kind of joy bubbled through her. They would get little Renee safely into the doctor's care. Then she and Pete could take some time to explore this new thing between them. This new thing that had grown from a seed that had been a part of her for as long as she could remember. Pete was still talking on the radio, but his eyes met hers and he smiled.

'Got all that,' he said.

Sarah had no idea what 'all that' was. She hadn't been paying attention to the voice on the radio. But Pete would have it. You could always rely on Pete.

'Fine. Get underway and get her in here as soon as you can. I'll be waiting.'

Pete handed the radio microphone back to Sarah. 'Adam thinks she's going to be fine, but he wants to see her at the hospital as soon as possible to check her out. I guess her parents will want to go too. They can travel with her. I can follow on behind in their motorhome, if they want me to.'

Sarah was letting the emotion of the moment run away with her. She knew she was. But at the same time, all she could think was how Pete was still willing to go that little bit further to help.

Before she could say anything, another voice came through the radio.

'Are you still there?'

'Yes,' she said.

'Mount Isa police back again. Can you get a message to one of the searchers? Pete Rankin.'

'He's right here,' Sarah said.

'Good. Tell him he needs to get back to Mount Isa as quickly as he can. To the hospital.'

Sarah's breath caught in her throat. Something was wrong. She impulsively reached out to touch Pete's hand, to give him a taste of the comfort he had given others, including her.

'He's listening,' she said, her voice catching in her throat in sudden unexplained fear.

'It's his girlfriend,' said the disembodied voice. 'There's a problem with the baby. He needs to come home.'

Chapter Twenty-Two

A problem with the baby.

Those awful words rang in Pete's ears. He grabbed the mike out of Sarah's hand. 'What problem? Is Linda all right? And the baby?'

'I don't have the details,' said the disembodied voice. 'Only a message for you to go to the hospital as soon as you can get back.'

Pete's head spun with terrible images of what might have happened.

'I'll leave right away. Can you tell Linda I'm coming but I'm almost ten hours away. I'll drive through the night and be there as soon as I can,' he said and dropped the handset back on the table. As he looked up, he saw Sarah.

Her face was white, and the light in her eyes was gone. She looked as if her whole world had suddenly shattered. Pete suddenly realised the impact of that radio call on the girl who, just minutes ago, had been in his arms.

'Sarah ...' he started to say.

She shook her head. Her eyes held his for a fraction of a second as emotion flared in their tawny depths. That look felt like a cold steel thrust into his heart. She was hurt and disappointed and angry – at him. With slow deliberate movements, she turned away and left the tent. She was limping because of her injured ankle, but obviously determined to get away from him as quickly as possible, despite the pain. He wanted to call her back, but what could he say that would change anything? He stood rooted to the spot as the cheerful congratulations of the search team still echoed around him.

He would have gone after her. That's what his heart told

him to do. To tell her everything and explain. He needed to make things right between the two of them if that was possible. But he couldn't. He had to get to Mount Isa, because Linda was carrying his child and she needed him.

He found Max and quickly passed on the doctor's instructions. Max needed to get the little girl to Coorah Creek as soon as he could. Without further explanation Pete then slipped away. He glanced at the Haywoods. They were still huddled together around Renee. He saw Dustin looking around, and Pete knew the boy was looking for him. He wanted to go and talk to him, if only to say goodbye, but there wasn't time. He hated to disappoint a child, but he had to leave.

In the car park, the searchers were beginning to make their way home. Pete quickly found someone with a spare seat who was willing to give him a lift back to the Creek. Pete slipped into the back seat of the car, hoping to avoid conversation. He leaned back and closed his eyes. All the searchers were exhausted. He hoped they would think he was asleep and leave him alone with his thoughts.

They were pretty uncomfortable thoughts.

The events of the past few days flashed through his brain in a kaleidoscope of sensations. He could feel the weight of young Renee in his arms as he helped Tia carry her home to her family. He could still hear a father crying for his child and Dustin's voice, quavering with emotion as he blamed himself for his sister's disappearance. If Pete closed his eyes he could see Sarah, determined to carry on the search despite her bad ankle. He could taste her lips and feel the touch of her fingers on his skin. His heart jumped at just the memory of that kiss. But most of all he could see the hurt in her eyes as she turned away from him. On top of all that, he was overwhelmed with concern for Linda and their baby. The child he had never wanted now seemed the most precious thing and the thought of losing it was almost too much to bear.

'Hey, Pete, wake up. We're back.'

Pete's eyes flashed open. The first thing he saw was his truck, still sitting where he had parked it what seemed like half a lifetime ago. They were back in Coorah Creek. He must have fallen asleep after all. He shook his head to gather his scattered wits.

'Thanks for the lift,' he said as he opened the door.

'No worries. We're going to the pub for a beer to celebrate. Come with us. Our shout for the hero of the day.'

'Thanks, but no. I've got to hit the road. And I'm no hero.'

'Next time. And good work, man. You saved that kid.'

'We all saved that kid,' Pete said.

He turned his back on the men and walked over to his rig. He fished the key out of his pocket and opened her up. A blast of heat poured out of the cabin into his face. He clambered aboard and hit the starter. The air-conditioning came on immediately. Pete took a second to inhale the blast of cool air, before slipping the truck into gear. The engine revved as the big rig started moving. Before he was out of the town limits, Pete had the radio in his hand and was calling his base.

'Hey, Pete. Good to hear from you. According to the ABC radio news, the little girl you were looking for has been found safe and well.'

Pete recognised the voice immediately. His mate Mick was obviously manning the office today, not driving.

'Yeah, she's good, Mick,' he said.

'Umm, Pete. We've been trying to get hold of you.' Mick sounded uncertain. 'It's about Linda.'

'Yeah. I got a message at the search camp. They said she was in hospital.'

'That's right.'

'Do you know how she is?'

'My missus went by to see how she was. Said she's doing okay.'

'And the baby?'

'There was a problem, but the doc says baby is okay too. I don't know any more than that.'

Relief surged through Pete. 'Say thanks to your missus for me,' he said. 'I'm on the road now. Just leaving Coorah Creek. Can you get a message to Linda that I'm on my way? I'll be there as soon as I can.'

'Sure, mate. Will do.'

'I didn't get much sleep last night, so at some point I'll have to stop for a while and get some shut-eye. I'll be there first thing in the morning.'

Pete signed off, thinking as he did that he hadn't sent a personal message to Linda. Hadn't told Mick to give her his love. Nothing like that. Because the truth was, he didn't love her. He loved Sarah. The little girl he had been so fond of had grown into a woman, and his feelings for her had grown too. They had shared just a couple of kisses – but those kisses had changed everything for him.

Almost everything.

It hadn't changed the fact that Linda was pregnant with his child.

A child. An image rose unbidden to his mind of the boy, young Dustin, who had cried for his sister. That boy had looked to Pete to fix everything. And he'd tried. He'd tried so very hard. One day his own child would need someone to make things better for him or her. Pete had to be there to do that. He would never be able to live with himself if he wasn't. It was the right thing to do.

But sometimes the right thing isn't always right. Sarah had said that. And he had come to see the truth in her words. How did she get to be that wise?

Night had fallen and his headlights and powerful spots emitted a long bright shaft of light that made the road ahead very clear.

If only his road was that clear.

Although it was very late by the time he left the Coorah Creek Hospital, Max went straight to his workshop. Despite two nights with very little sleep, he was wide awake. There was a mountain of paperwork waiting for him in his office, but he had no appetite for it.

Renee and her family were safely bedded down at the hospital. Never one for rules, Adam had decided they could all sleep there tonight. He wouldn't call it therapy, but that's what it was. After the trauma of the past three days, that family needed to be together. Adam was not willing to separate them. One of the searchers had driven the motorhome back into town and it was now in the hospital car park. But for Adam, that was still too far away from the bed where Renee lay sleeping deeply. Max had helped him drag another bed into the biggest of the rooms at the hospital, and the entire Haywood family was there now, probably sound asleep through emotional and physical exhaustion.

Chris Powell had taken charge of Grandpa Pindarri and his boys. Jess would fly them back to Warrina Downs in the morning, but in the meantime they were staying at the pub, where Trish no doubt had pulled out all the stops to give them a hearty dinner and make them comfortable.

Max knew he wasn't ready to sleep, but there was something he could do. He flicked on the workshop light, and started sorting through the timber stacked against the back wall. He knew exactly what he was looking for. At last he found the wood he wanted. He turned on the sound system, and after hesitating a moment, he selected the album 'Abbey Road'. As the first chords of 'Come Together' began, he settled himself on a stool and reached for his tools. As he sang softly under his breath, he smiled at the choice he'd made. The community of Coorah Creek had certainly come together when it was needed. What a remarkable group of people they were, and Max felt proud to be a part of them. Trish and Syd, Dan and Quinn, Adam and Jess. The trackers and the mine workers. Pete had helped, and he wasn't even a part of the town. Even young Steve, who was struggling to look after his own family ... all had played their part. That little girl owed her life to them.

He would never forget the sight of Tia walking out of the scrub with Renee in her arms. The little girl had been scratched and sunburned and filthy, but she was alive and the look on her face when she saw her family was a moment to be treasured. A look like that was the reason he had joined the force. That one moment more than made up for the bad parts of his job. Tia had also been dirty, her clothes stained by sweat and red earth. Her lovely red hair had been jammed under her hat and her skin too had been tinged with red from the sun. She'd been the most beautiful thing Max had ever seen. Her face had glowed with happiness as Renee ran into her parents' arms.

In the fuss of getting Renee to the hospital and breaking up the search, he hadn't had time to say more than a few words to Tia. But once things were back to normal, he would seek her out. Tomorrow couldn't come soon enough. He'd buy her that dinner he'd promised her.

His hands moved swiftly as he carved the wood. It was already beginning to take shape. There was a head and a body, strong hind legs and a long tail. He hoped Renee would like it.

After a moment's silence, another song began to float

across the workshop, bringing his thoughts right back to Tia. Something in the way she moved did attract him. And something in the way she smiled. In fact ... pretty much everything about her attracted him like no other. The Beatles had got it right again. And it was definitely time he did something about it.

'Hi.'

She was leaning against his door frame, the glow from the overhead light falling gently onto her face. She'd obviously taken a bit of time to recover from the day's searching. She looked clean and her clothes were fresh. The dampness of her hair made it seem an even darker shade of red. Almost crimson. She must have been tired, but her green eyes were bright.

'I thought you'd be asleep by now,' he said.

'I should be, but I don't seem to be tired.'

He nodded. 'Me neither.'

'What are you working on?' She stepped a little closer and held out her hand. Max gave her the partly finished carving. She turned it over and looked at it closely, running her finger along the lines of the wood.

'It's a kangaroo,' he said unnecessarily.

'Really?' She raised a mocking eyebrow. 'I would never have guessed.'

He smiled, less at her joke and more simply because she was there with him. That was enough.

'I didn't want Renee and Dustin to leave here with nothing but bad memories,' Max said slowly. 'I would hate to think they would never come back to the bush, or visit a national park again. It's probably a bit silly, but I thought a couple of toys ... the roo and maybe a galah or a cockatoo ... would at least give them one good memory of this trip. I guess it's not much compared to the sort of toys their parents can afford to buy them. But

I wanted them both to have something good to remember us all by.'

For a few moments, she didn't say anything. She turned the carving over in her hands. Then swiftly, almost shyly, she stepped forward. She was so close he could simply have pulled her into his arms. He wanted to. More than he had ever wanted anything in his life. But he was afraid that might chase her away. He sat stock-still, aware of her breath on his cheek. And then she brushed her lips gently over his.

'You are a good man, Max Delaney,' she said and then stepped back so quickly he could almost have imagined the kiss. But he hadn't. No imaginary kiss would have left his lips tingling like that, nor aroused such a longing in his heart and soul and body.

The world seemed to slow on its axis. There was no sound but the gentle rustle of the breeze in the trees outside.

'About that dinner,' Tia said softly. 'I have to go back to work tomorrow. The boss had a few blokes working overtime while the rest of us searched. Once I've had some sleep, I need to get back to the job so they can have a break. But Friday … I'm going to be free on Friday. That's if you still want to.'

Max's spirits soared. If he still wanted to? 'Friday it is,' he said, forcing his voice to echo the casual tone of hers.

She hesitated a moment as if to say something more, but then just handed the kangaroo back to him, nodded and silently vanished into the night.

Max sat himself back on the stool and resumed his work. The music wrapped gently around him, and he began to softly sing

'Here comes the sun. It's all right.'

Chapter Twenty-Three

The Mount Isa trucking depot was not the most attractive sight. There were several big warehouses made of unpainted corrugated iron and some were starting to rust. In the corners of the yard, an assortment of old fuel drums and rusting engine parts lay among the long brown tufts of wiry grass. The large parking area was finished in dull grey bitumen and usually held a few trucks. The whole place always seemed to smell of diesel fuel, grease and sweat. The site covered more than three hectares and was surrounded by a two metre high cyclone fence, the chain linked sections topped with barbed wire. To Pete, at this moment, it was a very welcome sight.

The sun was only just peeping over the horizon, but already the big swinging gates were open, and there were people moving around inside. The huge trucks were the lifeline of the outback, and they rarely sat still for long. Pete pulled his rig around to the back of the yard. With relief, he turned the engine off. The drive from the Creek had taken him more than ten hours. Coming on the back of the physical exertion of the search for Renee, he was totally shattered. Emotionally as well as physically. He probably shouldn't have been driving. He was over his hours. He had pulled over to get some sleep, but had simply lain in the sleeping compartment, staring out into the darkness. The turmoil raging in his mind made sleep impossible, so instead he'd driven on through the night.

He jumped down from the rig, and the first thing he saw was Mick walking towards him.

'G'day, Pete.'

'Mick. Any news from the hospital?'

'Not since last night. My missus dropped round and told Linda you were on your way. She said she was really happy about that. Cried a bit, according to the missus, but you know how women are.'

'And the baby is ...?'

'The docs still say everything is okay.'

Pete felt as if someone had lifted the Sydney Harbour Bridge off his shoulders. All night his head had been spinning with worry about his unborn child. When Linda first told him she was pregnant, he was shocked. He hadn't wanted the baby. But things had changed. During these last few days, he had changed. Ever since Dustin had placed his small hand inside Pete's bigger one, Pete had felt something stirring in his heart. This might not be how he planned to have a child, but he wanted that small one now. He would love that child and be the very best father he could be. He still wasn't sure what that meant for his relationship with Linda – or the feelings he had for Sarah. But he no longer doubted his feelings for his child.

'I've got to get to the hospital,' he said, running his fingers through his hair. 'Can I borrow your car?'

'Sure, mate, but don't you want to grab a shower and a cup of coffee first?'

'I ...' Pete hesitated and looked at his watch. It was not quite six thirty. Linda would hopefully still be asleep. The hospital might not even let him in this early. He probably looked like he'd been through a wringer – which he had. He was dirty and his shirt had been torn by some tree branch during the search. He didn't smell very good either. He probably shouldn't startle Linda by turning up looking like this.

'You're right. If we swing past my place I can clean up, and then take my own car to the hospital.'

The shower and change of clothes helped a lot, as did the

smell of the coffee Mick brewed. When Pete walked into the kitchen, his friend handed him a mug of the steaming black liquid. Neither sat down.

'Pete ...' Mick started hesitantly. 'Before this ... I didn't know. I mean about the baby and all.'

'We didn't tell anyone,' Pete said. 'Linda wanted to wait for a while just in case ...' He had been about to say in case something went wrong, but he couldn't finish the sentence.

'I knew the two of you were, you know, but I didn't think it was that serious.' Mick sipped his own coffee and avoided Pete's eyes.

'Well, a baby is pretty serious,' Pete said.

'And you're sure ...?'

'That we want to keep it? Yes, of course we're sure,' Pete said. 'And I'm going to love that kid and do the right thing by it.'

Mick hesitated a fraction of a second, as if he had something else to say. But then he nodded. 'Well, if you're all right, mate, I gotta go. I've got a load to take out this morning.'

'Yeah, Mick, I'm fine. Thanks for the lift.'

'Sure. No worries. Give Linda our best.'

There was no mistaking the smell of a hospital, Pete thought a short time later as he walked through the sliding glass doors. It was after seven thirty now, and the reception desk was open. Two women looked up as he approached. He asked after Linda, explaining why it had taken him this long to get to the hospital.

'Oh, we heard all about the search,' one of the women gushed. 'You were part of that? You helped save that poor little girl. There was such a lovely photo on the ABC website of her and her parents being reunited. How wonderful that you were part of that. It's not visiting hours yet, but I guess for a hero we can make an exception.'

Pete didn't argue. He listened to her directions and set off through the maze of almost deserted hospital corridors. At last he found the right ward, and carefully he entered.

Linda lay sleeping on one of the four beds, covered with just a light cotton sheet. The other beds were unoccupied and Pete was glad of the privacy. Careful not to wake Linda, he crossed the room and slid into a chair, from where he could watch her sleep.

Her face looked a bit pale, and her eyes were red as if she'd been crying. That was probably his fault, because he hadn't been there for her. As he looked at her face, he was swamped with guilt and more. He felt sympathy for Linda, facing this scare alone. He felt concern for her health and for the baby she carried. She stirred a little in her sleep, and her movement pulled the light sheet tighter around her body. For the first time, Pete imagined he could see a slight thickening of her waist. The beginnings of a baby bump. He knew that he would love that child, but he couldn't fool himself any longer. He didn't love Linda. He never would. Sarah had captured his heart a long, long time ago, and he was only just beginning to realise that he didn't ever want to get it back.

He didn't know if Sarah would have him. But even if she didn't, he could not marry Linda. It wouldn't be fair on her, or on their child. Linda was a good person who deserved someone to love her in a way that he never could. He would always be there for her, and for their child, but not as her husband.

It appeared he had made a decision. After all those hours of agonising, the decision had come to him in a moment, because it was the right decision. He knew that it was. Just as he knew that now wasn't the time to tell Linda. She needed all his support. And she would have it. When this crisis had passed and she was stronger, he'd tell her.

Then he would go to Sarah and explain everything. She was hurting. He'd seen that in her face those moments before she turned away from him. He hoped beyond everything that she would listen and forgive him.

His future was with her ... if she would have him, but in the meantime, he had Linda to care for.

She was still sleeping. Pete felt his own head nod. He shook it. He mustn't go to sleep. Tired as he was, he had to be there and awake when Linda woke up.

That was his last thought before his eyes fell shut and darkness claimed him.

Max waited until it was almost lunchtime. He wanted to give the Haywoods as much private time as he could. But duty called and he finally drove down to the hospital. The big motorhome was still in the car park, but it was locked up tight. He hoped it was a rental. He doubted that after the past few days the Haywoods would try another camping holiday.

Doctor Adam met him at the top of the stairs.

'How is Renee?' Max asked.

'She's doing fine,' said Adam. 'You know, kids amaze me. They are so much tougher than we give them credit for.'

'I need to talk to the family,' Max said. 'Paperwork and all that. It won't take long. Are they up for it?'

'Yeah. No worries.'

As both men turned to walk back into the hospital, they came face to face with Evan Haywood.

'Max!' Evan grabbed the policeman's hand and shook it. 'I was about to head into town to find you and say thank you. Thank you so much. I cannot begin to describe—'

'No thanks necessary,' Max interrupted him. 'Adam tells me Renee is doing well.'

'Yes. Yes. She is. She's wonderful.'

'That's good news. I need to talk to you and her, if that's all right. Just for the report I have to file. It will only take a few minutes.'

'Of course. Come on through.'

When he entered the hospital room, Max was delighted to see Renee sitting up in bed, her blonde head and her brother's almost touching as they peered at the screen of their computer tablet. The girl's skin was still red with sunburn, and the scratches stood out clearly, but her eyes were bright and when she laughed at something happening on the screen, it was one of the nicest sounds Max had ever heard. Their mother was also sharing the bed, and every few seconds she reached out to touch Renee's hair, as if to reassure herself that her little girl was still there. The bedraggled teddy bear was sitting on Renee's lap.

'Hello, Renee.'

The little girl looked up.

'Hello.'

'This is the policeman who helped bring you home,' her father said. 'Say thank you.'

'Thank you.'

'You are very welcome, sweetheart.' Max lowered himself into the room's only chair. 'Now, because I'm a policeman, I have to ask you some questions about how you got lost. Is that all right?'

Renee nodded warily.

'It won't take long, I promise.'

The little girl leaned back against her mother and pulled the teddy bear tight against her chest.

'Renee, honey, he's awfully dirty now. Why don't you give him to me, and Daddy will go and find you a nice new teddy. An even better one.'

Renee pursed her lips, shook her head and pulled the

190

bear closer. Max had a feeling it would be a very long time indeed before Renee let go of that bear. When the little girl was grown and had a daughter of her own, that bear would probably still be part of her family.

'You know, you felt better after a bath yesterday, didn't you?' Evan said. 'Well, teddy might feel better after a bath too. How about you and I give him a bath after the sergeant has finished asking his questions.'

'All right.'

'In the meantime,' Max said. 'I have something here.'

He stepped over to the bed. 'Close your eyes and hold out your hand.'

The little girl did as instructed and Max placed a carving on her open palm. Her eyes flashed open.

'Ooh. Look, Mummy. A kangaroo.'

'It's beautiful, darling. What do you say to the officer?'

'Thank you,' Renee said shyly.

'You're very welcome,' Max said. 'And, Dustin, I didn't forget you.' He handed the boy a wooden eagle, its wings spread in full flight.

'Wow. That's great,' Dustin said. 'Did you make this?'

'I did.'

'Cool. Thanks.'

As he opened his notebook, Max decided this family was going to be fine.

Chapter Twenty-Four

Sarah unlocked the front door of the shop and looked out into the deserted street. It was just gone nine o'clock in the morning, and things around Coorah Creek were starting to return to normal. For the past two nights, the pub had been overflowing with people talking about the search and the rescue of little Renee. Her parents had suggested Sarah go over and join the celebration, but she hadn't. Glad as she was for Renee and her family, there was nothing in Sarah's world to celebrate.

For the one thousandth time, her eyes turned towards the road north. The road leading to Mount Isa. She didn't expect to see the big blue and white Mercedes rig, but that didn't stop her heart from holding on to one last faint glimmer of hope. And she hated herself for that. Almost as much as she hated Pete.

He had a girlfriend and she was pregnant. Despite that he'd kissed Sarah. Allowed her to believe … And she had believed because that girlish crush had never gone away. Not even during those four big city years she'd joked about. Big city years in which she had dated her fair share of men. But not one of them had come close to touching her heart the way Pete had done without even trying.

But he'd deceived her. And deceived his girlfriend; his pregnant girlfriend. He was a coward and a liar and a cheat and … There were not enough insults in the English language to truly capture how she felt about him.

Because her heart was breaking.

She heard a noise behind her and turned back into the shop. Her mother was behind the counter, setting up for the day's trading. Theirs was no big city supermarket.

Their cash register was old. It didn't even have a bar code scanner. But that didn't matter. The people who shopped here were not in a big city kind of hurry. They stayed to chat while their groceries were rung up by hand. Shopping was still an outing in Coorah Creek – not a chore.

Unaware that Sarah was watching, her mother paused and closed her eyes, taking a low slow breath as if to try to muster enough energy for the day ahead. Sarah frowned. Her father was looking a little better now the chemo was over. But her mother wasn't. She still looked exhausted. That was not good. Sarah had come home to help, it was time she stopped mooning over a treacherous lying truckie, and started behaving like a loving daughter.

'Mum, why don't you head back to the house?' she said. 'I've got everything under control. Take a day off. Spend some time with Dad. If I need you, I can call.'

Gina's shoulders sagged. 'If you're sure …'

'I'm sure. Go.' Sarah sent her mother on her way with a quick hug. As she did, she saw the look of relief on a face far too lined with care. Her mother seemed to have aged ten years in the last few months.

Sarah finished preparing the counter for the day's trading, but it was still a bit early for customers. She made herself a cup of tea at the sink in the rear of the store, and then stepped out the front door again, telling herself she just wanted to watch the world go by. She wasn't waiting for anyone in particular.

The first people she saw were the Haywoods. The big gold motorhome was parked on the side of the road near the pub, exactly where it had been parked the first time Sarah had seen it. She smiled a little as she noticed a yellow teddy bear, looking newly washed and brushed, sitting in the window. It seemed such a very long time since she had sold that bear to the Haywoods. She was glad that little

Renee had at least had her new friend for comfort during those long scary hours alone in the bush.

The family were just alighting from the vehicle. Mrs Haywood was firmly holding Renee's hand. Sarah had a feeling it would be a long time before she felt easy about letting go. The icy-cold, well-groomed and fashionable blonde of a few days ago was nowhere to be seen. Mrs Haywood wore no make-up and her hair was caught in a ponytail. She laughed as she bent over to listen to something her daughter said. She and her husband shared a look and both smiled. Sarah wondered if maybe some good had come from all that trauma after all.

Seeing Sarah in the door of the store, the Haywoods crossed the road.

'Good morning,' she said as they approached. 'It's good to see Renee looking so well.'

The little girl looked up at hearing her name. The scratches on her face were healing, as was her sunburnt skin. Her brother was standing very close to her. Obviously the guilt Dustin felt at losing her was still fresh in his mind. She could only hope that time would heal him as it healed his sister.

'Hello,' Evan Haywood replied. 'You're Sarah, aren't you?'

'Yes.'

'You were out there with the searchers. I remember seeing you.'

'I was,' she said.

'Thank you,' Mrs Haywood said. 'If you, and all the others hadn't been there to help ...'

'Don't think about that,' Sarah said kindly. 'There were a lot of people out there. We had all the thanks we needed when we saw Tia and Pete carry Renee into the camp.'

'Is Pete here?' the boy asked.

'No,' she said, trying to keep her heartache out of her voice. 'He's off somewhere delivering a big load in his truck.'

'I wanted to say goodbye.'

'I'll tell him goodbye from you when I see him.' Sarah wondered if she would ever get the chance to keep her promise.

'All right.'

'And what about the girl who brought Renee back. Tia?' Haywood asked.

'I'll pass on your thanks to her,' Max said as he approached from the direction of the police station. 'She's on shift at the mine today, but I will be seeing her tomorrow.'

'Please make sure she knows how terribly grateful we are to her ... to the trackers. To everyone.'

'I will,' Max said.

'I would like to do something to show my gratitude,' Haywood continued. 'But I don't know what. Can you suggest something?'

'That's not necessary, you know,' Sarah said kindly.

'But still ...' Haywood said. 'I want to do something. Something for the whole town.'

'Come back some time. Bring the kids and have a good holiday here,' Sarah said. 'Make some good memories for them. That would be one way of saying thank you.'

Haywood nodded. 'I might just do that.'

He looked at his wife for agreement, but she said nothing. Sarah had a feeling this was the last time she would ever see the Haywoods. Not that she blamed them. Some things are so painful, you never want to go back and face the memories.

'Kids, we'd better go. We have a long trip in front of us,' Haywood said. He turned to Max and shook his hand. 'I cannot thank you enough. For everything.' Then, overcome with emotion, he clasped Max in a hug, pounding his back in an attempt to fight back his emotions. When Haywood finally released him, Max bent down to Renee, who was clutching a carved wooden kangaroo in her hand.

'Now, young lady,' Max said with mock severity. 'Do you promise me you won't wander off again?'

'I promise.'

'Good.' Max enveloped the child in a quick hug.

It was hard to watch the touching farewell. All Sarah could think about was Pete – soon to be a father. And the woman who would be his wife and the mother of his child. Soon they would be a family like the Haywoods. She wanted to wish Pete well, but she couldn't. It hurt too much. Instead she raised a hand in farewell and walked back into the shop.

Sarah tried to keep herself busy restocking shelves, but she was very pleased when, a short time later, the door opened to reveal her first customer of the day who was, mercifully, a stranger.

'What can I get you?' she asked.

'I need something cold and wet,' the man replied, reaching for a can of Coke in the fridge. 'And directions to the Goongalla mine.'

'I can help you with both,' Sarah said, thinking as she did that he didn't look like a miner. He was definitely a man from the city. Young and flashy, dressed in pointy-toed shoes, and a black shirt that could have been silk. The shirtsleeves were rolled up, revealing part of a tattoo on his arm. Sarah couldn't see it clearly, but it could almost be a Ned Kelly-style helmet, with crossed antique pistols beneath it.

'Thanks.'

His smile was a bit ... slimy. She certainly wouldn't

trust him. He was probably a con man. Or a criminal. She wondered what his business at the mine might be. Nothing good, she was sure of it.

Then Sarah caught herself. She was just transferring her anger and hurt with Pete onto this poor man, who was probably an accountant or something equally harmless. It was time she stopped building fantasies of her own devising about people. The world was not full of criminal masterminds and knights in shining armour. She had to grow up.

She handed over the change and gave the man directions to the mine.

Chapter Twenty-Five

'You didn't have to pick me up, you know.'

Max smiled. 'Yes, I did. This is a date. I wanted to do it properly.'

'But you didn't bring flowers.' She was teasing him. But that didn't stop him wishing that he had brought flowers. Roses. Armfuls of them.

'This is Coorah Creek,' he said. 'There aren't a lot of roses around here.'

She laughed softly at that and suddenly he was glad he had no roses. Roses were a cliché, and there was nothing about Tia that was clichéd. If not bringing her roses made her laugh like that, he'd willingly spend the rest of his life tearing rose bushes out of the ground with his bare hands.

'Well, I guess I'm ready.' She turned to lock the door and came down the metal stairs.

She looked amazing. For a woman who spent most of her time in protective work gear at the mine or in leathers on her bike, she certainly knew how to wear a short skirt. Max was still standing on the dry dust outside her trailer. And as she slowly came down those metal stairs, giving him a wonderful view of her long slim legs, he was glad she hadn't invited him inside.

When she stepped onto ground level with him, his eyes flashed to the neck of her blouse, searching for a hint of the tattoo that he had never seen clearly. He allowed himself a few moments to imagine what it might be. One day, maybe even tonight, he would find out. But he wasn't going to push. Tia's past was filled with men who had hurt her. He was not going to be one of them. Her future was going to be different. He was determined this would be the sort of date Tia deserved. With an overt display of gallantry, he opened the car door for her. In reality he was hoping for another look at those fabulous legs as she stepped up into the big four-wheel drive.

'You know, if you try to suddenly run out of petrol in some lonely lovers' lane, I'm not going to believe you,' Tia said as they drove away from the mine compound. 'I know you are far too organised to run out of petrol.'

'There's my entire plan shot to hell. I guess I'll have to buy you dinner instead.'

'That seems like a good idea. I'm starving.'

That made Max laugh.

'What?' she demanded.

'Most women wouldn't like to admit they're starving. They want their dates to think they eat like sparrows.'

'I'm not most women.'

Max didn't need reminding of that, but if he had, their entrance into the pub would have done it. Being Friday night, the pub was quite full. Coorah Creek was a town where very little happened, so even now the search and rescue was still the main topic of conversation. The minute he and Tia entered, a number of people shouted over for them to join their tables, offering to buy drinks and obviously wanting to talk about the search. In the minds of everyone there, Tia was very much the hero – or rather heroine – of the hour. Not only that, her short floaty skirt attracted more than a few not-so-covert glances from some of the men. Tia acknowledged the offers with a friendly grin and a shake of her head and followed Max to a quiet table in a far corner.

'It's going to take a little while for the excitement to die down,' Max said. 'But it will eventually.'

'That's okay. It feels kind of nice to be accepted like that.'

And that, thought Max, is what's different. Not too long ago, Tia wanted to remain distant from the town and from him. She'd finish her drink and ride off on the Harley whenever someone tried to talk to her. Especially him. Being part of the search for Renee had changed her feelings towards both the town and him. Perhaps it had also changed her feelings about herself. He hoped it had.

'It is nice to have a quiet table though,' Tia added as they took their seats. 'We were lucky to get a table on a Friday ...' She stopped and a smile twisted the corners of her mouth. 'No, we weren't lucky. You arranged this, didn't you?'

Max nodded. 'I wanted you all to myself.' He looked across the bar to see Trish Warren approaching. 'Or as much of you to myself as possible.'

'Tia. It's so good to see you. Don't you look pretty? I do believe this is the first time I have seen you in a dress. And Max. Looking handsome as always in civvies. I assume you are here to celebrate, like everyone else. Good news is always good for business. The other news is that Jack and Ellen are home from their visit back east. Missed all the excitement, but there you go. Ellen is helping me tonight. She's doing the cooking because Jack's behind the bar. And that gives me a chance to spend some time with those lovely children of theirs. She's done a lasagne. And there's the usual steak with her special pepper sauce. Dinner is on the house and ...' she held up her hand to silence Max before he could protest '... not a word from you, Max Delaney, you hear? Accepting a free meal from a friend is not police corruption. Nor is accepting the beer Jack is about to serve. Got it?'

'Yes, ma'am,' Max said with mock fear.

Trish grinned happily and walked away.

Tia was still giggling softly when Jack North appeared with a beer in each hand.

'Tia, I don't think you've met Jack,' Max said. 'He and his wife Ellen have been away for a few weeks with their kids. Jack is normally my right hand man when we've got trouble. I missed you, mate.' Jack put both beers on the table and clasped Max's hand.

'You managed fine without me, Sarge,' he said. 'Glad to meet you, Tia. I've heard a lot about you. You did good out there.'

'Don't believe everything you hear,' said Tia. 'I just happened to be in the right place at the right time. All the credit goes to Max for organising the search, and to the trackers who found her.'

'Don't worry, by the time this town has finished with the story, you will have swum the flooded river and plucked the girl from the very jaws of a saltwater croc,' Jack joked, his affection for the town clear in every word he spoke.

'Well, if they insist on turning me into a hero ...'

Jack chuckled as he returned to the bar, leaving Tia and Max alone.

'I am starting to see why you like this town so much,' Tia said.

'It's a good place. Good people.' Max raised his beer glass in a salute, which she returned. 'Does that mean you might think about staying here for a while?' He kept the question casual. If he let her see how much her answer mattered to him, he might frighten her away.

Tia glanced down at the beer glass in her hands, as if weighing his question. When she raised her eyes, she studied his face for a long moment before answering. 'I could be talked into it.'

'I'd like that.'

Trish appeared again to take their food order. Both Tia and Max opted for steak.

Max thought Tia looked as relaxed as he had ever seen

her. Perhaps some of the ghosts from her past had been exorcised. He was glad he had never traced her via the police systems. When she was ready to tell him about her past and the motorbike that wasn't hers, she would. In the meantime, if the past was a closed door for her, there was always the present. And if he was very lucky, perhaps a future.

'So, what's it like driving one of those big mine trucks?' he asked.

Tia could not remember a meal she had enjoyed this much. It wasn't just the steak that was good; although it was very, very good. It was a long time since she had talked this much. Or laughed this much. She and Max talked about anything and everything. Almost everything. They talked about her job at the mine and his work too. A disagreement over the best Beatles song was just another source for teasing. It seemed they liked some of the same films, although Max was more of a reader than she was. Max regaled her with funny stories from his days as a young beat cop, but not once during the evening did he ask about her past. She was grateful to him for that.

There was no doubt that Max was flirting with her. Catching her eye in a lingering glance. Touching her hand as he passed her another beer. A couple of times, he let his leg brush hers and she didn't pull away. It felt amazing to have someone like Max flirting with her. In her experience, men didn't flirt. They took what they wanted. This was something new and pretty wonderful. She felt her guard falling away as the evening passed. And it wasn't the beer doing it. She didn't need any help to relax around Max. She just needed Max.

They had moved from beer to coffee when Max finally glanced down at his watch.

'It's nearly closing time,' he said. 'We probably should go.'

'I guess we should.' Her own reluctance surprised her. 'It probably wouldn't do for you to be caught drinking out of hours in the pub.'

Max grinned that same cheeky grin that had held her spellbound all night. 'And who is going to catch me?'

They managed to escape with no more than a few words with Trish. Outside, the night was dark and quiet. Tia raised her face to the sky, taking in the twinkling of the stars in the inky blackness. It was the sort of night she liked to take the bike out on the highway and feel the freedom of being her own person. To revel in being alone. Tonight however was different. She didn't want the evening to end. She didn't want to say goodnight to Max and she didn't want to be alone.

'There's something I want to show you,' Max said. 'And I promise no running out of petrol in lovers' lane.'

A tiny part of her was disappointed to hear that.

'Okay.'

They drove out of town a short distance, then Max turned off the main road onto a graded gravel road. A short time later, they abandoned the gravel and turned onto what was little more than two wheel ruts, barely visible in the red earth. Tia could hear Max humming softly to himself as he drove towards the big red sandstone bluff that overlooked the town. She smiled as she recognised the song, wondering if the lonely hearts he was thinking of were theirs.

If Tia had been expecting the track to climb to the top of the bluff, to some spectacular outlook, she was wrong. When Max parked the car, they were still surrounded by scrubby trees. He got out of the car, closing the door quietly. She followed his example. He held out his hand,

and she took it without hesitation and followed where he lead.

They walked along a narrow track that looked as if it had only recently been pushed through the long dry grass that came almost to Tia's knees. About them, the tall gums reached leafy fingers up into the sky. Somewhere she heard the high sharp call of a night bird. Wherever they were it wasn't lovers' lane. Tia's survival instinct started to kick into high gear. She was alone with a man she barely knew, in this hidden place where clearly no one ever came. In the city, she would be in danger. In the city, she had never allowed herself to be this vulnerable. That this man was a cop meant nothing. She knew more about some cops that she wanted to. This was Max, and she wanted to trust him, but her past began closing in around her. She felt her feet hesitate.

Max stopped and turned to her. 'It's not much further.'

Her instincts told her to turn and try to get away, until she looked into Max's open and honest face. Something deep in her heart wanted to believe in him.

Another few steps and they emerged from the scrub into a clearing.

It wasn't the spectacular view she had expected, but it was lovely none the less.

The land sloped gently down from where they stood to the creek. The water glistened in the moonlight. All around them, the stately gums stretched into the night sky, and above them the stars seemed so close, Tia felt as if she could reach out and touch them. There was no light here, other than that provided by nature. It softened the harshness of the land, and created an ethereal beauty.

A slight stirring of breeze rustled the grass and the leaves of the trees above, but other than that, there was no sound except for the occasional chirp of a cicada. Tia's world had never been silent. There had always been something, from the harsh sounds of the city and of other people, to the roar of the Harley or her mine truck. Noise had helped drown out her thoughts and the memories that haunted her. Until this moment, she had never really felt at peace with the world, or with herself. And never had she even thought to share a moment like this with anyone.

'How beautiful it is,' Tia said softly. 'It's as if we are the first people ever to come here. That the land is as it was before ... well ... before people came and started changing things.'

'When I come here, I think I catch just a hint of what the aboriginal people call The Dreaming. I will never have Grandpa Pindarri's connection to the land, but here I feel ... I'm not sure what. But I do know it's very special.'

Tia knew exactly what he meant. 'So what is this place? Part of the National Park?'

'No. This is my place.'

Tia dragged her eyes away from the scene before her. 'Your place?'

Max glanced around him, something like pride on his face. 'Yes. I bought this land a few months ago. I think it would be a fine place to build a house.'

Tia nodded slowly. 'I think so too. But you haven't started building yet?'

'No. The station residence is fine for me. A home I made here would be for a family.'

The word hung silently in the air between them, but it wasn't an uncomfortable silence. Tia felt a surge of longing for something she hadn't had in a very long time. Images played through her mind. A large home with big wide verandas built on this spot. There were kids playing in the yard, perhaps with a dog or a pony. Family meals would be served around a huge wooden table, probably one that

Max had made himself. At the centre of all those images was Max, with his easy smile and those gentle hands that were also strong enough to turn a lump of old wood into something beautiful. There was something missing from the images inside Tia's head. Max needed a woman by his side. A wife to him and a mother to those children.

How she longed to be that woman.

It was time she told him. If she could. She turned to gaze back out over the creek, because she didn't want to see Max's face as she talked. She didn't want to see the disgust and condemnation there.

'I ran away from home when I was just fifteen,' she said softly. 'My father was long gone and my mother's boyfriend … well … he was getting a bit too interested in me. Especially when Mum wasn't there.'

Max's fingers closed around hers. Amazing how such a little thing could bring such a sense of understanding and support.

'I lived on the streets for a while. I shoplifted. Food, mostly, because I was hungry. I was on my own and I was lonely and frightened. Then a gang took me in. Funny – I found myself doing the very thing I had run away from home to avoid. But at least it wasn't my mother's boyfriend.'

She waited for him to say something. Or at least remove his hand from hers. But he didn't. That gave her the courage to go on.

'We lived in the squats. Stole for a living. Not just food, but we robbed people and houses. And if the cops found out …' Tia took a slow deep breath and closed her eyes. This was going to be hard to say. 'If the cops found out, I would persuade them not to report us.'

Once again, the words hung in the air between them. 'I am so sorry.'

'There's no need for you to say that, Max. It wasn't you.

If there's one thing I have learned from the last ten years, it's that there are men like that everywhere. And really good men are very few and hard to find.' She hoped he understood what she was saying to him.

'There was a gang leader. He ... well, I was his.' Now was the time to confess everything. To tell Max the whole story and ask for his help. But she couldn't do it. It was one step too far. But for the first time, she was beginning to believe that one day, and one day soon, she would be able to tell him everything. 'Let's just say, I learned things about him. And so I had to run away.'

'The Harley. It's his.' Max wasn't asking a question.

'Yes. I took it. I guess it was reported stolen.'

'Actually, it wasn't.'

Max took her by the shoulders and turned her to face him. She looked into his face and saw nothing there but honest concern.

'Tia, I know there's something you are not telling me. And that's fine. Whenever you are ready, I'm here to help you, in whatever way I can. You have to know that.'

The depth of feeling in his words almost made her tell him. Instead, she nodded and stood on the tips of her toes to lightly brush her lips against his cheek. 'I know.'

She made as if to step back, but he didn't let her go. Slowly and gently he pulled her to him. She knew that he would never touch her against her will. If she wanted to, she could say no – something she had never had the chance to do before. For the first time, she didn't want to say no.

He kissed her. It was a gentle kiss. Light and full of promise.

All that had gone before ceased to matter. The other men were nothing. Not even memories any more. This kiss was her first kiss and the sweetest thing she had ever known.

When at last he let her go, Max ran a finger ever so

lightly down her cheek. He took her hand and led her back to the car, away from his small plot in the wilderness, but not from a hope for the future.

The mine compound was silent when Max pulled up next to her trailer. He got out and moved quickly to open the car door for her. It was the last act in an evening full of wonderful new experiences.

Tia hesitated, not certain if she should invite him inside. She didn't want him to leave, but nor did she want to tarnish the most amazing evening of her life.

'I'll go now,' Max said, relieving her of the decision.

'Most of the men I've known would want—'

He reached up and gently touched one finger to her lips to silence her.

'I do want. But I'm not most men. I can wait.'

He smiled at her, a smile that warmed her heart and soul, and then he turned and got back into his car. She watched his tail light vanish through the compound gates before opening the door to her trailer. Her mind was spinning with so many joyous thoughts, that for a few seconds she didn't see what lay on her small table. Then she froze.

It was a newspaper cutting. The story was about the search for little Renee Haywood. It wasn't the story that made her breath catch in her throat. It was the photograph. It showed the happy moment of reunion between Renee and her family at the search site. But there, looking on and smiling, was Tia, her face clearly visible.

Someone had broken into her trailer and put it there. But first that person had drawn an angry slash across her face in thick red ink.

Chapter Twenty-Six

Pete hated the smell of the hospital. He had no particular reason for his irrational hatred. As a kid he'd been to hospital once with a broken arm after a foolish tree-climbing accident. That hadn't been particularly traumatic and he rarely, if ever, thought about it. This hatred of hospitals obviously stemmed from somewhere else that he couldn't remember. Or maybe he just did not want to go into this particular hospital.

He took a last deep breath of the warm early evening air and then climbed the steps to the main entrance. The glass doors sliding closed behind him felt almost like the doors of a prison cell. He had spent most of the past three days at the hospital, or ferrying Linda's mother between her home and her daughter's bedside.

Linda was doing fine now, as was the baby. The bleeding that had so panicked her had stopped. And so had the pain. The doctors wanted her to put her feet up for a few days and rest, but they were happy for her to go home tomorrow. And therein lay his problem.

Pete didn't want to take Linda to his home. He had taken the past few days off work to be with her, but he had to go back. He couldn't afford not to. He didn't want to leave Linda at his house alone, in case there was another scare. The doctors said that was unlikely, but he didn't want to take the risk. She would be far better off staying with her mother.

What Pete couldn't say to Linda, and in fact could barely admit to himself, was that he didn't want Linda to go home *with him*. To have her in his home and in his bed, when he felt as he did for Sarah, would be dishonest. It could only hurt everyone concerned. But how could he break her heart when she was still in recovery from the terrible fear of losing their child? She was still frightened and upset and he couldn't do anything to delay her recovery. He had to do the right thing by her.

What had Sarah said – sometimes what is right isn't the right thing to do?

He allowed himself one lingering thought of Sarah, then pushed her away as he walked down the long echoing corridor towards the ward where Linda lay.

She wasn't alone.

Pete hesitated in the doorway. There was a man seated on a chair beside Linda's bed. He was holding her hand and they were obviously in the middle of some intense and private conversation. So much so, they didn't see or hear him. Instinctively he stepped back, not wishing to interrupt them.

He felt like a fool standing there wondering who the man was, so after a few moments, he re-entered the room as noisily as he could without making it too obvious. Linda and her visitor turned as he walked in. Linda's eyes were shining with tears.

'Linda? Are you all right? What—'

'You must be Pete.' The man got to his feet and held out his hand. 'I am Guy Raymond. Linda has told me a lot about you.'

Pete took his hand warily. Guy was about his own age, but shorter and well-groomed. His short brown hair and tailored shirt and trousers clearly marked him as a city man – as did his handshake. There were no callouses on those manicured hands. Everything about him said travelling salesman. Pete had to fight back a feeling of instant dislike for the man.

'Pete, sit down. I've got something to tell you,' Linda said.

Pete looked from Linda to Guy and back again, suspicion starting to form in his mind.

'What's this about?' he asked slowly, remaining where he stood.

Linda and Guy shared a look. Guy nodded. 'I'll be back shortly,' he said.

When they were alone, Pete sat down and looked at Linda. Her eyes were red. She had been crying, but nothing about her demeanour was sad. In fact, she looked radiant.

'Linda, what's going on?'

'Pete, I really don't know how to say this. I am so sorry. I've been lying to you.'

'About what?'

Linda hesitated and Pete suddenly knew exactly what she was about to say.

'The baby. It's not yours.'

The words struck him like a physical blow.

'How do you know it's not mine? You've been with someone else?'

'Yes. Guy.'

Strangely enough, that didn't hurt so much.

'And you know it's his baby because of ... what? The timing?'

'Yes. I'm further along than I told you. Remember, when you were away on that long haul to Western Australia. You were gone for over a month. That's when Guy and I ...'

Linda's voice trailed off and he saw a glimmer of tears in her eyes.

Pete couldn't look at her. He got to his feet and crossed the room to stare out of the window. Out there the world was still spinning on its axis and people were going about their daily business. But inside this room, everything had changed. He felt as if he had lost something very important. He hadn't ever wanted this baby, but over the past few weeks the child had become very real to him. As real as little Dustin Haywood placing a small hand in his, looking for comfort. Linda's words ripped a huge hole in his heart, where the unborn child had begun to make its home. It hurt.

Tears began to fall down Linda's cheeks. 'Oh, Pete, I'm so sorry. I never meant to hurt you.'

'Then why did you tell me it was my baby? You were trying to trick me into marrying you.'

'It wasn't like that, Pete. Honestly. I told Guy I was pregnant, but he left me. I couldn't face being a single mum. So I told you it was yours. I knew you would be good to me and the baby. I know it was wrong but I was desperate.'

Pete suddenly remembered Mick's words. He had asked Pete if he was sure, but he hadn't meant about marrying Linda. He had been asking if he was sure the baby was his. Mick had known she was sleeping with someone else. He wondered if all his other mates knew too. Pete felt like a fool. He should be angry, but he wasn't. He was more confused and hurt than anything else. After struggling so hard to accept the new reality of his life, it had changed again.

A hand touched his arm. He turned to find Linda standing beside him. In her hospital gown, with a face devoid of make-up she looked younger – and in some ways more beautiful than she ever had before.

'I'm sorry, Pete. You have to believe me. But today Guy came back. He wants us to make a go of it. As a family. He says he loves me, and I know you don't.'

She must have seen the frown creasing his forehead.

'Oh, Pete,' she said. 'You are such a good man. You were going to do the right thing, even though you didn't want to. I love you a little for that.' She reached up and kissed him on the cheek. 'But you don't have to. Not any more. I'm ...' she hesitated and placed one hand gently on her stomach '... we are going to be all right.'

His anger faded, and all that was left behind was that aching hole in his heart.   Behind them, the sound of returning footsteps told Pete that it was time for him to go. He turned and shook Guy's hand.

'You are a lucky man.' He meant it.

'I know.'

'You take good care of them, you hear?'

'I intend to.'

Pete left them.

The walk down the grey hospital corridor seemed endless as he came to terms with the loss of something that had become important to him, even though it had really never been his. But as he walked, his step became lighter, as if a burden had been removed from his shoulders. As the sliding glass doors released him back into the sunlight, he knew where he had to go.

Back at the depot, he looked for Mick, but his friend was out on the road. Men who spend much of their time alone do like to gossip, and most of the drivers knew Linda. Pete deftly turned aside their questions as he headed for the office. He needed a load. Not just any load. He needed a load for Coorah Creek.

'Stop fussing, daughter. I am perfectly capable of stacking a few shelves.'

'I know you are, Dad,' Sarah said with a sigh. 'But you don't want to do too much.'

'You heard what Doctor Adam said,' her father reminded her. 'He said my bloods are looking much better.'

'But you've still got more tests to do,' Sarah reminded him.

Ken put the tinned fruit he was holding on the shelves and sighed. 'I know I have. But I feel the best I have in months,' he said. 'Please, Sarah, don't fuss. Let me enjoy a day that feels like every day used to.'

Sarah threw her arms around her father in a hug that was filled with contrition and very gentle love.

'Sorry, Dad.'

Ken hugged her back. 'And I'm sorry too. I know I've been pretty hard to live with these past few months. I am so grateful you came home. Your mother is strong, but having you here too was a great help to her.'

'I am so glad I was here when you both needed me,' Sarah said slowly.

Her father extricated himself from her hug, and looked at her intently. 'Are you thinking of going back?'

That was the big question, wasn't it? Sarah had to think for a few seconds, to make sure she phrased the answer the right way.

'I wouldn't go if you still needed me. But as you are so quick to point out, you're getting better. At some point I guess I have to get on with my life.'

Ken nodded. 'I understand. But your mother and I were hoping you'd stay. Find a job in town, or even take over the store so we could retire.'

Sarah chuckled. 'Retire? Dad you are never going to retire.'

'Maybe not.' Ken hesitated and Sarah knew exactly what he was going to say next. 'I thought that maybe you wanted to stay around because of Pete.'

There it was. The thing she had been avoiding for several days. There was no hiding now – not from her father and not from herself.

'No. That's not going to work,' she said, doing her best to keep her voice neutral.

'Oh. I thought …'

'No.'

'I'm sorry, honey.'

'That's all right, Dad. It was only a child's crush after all. I've grown up a lot since then. That's why I think going away is probably the best thing for me. But I promise it won't be so long between visits in the future.'

Sarah busied herself stacking the shelves. She didn't want her father to see the glint of tears in her eyes. But he understood. Her father always had.

'Let me go and see if your mother and I can organise some lunch. And a cuppa. How does that sound?'

'Great,' Sarah said. She wasn't hungry, but a few minutes alone would give her a chance to try to shift the wave of sadness that had settled about her like a cloak at the mention of Pete's name.

She had to forget about him. He had a girlfriend and a child on the way. He hadn't lied to her, but he hadn't told her the truth either. That kiss they had shared while searching for Renee had been the sweetest moment of her life. And now it was lost. She could almost hate him for that.

A crash from the storeroom behind the shop made her jump.

'Dad!'

She dropped the tins she was stacking and ran the length of the store to the open doorway at the back. But it wasn't her father lying on the floor surrounded by shattered tea mugs. It was her mother. Before Sarah could reach her, Ken appeared from the direction of the house and flung himself down beside his wife.

'Gina? Gina? Talk to me.'

But his wife remained unmoving, her eyes shut and her chest rising and falling so slowly Sarah could barely see it.

'Call Doctor Adam!'

Before the words were even out of her father's mouth, Sarah was reaching for the phone.

Adam seemed to take forever to get there. Sarah stood rooted to the spot, unable to move. Her father sat on the floor beside his wife, speaking to her softly and holding her hand. His face was stricken. Sarah saw more anguish on his face than she had at even the worst moments of his own illness. It was easier for him to face his own mortality than to face a future without the woman who had been the centre of his life for thirty years. The love Sarah saw on his face was as humbling as it was heartbreaking.

At Adam's instructions, they hadn't tried to move her. All Sarah wanted to do was put a pillow under her mother's head, and straighten her skirt. Gina was a neat and tidy person. She would not have approved of the way she was lying there, limbs all awry.

The front door of the shop opened and Adam dashed in. He saw Sarah in the storeroom doorway and came straight to her. He placed his emergency bag down and knelt next to Gina.

'Ken, you have to let me do my job,' Adam said gently as he eased Gina's hand away from her husband's grasp. Ken sat back a fraction, but his eyes never left Gina's still face.

Sarah leaned against the doorway for support as Adam took her mother's pulse and listened to her chest. Then she heard a murmur, and her mother's eyes flickered open.

'Gina, it's Adam Gilmore. You passed out. But I'm here now and we are going to take good care of you.'

Her mother's lips moved, but no sound came out. She began to move one hand as if searching for something. She fell still again when her husband cradled her hand in his.

'Sarah, get your mother some water,' Adam instructed without looking around. Sarah raced into the shop to grab

216

a water bottle and was back in a flash. By then Adam had helped Gina into a sitting position, supported by both her doctor and her husband.

'I am going to take you to the hospital,' Adam said as he assisted Gina to take a mouthful of water. 'I don't think we need to go to the Isa yet. Let's see how you are doing in an hour or so. I'll have Jess and the plane on standby, though, just in case. Okay?'

Gina nodded slowly.

'Right.'

Behind her, Sarah heard the door to the shop open and then crash shut. Whoever it was, they were going to have to go away. She turned to tell them to do just that, and saw Pete standing there, his face a still mask of concern.

'What's wrong?'

She wanted to run to him. Her knight. She wanted to bury her face in his chest and ask him to make everything all right for her. But his armour was tarnished now and she was no longer a little girl waiting for his truck to appear on the road.

'Mum collapsed,' she said shortly. 'Doctor Adam wants to take her to the hospital.'

'Do you need any help?'

'Is that you, Pete?' Adam's voice called from inside the storeroom. 'We could use a pair of strong arms.'

Sarah stood back as Pete walked through into the storeroom. In a few seconds he had scooped Gina up in his arms and was carrying her through the store to Adam's car, where he placed her in the back seat, as gently as if she were made of glass.

'Ken, stay with me,' Gina called in a weak voice. Sarah's father darted around the car to get in next to his wife.

'You let her lean on you,' Adam instructed. 'Get in, Sarah. We have to get going.'

Sarah hesitated and glanced back at the shop. They couldn't just leave it unlocked and open.

'Forget it,' Pete said, obviously understanding the look. 'You go with your parents. I've got this.'

Sarah met his eyes then for the first time. She wanted him to know how grateful she was. Then she leaped into Adam's car. The doctor was already behind the wheel, and within a few seconds they had pulled away from the store.

Sarah glanced in a side mirror. This time, she was the one driving away and Pete was left standing beside the road.

Chapter Twenty-Seven

The ringing just wouldn't stop. Max rolled over and glanced at the bedside clock. The glowing numbers told him it was a few minutes after two o'clock. And his phone was ringing. He instantly snapped awake. This had to be work.

'Delaney,' he said as he picked up the phone.

'Mount Isa Dispatch,' a woman's voice at the other end told him. 'We have a call out in Coorah Creek.'

Max had expected as much. When he was off duty the local phone diverted through to the regional HQ in Mount Isa, which was manned twenty-four hours a day. And they would only disturb him in the middle of the night if it was something urgent.

His first thought was for the Travers' family. Gina had been taken to the hospital earlier that day, after collapsing in the shop. Surely she hadn't …

'We have a 141 with a possible 301. Code two.'

Max was out of bed before she finished speaking. A prowler. Possibly armed. This was an urgent matter.

'Location?' He flung open his wardrobe and reached for his uniform.

'Goongalla Mine. The workers' compound. A trailer home set towards the back of the compound.'

Tia!

'On the way.'

He slammed the phone down and threw on his uniform. He buckled on his belt, his weapon in its holster. He'd never used the weapon in anger. Hoped he never would. But he was prepared to, if it was necessary.

He was in his car within a couple of minutes of waking.

The Code two classification allowed him to use his lights and siren at his discretion. He chose not to. At this hour there would be little or no traffic between his house and the mine, so he didn't need them. He didn't want to wake the whole town, but more importantly, he didn't want to alert whoever was prowling the mine compound to his approach. But that didn't stop him from breaking several speed limits as he raced towards the mine.

The mine itself was heavily protected by a high fence topped with barbed wire, with heavy iron gates manned around the clock. That was standard practise at any mine, but particularly a uranium mine. The accommodation compound, however, was outside the main security perimeter. It was fenced, of course, but its gates were usually wide open. That had never been a problem – until now.

As he approached the compound, Max let his speed drop and turned off his headlights. He knew this road well enough to continue by the faint light shed by the security lights along the mine fences. The moonlight helped too. He pulled his car through the gates and parked in the dark shadow of a row of dongas.

He flicked off his interior light and cautiously got out, leaving his door open. He stood perfectly still, listening. At first he heard nothing but the normal sounds of night in the bush. But then something out of place. Footsteps. He tilted his head to try to determine their source, when he heard loud angry voices and a grunt of pain.

With one hand on his gun, and the other pulling a powerful torch from his belt, Max began to run towards the rear of the compound, where Tia's trailer was set.

The sounds got louder. This was some sort of a scuffle involving several people. He swung the torch around and the beam caught a flash of a running figure disappearing behind the mess building. He sprinted after it, only to find himself joined by a couple of mine workers.

'He went that way,' one of them shouted.

'You lot stay out of it,' Max told them as he set off in that direction at a run.

'Not bloody likely, mate,' was the reply as the others joined him.

As a group, they followed the shadow Max had seen. At the other side of the mess, Max paused and shone his torch around. Nothing. He sprinted in the direction of the perimeter fence. There, his torch revealed a hole cut in the wire. He shone his torch into the trees beyond the wire. Nothing. No sign of the prowler and no way to know in which direction he had gone.

Max let his hand fall away from his gun. This was over – for now.

He led the men back towards the mess. 'Tell me what happened?'

'I was just getting back after working late,' one man said. 'I saw someone skulking around Tia's trailer and the bike. I grabbed him and called for someone to ring you.'

'Is Tia here?' Max asked, his heart beating harder at the thought of the danger she might have been in.

'No. She's on shift until six.'

'I got a message that this guy might have been armed.'

'That was me,' a second man said. 'I saw him and Blue wrestling through the window of my donga. He was holding something. It might have been a gun ...' The man paused and looked a bit bashful. 'But I'd fallen asleep watching some crime show, so maybe it wasn't.'

'I thought I had him, but then he clocked me one,' Blue said ruefully, rubbing his chin. 'And I let him go. That's when you arrived.'

'Okay. Thanks, guys,' Max said. 'He's gone now. He

probably won't come back, but I'll hang around anyway. Just in case.'

'Do you need a hand?' Blue asked. 'I wouldn't mind a chance to give back what he gave me.'

'No, thanks.' Max smiled and slapped the man's back. 'Get some sleep. If I need you, I'll let you know. And next time, if there is a next time, don't go off all half-cocked. Call me first and let me deal with him. Especially if you think he's armed. All right?'

The men nodded reluctantly.

Max took down a few more details of the incident, and a description, vague though it was, of the intruder. The yawning miners, their adrenaline rush fading, headed to their beds.

Max walked over to Tia's trailer and walked around it, shining his light carefully on the door and windows. There was no sign of any attempt to break in. The Harley sat in its usual spot near the door, and it too appeared untouched. He didn't like this, not one bit. His gut told him that Tia's past had found her. He didn't know what it was, but his instincts also told him it was dangerous. If he was going to protect her, he had to know what this was all about.

He walked slowly back to his car and moved it to a place from where he had a good view of the trailer and the Harley. He wound the window down to let in some fresh air and settled low in the seat. It was going to be a long night.

Tia stretched, feeling cramped muscles crack as the tension dropped from her shoulders. Ten hours behind the wheel of a machine bigger than a house took their toll. She removed her helmet and pulled the band from her hair, shaking it out with a toss of her head.

'Long night,' another driver said as he walked towards the office to clock out.

'You got that right,' Tia said, falling into step beside him.

'I hear there was some sort of scuffle at the mess last night.'

'Really?' Tia wasn't really interested. Tempers occasionally flared at the mess. It was no concern of hers.

'Yeah. A burglar or something.'

Tia forced herself to keep walking. 'What did he break into?' she asked, her voice much calmer than she was.

'Dunno. I think they chased him off before he got whatever he was looking for. Probably just looking to lift a laptop. Or maybe he was thirsty and looking for beer. Nothing to worry about.'

Oh, but it was something to worry about. The newspaper cutting she had found after her date with Max was safely stowed in the rucksack under the bench in her trailer. She'd been expecting the next move ever since. Now here it was. Tia let her steps slow and the rest of her shift drew ahead of her. They were eagerly discussing the events of the night before, spurred on by details told to them by the incoming shift. Tia wanted no part of the discussion, but she knew better than they did what this was all about.

Most of the others headed straight for the mess when they arrived at the compound. Tia turned towards her trailer, her heart in her mouth. Wondering what – or who – she might find there. It was just after six o'clock and the day was still cool; or rather what passed for cool at this time of the year. The early morning light, however, was clear and in that clear light she had no difficulty recognising the blue and white checks on the four-wheel drive parked under a tree near her trailer.

Max had staked out her trailer? She wasn't sure whether

to be pleased he cared enough to do that or be angry at him for spying on her. She was also a little afraid. If Max and Ned came face to face, there was no good way for the confrontation to end.

She approached the car, and noticed that Max's head had slumped back against the headrest. His eyes were closed and his long dark eyelashes fluttered against his cheek. He was snoring ever so softly. Tia felt a smile twist the corners of her mouth. Tired as she was, she could imagine how good it would feel to lay her head against his shoulder and join him in slumber. He looked so cute when he was asleep.

But he was also vulnerable, and he had no idea who and what had been out there in the darkness last night.

'Hey, Max. Wake up.'

His eyes blinked open. In those few waking moments, as he first saw her, the look of pleasure on his face was enough to melt her heart, but not her resolve.

'Tia.' A moment later he was fully awake, his eyes searching the compound for any signs that something was amiss.

'Everything's fine,' she said. At least she hoped everything was fine. She hadn't been inside her trailer yet.

'I don't usually fall asleep on the job,' Max said. 'But I didn't have time to grab a coffee before I came out.'

She could hardly ignore the hint. Or suggest they go to the mess. Max wanted to talk to her about last night. That was obvious. And the conversation was best had in private. With a tilt of her head in invitation, she turned and headed for her front door, noting as she did that the Harley was parked where she had left it. She also noticed that someone had brushed away the layer of dust that had accumulated on the seat. When she opened her door, she looked carefully around her home, searching for any signs that someone had been there. It seemed exactly as she had left it. Max and the miners had interrupted her uninvited guest before he could get inside.

But she had no doubt who it was or what he wanted.

She walked inside and Max followed her. She felt very self-conscious having him here, in her private space. He was the first person she had invited inside. The trailer was clean and tidy, but it was pretty bare. A few books lay on a shelf, and the motorcycle helmet was in its usual spot. But Tia was acutely aware that the trailer had no photos or small trinkets, the sort of personal possessions that made a home. She was also acutely aware of what lay in the rucksack in the cupboard under the bench seat.

She busied herself making coffee, while Max sat and waited patiently. It wasn't the coffee he was waiting for and they both knew it. At last she sat down opposite him at the little table, two steaming mugs between them.

'It's someone from your past, isn't it?' Max's voice was gentle.

She nodded.

'Tell me.'

'I can't. He's dangerous.'

'If you tell me, I can protect you. But if I don't know what's going on, or what he's likely to do, that only makes it harder.'

'I can't tell you. I wish I could, but I just can't.'

Max covered her hand with his. 'Tia, you can tell me anything. I know I'm a cop, and I suspect over the years you have had little reason to trust cops, but you can trust me.'

'I know I can.'

'And whatever it is in your past that you are so afraid of, it won't change the way I feel about you.'

'You can't know that.' Half of her wanted to just let go and tell him the truth, but the other half, the honest half, knew that she couldn't.

'I do know that. I am your friend, Tia. Always.'

'I know. But it would be safer if you weren't.'

'Safer?' His brow furrowed. 'Tia, I won't let him hurt you. I will keep you safe. I promise you that.'

She shook her head, her heart nearly breaking. 'No. He won't hurt me. I meant it would be safer for you.'

Chapter Twenty-Eight

The big blue and white rig was parked close to the store. The door was open and Pete was sitting sideways in the seat, drinking orange juice from a plastic bottle. He was the last person Sarah wanted to see, but it looked as if she had very little choice. Doctor Adam's wife, Jess, had offered Sarah a lift home after the long night at the hospital, and she pulled her car over to the side of the road without switching the engine off.

'Are you going to be all right?' Jess asked, with a glance in Pete's direction.

'I'll be fine. Thanks for the lift.' Sarah got out of the car.

Pete immediately jumped down from his seat, and regarded Sarah through eyes dark with worry.

'How's your mother?'

For the merest fraction of a second, Sarah was almost overwhelmed by a desire to fling herself into Pete's arms and let go. To stop being strong and cry out all the fears and tension of the past twenty-four hours. She wanted Pete to scoop her up in his arms, much as he had lifted her mother the day before and rock her like a child until the pain went away.

But she wasn't going to do that. She had grown up a lot in the past few days. And she'd come to realise that her knight's armour was irrevocably tarnished.

'Did you spend the night here?' she asked in a voice that was totally devoid of all emotion.

He nodded. 'I wasn't sure if the shop and house were locked, so I wanted to keep an eye on things for you. Besides, I couldn't leave without knowing ...'

'Mum is okay,' she said quickly. Whatever Pete had

227

done to her, he was still a friend to her family. 'Doctor Adam says it was just exhaustion and stress. She was so busy taking care of Dad, she didn't look after herself. None of us looked after her. But that's going to change now.'

She saw the relief cross Pete's face.

'Dad's still at the hospital with her. I expect Adam will let her come home later today. I need to get things ready for her, to make sure she does absolutely nothing when she gets back. Doesn't lift one finger. Not even if she wants to.'

'She's lucky to have you here to take care of her. They both are.'

'Thank you for helping us yesterday. And for keeping an eye on the shop,' Sarah said, struggling to keep her voice polite but impersonal. 'You've been a good friend to us, Pete. We appreciate it.'

'That was nothing.' He paused for a moment, and then lifted his eyes to look her full in the face. 'Sarah we need to talk about—'

Sarah shook her head. 'No, Pete. Not now.'

His face fell, but Sarah did not have the emotional strength left to feel anything and certainly not sympathy for a man who had lied to her. Well, perhaps not lied, but certainly not told her the truth. There was nothing she could say to him right now, and there was certainly nothing he could say that would change the way she felt. She simply turned and walked into the shop.

She locked the door behind her, and turned the hanging sign to say 'Closed'. Not that she expected customers. Trish Warren would have made certain the whole town knew to stay away from the shop today. For once she was grateful for the Coorah Creek grapevine.

Slowly she walked through the house to be greeted by a loud wail of protest from Meggs. The cat was waiting for her just inside the kitchen door, sitting next to his empty food bowl. He glared up at her in an accusing manner. The remains of a smashed plate still lay where her father had dropped it the previous afternoon in his rush to get to his wife's side. She should clean that up, but not now. She didn't have the strength. It took all of her willpower to retrieve a can of cat food from the fridge and dispense breakfast for her hungry feline.

Sarah walked through to her bedroom. On her return from college, she had moved back into the room she'd used as a child. A few of her prized childhood possessions were still there. Some books. A somewhat battered stuffed elephant. A poster of some long forgotten pop idol. She flung herself down on the bed. Despite the bone weariness she felt after being awake all night, she did not feel like sleeping. Instead she opened the top drawer of her bedside table and removed the faded old photograph she had found in the dusty box in the storeroom. The afternoon she had found it now seemed years ago, almost as many years ago as the day the photo had been taken.

How young she had been. How innocent. As she sat there at the wheel of Pete's big truck, she had honestly believed in the happy ever after of the fairy tales she read. She had pictured herself, all grown up, driving away into the sunset with Pete. She'd grown out of that, of course, when she went away. But then fallen straight back into the same trap the moment she laid eyes on him again.

It was about time she stopped believing in fairy tales.

She did still believe in love. Her parents had shown her that real love could exist. Sitting in the hospital last night, as her father held the hand of the woman he still loved after all these years, Sarah knew that she wanted to find a similar love.

But it just wasn't going to be with Pete.

She was too tired to get off the bed to throw the photo in

the bin. Instead, she tossed it carelessly away, not bothering to look where it fell.

'I am an idiot,' Pete cursed himself softly under his breath as he watched the mine team unloading his truck. This was the load he should have delivered the night before. He had stopped at the shop first because he was desperate to see Sarah and tell her the truth. He was glad he had been there to help, but he wished things were different.

'As if she wants to talk about me, with her mother sick in the hospital. And her father too, for that matter. What was I thinking?'

He took another swig from the water bottle and looked up at the sun. At this rate, the unloading would be finished very soon. There was plenty of daylight left. He would drive back to the Isa immediately and try to see if there was another load waiting for him. He had to make up some of the money he'd lost during the search and those long days at the hospital with Linda, although that seemed less important now that he no longer had to think about supporting a family.

A short distance away, some workers were coming off shift. He saw Tia immediately. Her height and the femininity that she exuded even in protective work gear made her stand out from her workmates. As she always seemed to be, she was walking a little away from the others.

He raised a hand to catch her eye and she walked over to him.

'Hi, partner,' he said.

'Hi. How's things?'

'All right,' he said. 'Did you get a chance to say goodbye to the Haywoods? I didn't and I'm sorry I missed them.'

'I missed them too,' Tia said. 'Max said they dropped by to say goodbye and sent their thanks to both of us.'

'That was nice of them.'

The two of them stood in silence for a few seconds, watching the last of the load being removed from Pete's trailer.

'So, life is back to normal around here,' Pete said.

'I guess. But there are times I wonder what normal really is.'

With that she walked away. Pete watched her go, wondering if he too really had any idea of what normal was. His life had been a rollercoaster for the past few weeks. It wasn't like being physically tired. He worked hard and knew what exhaustion felt like. This was worse. This was an emotional burnout. He couldn't see any joy in the days, weeks and months ahead, if he couldn't find a way to mend his bridges with Sarah. One thing he did know, any life that didn't include her was not going to be a happy one.

Chapter Twenty-Nine

Tia removed the rucksack from its hiding place and put it on the table next to the newspaper cutting with the garish red slash across the photograph. She opened the bag and the old Christmas card fell out. The colours had faded over the years and now it looked more sad than cheerful as it lay on the Formica tabletop. Tia picked it up and looked inside. The writing had faded too. The card represented her last contact with her mother. The day after she received it, Tia had run away from home and never returned. If she had known then what she knew now, perhaps she might not have run so quickly. Or so far.

She set the card to one side and emptied the rest of the rucksack's contents onto the table.

Even encased in its plastic bag, the gun lay there looking exactly what it was. Deadly. A threat to her and everyone close to her. She glanced nervously over her shoulder. The light inside her trailer was dim, due to the closed curtains. She was safe from the prying eyes of her workmates. But not from Ned. She had no doubt the prowler disturbed the previous night was her former boyfriend. Well, boyfriend wasn't the right word. He was a gang leader who ruled his gang with an iron fist, and he had decided she was his. She'd had no say in the matter. Not that she would have said no. At the time, she had been thrilled and flattered to be the gang leader's girl. That gave her some power and prestige. More than she'd ever had before in her life. To a teenage runaway, that was important. She hadn't seen the dark side then.

She was equally certain Ned had left the newspaper cutting. It was his way of telling her how he had found her. His way of telling her she had been careless.

She opened the small velvet box lying next to the gun. All those months at the bottom of the rucksack had not dulled the ring's glamour. The huge square-cut diamond shone like a star even in the dim light. How Ned had coveted this ring. From the moment he'd seen it in the window of an exclusive jewellery store, he had wanted it with an obsessive passion. He said it would give him the status he demanded. Like some American gangsta leader. It hadn't taken Ned long to decide to acquire it the only way he knew how. With violence.

Which was where the gun came in.

Tia flinched as the memories of that day came crowding back. The shop and the terrified faces of the staff and customers. The triumph and joy on Ned's face as he pulled the trigger and the deafening sound as the shot echoed around them. If she closed her eyes, she could still see the red blood against the cream marble floor. Lying in her bed in the silent darkness of the small hours of the morning, she had relived those traumatic moments a thousand times.

And she had run away. Escaping from Ned and his gang had been as terrifying and dangerous as that day in the jewellery store. Running away now would be easy by comparison. But she was no longer the frightened girl she had been back then. She had changed, and a large part of the change was due to this town and the people in it. Especially Max. She wasn't going to run away again. Ever.

Tia thrust everything back into the rucksack and returned it to its hiding place. It was time she told Max the whole story.

As she left, she locked the trailer behind her. Not that a simple lock would ever stop Ned. But it might discourage him, at least while the sun was shining and other people were moving around the compound. She decided then that whatever happened, she did not want to be alone in her trailer tonight.

It would be far too dangerous.

Forcing herself not to look over her shoulder, she slipped her helmet on and swung her leg over the Harley. As she pressed the starter, she couldn't help but wonder if Ned was out there somewhere watching her. The distinctive sound of the bike's engine would no doubt add to his fury, making him even more dangerous. She slipped the bike into gear and headed into town.

As she approached the police station, she noticed several cars parked in and around the town square. The police station itself was overflowing with people and it seemed tempers were running a little high. Tia paused just outside the door.

'... his fault. He was tailgating me. Then when the roo jumped out—'

'I was not! Your brake lights—'

'Enough!' Max's voice cut through the hubbub. 'We will sort this out, but I am only going to listen to one of you at a time. So, Mr Taylor, go and sit over there and be quiet! Mr Coupland, that chair there. If I catch either one of you even looking like talking, it will be the cells for both of you. Got it?'

The silence that followed seemed to indicate they had.

'Good. Now, ladies. Please go and sit by your husbands and join them in their silent meditation.'

'But—'

'No buts. Go and sit down. Everyone will get a chance to say their piece, but one at a time and when I ask them to.'

Tia stepped through the doorway to see Max standing at his desk dividing his attention between two smartly dressed middle-aged couples, who were seating themselves at opposite ends of the room. There was a definite chill in the air between them. Max glanced over to the doorway and when he saw Tia, his face lit up.

'Right. Nobody so much as move. I'll be back in a minute.'

He stepped to the door and gently eased himself and Tia outside, but not so far away that he couldn't keep a watchful eye on proceedings inside the police station.

'What's that all about?' Tia asked.

'A couple of dents and some scratched paintwork,' Max said, shaking his head. 'Unfortunately both men are classic car buffs, so the cars concerned are apparently worth a lot of money. They are at each other's throats over who is to blame. And the wives aren't helping either. The silly thing is, they are all friends and this accident happened during a long drive they were taking together.'

'I'm sure you'll sort them out,' Tia said.

'I will, but it may take a while. Was this business?' His eyes twinkled. 'Or did you come here to ask me out to dinner tonight?'

How she wished it was just the latter.

'Actually it is business.'

Max nodded. 'I did want to talk some more about that prowler. '

'Yes. It's about that.' It wasn't a lie. But there was more to it than Max could even begin to guess.

Max glanced at his watch. 'It'll probably take me an hour or more to sort this lot out. Why don't I come around to see you after that? It'll be about five-ish, I guess. We can get the business part done, and then maybe share a meal. I can cook if you don't want to. And I'll bring a bottle of wine.'

That sounded so good. Like a normal date. The sort of date she had never had.

'And,' Max continued, 'To be honest, I'd like to check out your security. I could set up a stakeout outside in my car, but I'd rather be inside. With you. For your own safety, of course.' He actually winked at her.

'All right,' she said. 'I'm fairly new to cooking, but if you are willing to take a risk, I can try to make us an edible meal.'

As she spoke, another shouting match began inside the police station. Max raised his eyes to the heavens with a sigh. 'I have to go. I'll see you later.'

Tia left him returning to his role as referee and walked towards the store. She was a bit confused. Was the evening going to be her confessing to a policeman? Or was it going to be her telling her … whatever Max was to her … about her past? Both had to be done. Would blurring the lines make it easier or harder, she wondered?

Sarah was counting the cash in the register when the door opened and Tia walked in. She put the cash back and shut the money drawer.

'Hi, Tia. I haven't seen you for a couple of days.'

'I've been doing extra time at the mine. Giving a break to the guys who worked double shifts during the search.'

'I heard there was some sort of problem out there. A prowler. In the accommodation compound. Were you there?'

'No. I was working.'

'I also hear Max was out there all night. I wondered if maybe you had something to do with that?' Sarah watched Tia's face closely, and was rewarded with a faint glow of colour.

'You're blushing,' Sarah said triumphantly. 'Trish was right. Of course. When is Trish ever wrong?'

'He's coming out after work tonight – to talk about the

236

prowler,' Tia said. 'I thought it would be nice to cook him dinner.'

'Well, at least things are working out for the two of you.' The bitter words were out before Sarah could stop them.

Tia frowned. 'You and Pete … it's not …'

'It's not anything.' Sarah sighed. 'When I was a little girl, all I wanted was a knight in shining armour to come driving down that road and sweep me away. Like in the fairy tales. There was a time I thought Pete was that man. I was wrong. That sort of thing only happens in fairy tales. Real life isn't like that.'

'Don't say that. I want to think maybe it can be,' Tia said softly.

Sarah hid her surprise. Something had certainly changed for Tia, and she was sure Max was responsible. She'd seen the way the two of them had looked at each other out there during the search. She was glad for them both. And a little bit envious.

'So, dinner,' she said, trying to send the conversation in a direction that would not threaten her own composure. 'I suppose a tuna casserole is not quite what you are looking for.'

'No. It's not.' Tia smiled.

'Good. I'm sure I can help you do better than that. We have some candles, too, if you want them.'

No sooner had Tia left than the front door of the shop opened again. Sarah felt her heart skip a beat as she instantly recognised the tall figure blocking most of the sunlight in the doorway.

'Hi, Sarah.' His voice was hesitant. 'I wanted to see how your mum was doing.'

'She's doing much better now, thanks. She's home. I would have thought you would be back in the Isa by now.'

'No. I hung around. I need to talk to you. But if this is still a bad time, I can wait.'

He was inside the shop now, and she could see his face clearly. The look he wore was a mixture of pleading, determination and something else. The same something she had seen on him during the search. In the moments before he kissed her. That look was tugging at her heartstrings. But she was a grown woman now, not a child. She had to deal with reality.

'I haven't asked you, Pete. How is your girlfriend? And the baby? I hope everything is all right.' She didn't even try to disguise the bitterness in her voice.

'That's what I need to talk to you about.'

'Pete. You don't have to explain anything. It was just a kiss.' A kiss that had changed everything for her. 'You don't owe me anything—'

'Sarah. Stop. Listen. It's not my baby.' He blurted it out and then stopped, his eyes searching her face as the words seemed to hang in the air between them.

Sarah blinked, struggling to fully understand what he was saying.

'Not your baby? But your girlfriend—?'

'She told me it was my baby. But it's not. She was ... well, it's enough to say that the real father is back with her. They are going to make a life together.'

She tried to speak, but there were no words. Her mind was blank.

'I'm glad things have worked out for them,' Pete continued, his eyes never leaving her face. 'I know I should never have kissed you like that. Not without telling you what was happening. I guess it wasn't a lie as such. But to me it felt like one. These past few weeks have taught me two things. The first is that I like the idea of being a dad. My mother will be so pleased to hear me say that. She's been on at me for ages about settling down. I think maybe it's time. I was ready to take responsibility for the baby. Be there to support Linda and the baby financially and any other support I could give them. But any future I plan has to be with the right person. I was going to tell Linda that she was the wrong person. But she told me her truth first.'

'Oh.' Sarah shook her head, trying to take in everything he was saying. Pete wasn't normally a big talker. But now, it was as if he couldn't stop. Maybe he'd been holding all this inside for too long.

'When I settle down, I want the sort of life my parents have. Your parents, too. That's why I'm here, Sarah. Because you are the right person for me. You were the little girl I was fond of, and somehow you've become the woman I'm in love with. I want to take the time to be with you and see where these feelings lead me. Lead us.'

He paused then, waiting for her to say something. Her mind was racing but somewhere deep inside her, joy was beginning to wash away the despair of the past few days. She was still struggling for words, and slowly she began to shake her head.

She took a deep breath, but before she could speak the door of the store swung open, and a mother with kids in tow walked in.

'I guess I'd better ...' Sarah said, indicating her customers.

'I know. Look, think about what I said. I'll be across the road. Waiting for you. If you don't come, I'll have my answer.'

'I ...' She already knew what her answer would be.

A woman's voice interrupted her. 'Sorry to butt in, Sarah, but can you tell me which is the better brand of dry cat food?'

Pete turned and left her to her customers.

Chapter Thirty

For the very first time in her life, Tia was cooking dinner for a guest. Not just any guest: a man. A good man who had never hurt her or used her or caused her to cry.

She was cooking for Max.

She was excited and nervous. This must be how it felt to be a schoolgirl on a first date. That was just one of the experiences denied her. Until now. It felt good.

The dinner ingredients she had bought from Sarah at the store were all laid out in her tiny kitchen. Since coming to Coorah Creek and having a home of her own, Tia had discovered that not only did she like cooking, she was actually pretty good at it. Especially considering her late introduction to the culinary arts. At least, she hoped she was pretty good at it. The meals she had cooked for herself were always tasty and filling. But cooking a meal for Max was still a bit scary. Would he like what she made? It seemed very important that he did.

She laid out the piece of lamb on her small work surface and began rubbing the dried rosemary and garlic that would add some Greek flavours to the skin. There would be lemon and rosemary potatoes to go with it. And Max was bringing wine. Red wine would make this a proper Greek meal. Her very first. She'd really love to go to Greece one day. See the ruins she had read about. The thought caused her to pause in her work. That was another first for her. The idea that one day she might actually travel to somewhere like Greece. She might visit places she had seen on TV. There was a whole world out there that she could now believe was waiting for her.

All she had to do was break free of her past. And the first step was to talk to Max.

She turned around and looked at the rucksack that was waiting on the table. Lying next to it was the newspaper cutting with the vivid red slash. She had put them there so they would be the first thing Max saw when he walked in the door. Then she wouldn't be able to back down. She would have to go through with it.

She returned to her task, and placed the lamb in a baking dish. Then she turned on her small oven and slid the dish inside. She had a few minutes to kill before she needed to start on the potatoes. Maybe she should change out of her jeans into something more ... what? Something sexier? That wasn't what this evening was about. It was about her confession.

But after she confessed, would they even get to eat the lamb? It suddenly dawned on her that Max might arrest her. After all, she was confessing to a crime. Several crimes, in fact; some of them very serious. He was an honest cop and he couldn't just turn a blind eye to what she had done. She hadn't even considered that.

She took a couple of slow breaths.

No. She wasn't going to let anything destroy her chance for even an hour of happiness. This one evening, she was going to be normal and have the things that other women had. She would have this one taste of those dreams, because it might be her only chance. Ever. What happened after that would depend on Max and how he reacted to her confession.

She grabbed the rucksack and tossed it into a cupboard, slamming the door solidly behind it. She also picked up the cutting and slid it under a book on the shelf in what she grandly called her living room. Then she darted into her bedroom and began riffling through her clothes, looking for something more appealing than her jeans and T-shirt.

'You look great.' Max meant it too. Tia was wearing a short denim skirt and a light creamy blouse, open at the neck to reveal a hint of that tantalising tattoo. Standing as he was on the lower rung of the trailer's stairs, he had a wonderful view of the shapely curves of her legs, and the small, almost elegant, bare feet.

'Thank you.' Tia stepped back from the doorway and Max followed her into the trailer. It looked much the same as on his last visit. Clean and tidy, but bare. The dog-eared books on the shelf were the only personal possessions he could see. He looked at the titles. There were history books and travel books, and the sort of classic novels that were required reading at school. It suddenly occurred to him that Tia was trying to catch up on the schooling she had missed when she ran away from home. That was just another thing to admire about her.

Then he noticed the amazing aroma coming from her oven.

'Is that dinner?' he asked.

Tia nodded, grinning shyly. 'I'm making Greek style lamb and potatoes. I've never cooked it before. I hope it will be okay.'

'If it's half as good as it smells, it will be great,' Max assured her. 'By the way, I brought us wine. I wasn't sure if you liked white or red, so I brought both.'

Tia took the bottles he offered and grinned. 'To be honest, I really don't know. I haven't ever drunk much wine. I'm more a beer sort of a girl.'

'Oh. Sorry.'

'No. I'd like to give it a try. Shall we open a bottle?'

Max hesitated. He wanted to say yes. He wanted to

242

forget about the work-related reasons he was there. The last thing he wanted to do was worry Tia with thoughts about the prowler. But he wanted to make sure she was safe. If he did that first, then he could consider himself off duty for the rest of the evening and just be himself and enjoy spending time with the most attractive and intriguing woman he had ever met.

'I'd like to get the business part of this done first,' he said. 'I'll take a look around outside and see if I can see any more signs of that prowler. And I'll have a look at the locks on your windows too.'

'Oh.' She looked disappointed. 'Sure. You should do that. Thanks.'

Max stepped outside and walked around the trailer. He checked the windows for signs that someone had tried to break in, but he saw nothing. But when he examined the door lock, there were some scratches in the metal around the keyhole, as if someone had tried to pick it. Or possibly even succeeded. He didn't like the look of that at all.

He walked to a nearby stand of trees, and there he found what he expected. The dirt was scuffed and there were several cigarette butts. Someone had been watching Tia's trailer. Was this person a lonely miner or a peeping tom? Or was there something more sinister here? The thought of danger to Tia was enough to set his blood boiling.

Max glanced around him. He wasn't sure where tonight was leading for him and Tia, but he was not going to leave her alone tonight. His car was parked a short distance from her trailer, pretty much hidden among the dongas and the other cars. Most people wouldn't see it. If necessary, he was prepared to spend another night sitting there. Keeping watch. Keeping Tia safe. But he couldn't stay here every night. He needed to talk to Chris Powell. As mine manager,

Chris was responsible for this compound. He needed to beef up his security here.

When Max walked back into the trailer, Tia was sitting at the dining table. An open rucksack sat in front of her. There was a newspaper cutting next to it.

'Tia?'

'Sit down, Max. I need to talk to you. And to show you some things. I was going to wait until after dinner, but you're right. We need to do this now.'

'Sure.'

He sat down. Silently, Tia pushed the cutting towards him. He was shocked to see the angry red slash across the image of Tia.

'Where did this come from?' he asked.

'I found it after we had dinner in the pub. When you dropped me off, it was waiting here for me. On the table.'

'Someone had broken in? Tia, why didn't you call me back? This looks like a threat to me. And now there's that prowler. You shouldn't be here on your own.'

He reached out to hold her hand. He wasn't surprised to find it was shaking. He squeezed it gently, hoping the need to comfort Tia would control the anger that was surging inside him at the thought of someone invading her home.

'I know who it was,' she said in a very tiny voice.

He could feel her fear. Was it the echo of fears from her past, or was it a present fear? There was nothing he could do about the past, but he would not have her sitting alone and afraid. Not while he was around.

'Who was it?'

Tia's fingers gripped his hand so hard it was as if she wanted to break his bones. He didn't flinch.

'It's a long story, Max. I have been wanting to tell you, but I was too afraid of what you would think of me when I did.'

'Tia, I won't think—'

'Stop.' She held up a hand to silence him. 'Please, just let me tell you everything. Don't say a word until I'm finished. I may never find the courage to do this again.'

He did the only thing he could. He nodded, holding her hand tightly as she began her tale.

'You know I was a runaway. And that I lived in squats. And I told you about the gang I joined. I was sixteen then. The gang leader was a few years older. I thought he was so handsome. And he had this power and charisma about him. His name was Andrew Kelly – he called himself Ned Kelly – after the bushranger. I think that's how he saw himself, as some sort of cult hero. He had a girlfriend when I joined. But he got rid of her and chose me instead. He was the one who made me get this.'

Tia pulled open her shirt to reveal the tattoo that had so tantalised Max. For the first time he could see it clearly. It was a highly stylised image of a man with a rifle. A man wearing an iconic metal helmet. Max felt his stomach clench in revulsion. How could he have been teased by this? Or thought it sexy?

'He branded you?'

Tia nodded.

'I thought it was cool at first, but I soon figured out just the sort of person he was. He used me ... in a lot of ways.'

Max tightened his fingers around hers again, feeling a surge of hatred the strength of which shocked him. How could someone do that? To the young and vulnerable girl Tia had once been. His heart cried for her while his fingers itched to grab the man's throat.

'I stayed because I had nowhere else to go. I stayed because I was afraid that if I left, he would track me down and drag me back. I didn't think there could be a better life for someone like me. I did drugs sometimes. When I had to.

To blend in with the others. Or to escape reality. But never the hard stuff. I wasn't quite that much of a mess. And I wasn't a dealer either.

'We had always stolen – food, booze and a bit of money when we could. But he started taking the whole Ned Kelly thing too seriously. They started mugging people. Sometimes they beat the victim up. Max, I didn't ever do that. You have to believe me.'

Her lovely green eyes pleaded with him. In his heart, he knew she wasn't lying. And even if she had been, he was not going to lay any blame at her door for the sort of life that no young girl should ever have to experience.

'Of course I believe you,' he said gently.

'They had guns and started robbing stores. Ned got greedy. Every time they got away with it, he wanted more. Then one day, while we were walking through town, he saw this.'

She reached into the rucksack and pulled out a small black velvet box. She put it on the table and left it for Max to open. He was shocked to see a man's diamond ring nestled in its velvet holder. He lifted the box and looked more closely at it. He was no expert, but his every instinct told him this was a valuable piece. He closed the lid and turned the box over. The jeweller's name almost leaped out at him.

'This is from that hold-up last year. The one where—'

'—a cop was killed.' Tia finished the sentence for him. 'Yes, it is.'

Max remembered the incident. He was a cop, and any crime where another officer was killed struck home with great force. The hold-up had taken place at the very end of the business day. Three men; all armed. The local beat cop had just happened to walk past in the middle of the hold-up. He'd tried to stop the robbery, and lost his life.

The reports said the killer had laughed as he walked out of the door.

'I was there, Max. Ned made me go with them to grab as much jewellery as I could, then carry it while the others took care of the staff and witnesses. I wasn't part of the shooting. I didn't know that was going to happen.'

'I saw the reports. They were looking for three men, all armed, and a female accomplice. That was you?'

She nodded. 'One of the men was Ned. He was the one who did the shooting. He was proud of it. Boasted about it. Thought it made him such a big man. That's when I knew I had to get out. I waited for my chance and took off.'

'Why did you take the ring?'

'I don't know. I guess I didn't want him to have it.'

'So you stole the Harley and took off?'

'That wasn't the only thing I stole.'

Tia reached into the rucksack once more. Max heard the rustling of the plastic bag, but it wasn't until it was lying on the table in front of him that he realised what he was looking at.

'This is the gun that killed that constable,' he said.

'Yes. It's Ned's gun. I put it in a plastic bag to preserve the fingerprints, or whatever. I thought if he ever found me, I could trade this and the ring. Give it back if he promised to let me go.'

Max carefully picked up the gun. He looked at it through the plastic. The safety was off. He weighed it in his hand.

'This is loaded?'

'I guess so. I don't know anything about guns. I just took it and threw it in my bag. I didn't ever want to use it. Or even look at it.' Tia took a long slow breath. 'I guess Ned saw that piece in the newspaper and came looking for me. Just when I was starting to think I was safe from him.

Not that I regret helping find little Renee, but I wish that reporter had used a different photo.'

'But it's good that you've told me,' Max said. 'You really can't spend the rest of your life running from this guy. And carrying all this with you.'

'I know I can't.' Tia took a deep breath and exhaled slowly, as if she was pleased to have finally broken her silence. 'So what happens now? I guess you arrest me.'

'No!' The word came out far more vehemently than Max intended. He paused for a second to calm himself. 'You are not the criminal here. You're a victim. And you're a witness too. You need to give evidence against him. Then we can put him away and you'll be safe.'

'Really?' The question in her eyes almost broke his heart. Max got to his feet and pulled her into his arms. He held her close, as if he would never let her go.

'Yes, really. Tia, you've overcome the most shocking past. And you've made a new life for yourself. I will not let anything destroy what you have accomplished.'

'Well, isn't that just lovely,' the sarcastic sneer from the doorway took them both by surprise.

Max spun to face the intruder, pushing Tia behind him to shelter her with his own body. The man standing in the doorway wasn't as tall as Max, but he was heavily built. His clothes were stylish and his hair was neatly cropped. There was a tattoo on his arm. In an instant, Max knew who he was. The gang boss wasn't holding a gun, but he exuded danger all the same.

'Take it easy,' Ned said. 'We don't want anyone to get hurt now, do we?'

The explicit threat to Tia made the hairs on the back of Max's neck stand up. He cursed himself for leaving his own weapon back at the station, but he'd been coming off duty and this was supposed to be a date.

'This doesn't need to get nasty,' Ned continued in that same sneering tone as he studied the items lying on the table. 'I came to get what's mine. The bike. That ring. The gun.'

Max opened his mouth to reply ... then froze as Ned continued. 'And her too, of course.'

Chapter Thirty-One

He shouldn't stare at the pub door. That wasn't going to make Sarah appear. Pete lowered his eyes back to the beer in his hand. It was his first and he'd been sitting there not drinking it for almost an hour now.

She wasn't coming. That was becoming very clear. He should have realised that when he saw her shake her head just before they were interrupted in the store.

He ran his finger down the damp side of the beer glass, watching the droplets slide down the glass onto the red and gold beer mat underneath. He should just go. Maybe if he gave her some time – a few days, a few weeks, maybe – she might forgive him. He was willing to wait as long as it took.

'Is there something wrong with the beer, mate?' Behind the bar Jack North was stacking clean glasses from the washer.

'No. I guess I'm just not in the mood,' Pete said.

'Are you sure?' Jack nodded in the direction of the door.

Pete looked up. Sarah was there, looking straight at him. He moved as if to rise from his bar stool, but before he could, Sarah slid onto the stool next to him.

'Do you also want a beer that you don't drink and leave on the bar to get hot and flat?' Jack asked.

'Yes, please.'

Sarah and Pete sat in silence until after Jack had done his duty and moved away to the other end of the bar.

'I thought you weren't coming,' Pete said quietly.

'I knew I was. You just won't believe how long those people took to buy some cat food. It must be a pretty fussy cat.'

Pete blinked a little. Sarah was smiling at him. Joking. This wasn't how he had imagined their next encounter. He had been sitting here trying to find the words that would convince her to give him another chance. The words he'd rehearsed now seemed totally inadequate, and had all vanished from his mind.

'Look, Pete,' Sarah continued. 'I've known you since I was ten years old. In all that time, you have always been straight with me. And you have never done anything to harm me – or anyone else – as far as I know. You always did the right thing by everyone.'

'But sometimes the right thing isn't right,' he said, with a slow smile as the memory of the first time she had said those words came back to him. 'A very wise woman told me that once.'

'And I was right.' Sarah reached out to lay her hand over his. 'Pete, I know you wanted to help Linda and the baby. But even if it had been your child, marrying her for the wrong reasons would only have hurt both of you, and the child, in the end. A child deserves to have parents who love each other and can be a proper family. I am so glad you finally recognised that. Should you have kissed me? Yes. Of course you should, because that was a moment of absolute honesty. For both of us.'

As she looked up at him from under her eyelashes, Pete felt the world shift once more. The earth was back on its proper axis. He let out a long slow breath.

'So,' he said barely able to believe what was happening, 'if I was to suggest that we go out together some time. You'd say...?'

'Yes.'

When it was right, it really was as simple as that.

'And if I was to ask you to stay and have dinner with me tonight before I head back to the Isa?'

'That would be a yes too. And before you ask, if you wanted to kiss me again before you left, that would also be a yes.'

Pete smiled as happiness replaced the uncertainty that he had been wearing like a cloak. He reached out to take Sarah's hand. It felt so right in his. Their fingers twined together and, oblivious to the watchful eyes around the bar, he lifted her hand and touched his lips ever so gently to her skin.

He let go of her hand and only then did he finally lift his beer and take a drink. Sarah smiled and did the same with hers.

The phone at the end of the bar rang. Trish Warren appeared from the direction of the kitchen and answered it.

'What? No. He's not here. I don't know where he is. Hang on, I'll ask.' She held the phone aside. 'Does anyone know where Max is?' she asked the bar in general.

'Yes,' said Sarah. 'He's having dinner with Tia. At her place in the mine compound.'

'That can't be right,' Trish said, frowning. 'I've got Blue here from the mine. He says that prowler is back hanging around the dongas. Near Tia's trailer. He's looking for Max. But if Max is already there, wouldn't he—'

Sarah and Pete exchanged a look.

'Can I talk to him for a second?' Pete said.

Trish handed over the phone.

'Are you sure you can't see Max's car?' he asked the man on the other end of the line.

'I can't see it,' Blue said. 'But if he's put it under the trees where he kept watch last time, I might not. Maybe I should go and have a look. But last time, Max said to get in touch with him before doing anything.'

Pete thought for a moment. Everything about this

sounded wrong. He didn't have Max's police training to guide him, but some things don't need that sort of training.

'No, don't go near Tia's trailer or the car. If there is something wrong, you might make it worse. A couple of us are heading your way right now. Don't do anything until we get there.'

'All right.'

Pete handed the phone back to Trish. He looked around the room. Jack had already put down the glasses he was stacking and come out from behind the bar. Pete looked at him and nodded. They were obviously both thinking the same thing. They were the only ones present who had not been drinking all evening.

'And I'm coming with you,' Sarah said, getting to her feet.

'No. You stay here. If there's trouble …' Pete started to say, but Sarah was one step ahead of him.

'If there's trouble, Tia will need a friend.' She led the way out the door.

'She's not going anywhere. You will never lay a hand on her again.' Max's voice was steel.

Tia loved him for those words, but he had no idea what he was up against. He was still holding her behind him, using his own body as a shield between her and the intruder. Cold fear clutched at Tia's heart. Ned wasn't holding a gun, but that meant nothing. He'd killed one policeman and boasted about it. He wouldn't hesitate to do it a second time. The thought of Max being hurt was more than she could stand. He was the one good man she had ever known … and if he was hurt or died because of her, she would never forgive herself.

Ned had changed since she last saw him. He was better dressed and more confident. Killing a cop had obviously turned him from the leader of a street gang into something bigger; a more seasoned criminal and a more dangerous man than he'd been back then. She looked at his face, and the almost maniac shine in his eyes, and felt an icy shiver through her soul. Ned was no longer just a nasty piece of work – he had progressed to truly evil. He wouldn't need much provocation to kill again. He would probably enjoy it. Giving him back the things she had stolen would never be enough. There was only one way she could keep Max safe.

'All right, Ned. I'll come with you. Let's just go.'

She felt Max's body stiffen as she spoke.

'No.' Max began to move but in a heartbeat a gun materialised in Ned's hand.

'Sit down,' he snarled.

Max froze and then slowly took a step backwards and lowered himself onto a chair.

Tia stared at the gun. It was pointed straight at Max and it was as steady as a rock. Ned saw her glance.

'You didn't think you took my only one, did you?' he asked.

Tia knew from bitter experience what he expected. 'No, Ned,' she said in a quiet and submissive voice.

'Now, be a good girl and pass me my things,' he said.

'All right.'

Tia reached out one hand to pick up the black velvet box. She snapped it shut and passed it to Ned. Never taking his eyes off Max, Ned took it. She flinched as his fingers touched hers. He slipped the box into his pocket.

'And now the gun.'

Tia kept her eyes lowered as she reached for the gun. She deliberately avoided looking at Max. She didn't want to see the disappointment on his face. Or even worse, acceptance.

'No. Tia, don't.' Max's voice was strong and defiant.

'Look, Kelly. Quit while you can. You can take the Harley and the ring and run as far and as fast as you can.'

'I'm not going without my gun.'

'You know I can't let you take the gun.'

'And I am not going without her.'

'If you take her, I will come after you. Nothing will save you.' Max's voice was cold, hard steel. In that moment, Tia understood that in his own way, Max was dangerous too. 'It doesn't matter where you go. It doesn't matter how long it takes. I will find you. And God help me, if you have hurt her, I will kill you.'

Max spoke the words in a cold matter of fact tone that terrified Tia. She wanted to scream at him to stop. He was deliberately goading Ned. She knew only too well what happened when the gang boss lost control.

'Oh, really,' Ned sneered and the gun pointing at Max never wavered. 'You don't scare me. I've killed one cop. What makes you think I won't kill another one? And way out here, there's no one to stop me. I checked this place out. You're the only cop. With you gone, I could just walk away. And I'd take her with me. I'm sure I'd find a use for her.'

The implication in his words made Tia's stomach churn.

'Please, Ned.' She had to stop this. Now. Max would goad Ned into pulling the trigger. That hot lead would tear through Max's flesh, taking his life. Her own life would end in the same moment, whether or not Ned pulled the trigger a second time. She would not let Max die because of her!

She took a step towards Ned. 'I'll go with you, Ned. I'll do anything you want. Come on. Let's go.'

'Tia. No!' Max's voice was a ragged cry.

Ned's eyes flashed from one to the other. 'Oh. So that's how it is? Tia, you replaced me with a pig. Still, he's not your first, is he? I always thought you liked it when I sent you to do them.'

Bitterness rose in Tia's throat.

'Come on then, girl. Bring me the gun.'

She couldn't look at Max. She took the plastic bag with the gun from the table and handed it to Ned. He kept his eyes glued on Max as he tossed the gun gently in his hand, then tucked it into his belt.

'All right. Now for the bike. Keys.'

Tia pointed to the shelf where the keys lay.

'Well, get them. Go on.'

She did as she was told. The room quivered with tension. She wanted to scream. But she had to hold it together. She had to get Ned away from here before he snapped. Because when he did, Max would die. And she would be to blame.

'Let's go,' she said. 'Let's get away from here. The bike's just outside. We can go now.'

'Yeah. Let's go.' Ned grabbed her arm and pulled her close to him. Across the room, Max tensed and started to rise from his seat.

Ned jammed the gun into Tia's neck. She bit back a scream.

'Listen to me. Both of you,' Ned said. 'Let's keep this nice and quiet. We don't want to attract any attention. That would get messy. I've got more than enough bullets for everyone. Tia, baby, it's good to have you back.' Ned's eyes never left Max, but he ran his hands over her body in a way that brought bile rising in her throat. 'You are going to lead the way. I want you to open that door and slowly step outside. One false move from you, and I shoot the cop. And you.' He glared at Max. 'You will stay right where you are. If I see your face in that doorway, I'll put a bullet in her. Do you understand?'

Tia wasn't sure she could walk down the stairs. Her

knees were shaking too badly. She risked one last glance at Max. His face was calm but cold. His eyes steely and fixed on Ned. She would never see him again, but at least she would not have to blame herself for his death.

She put one foot on the top step.

'Slowly now, bitch,' Ned said as he hovered in the doorway. 'You don't want to make my finger twitch, do you?'

Tia lifted her foot. Her head still turned towards the interior of her trailer, she felt down for the next step.

Suddenly hands reached for her out of the darkness. They grabbed her arm and yanked her forward. As she fell her shoulder hit the edge of the metal door, sending a shaft of agony through her left side. Then the air around her exploded with the deafening sound of a gunshot.

Tia screamed.

Chapter Thirty-Two

Max felt the bullet pass very close to his cheek as he flung himself across the room, his ears ringing from the gunshot in such an enclosed space. The moment that Tia had fallen, Ned's gun had wavered just for an instant, but an instant was all Max needed.

His shoulder hit Ned's legs just above his knees, his hands groping for the second gun tucked into the man's belt. Ned staggered with the force of the impact, and together they tumbled backwards, through the open door and down the trailer steps. He heard Ned grunt with pain as his ribs slammed against the metal edges of the stairs. As they fell, Ned twisted and Max hit the earth first with a bone jarring crash that knocked the breath from his body. He didn't care. All he wanted to do was stop this creep from ever touching Tia again.

Ned was still clutching his weapon. But there was another one. Max had to get that gun.

Ned was on top of him, his weight crushing Max's chest. With both of his hands, he grabbed the hand holding the gun and began to force the arm back. Ned was strong, but Max fought him with every fibre of his being. Tia was out there somewhere. It didn't matter what Ned did to him, as long as Tia had time to get away. The weight on his chest was making it hard to breathe. He knew he had only a few moments before the lack of air began to drain his strength.

Something made Ned turn his head, giving Max the chance he needed. Letting go of Ned's wrist, he slammed the heel of his hand hard into Ned's chin, putting all of his anger and fear and determination into a single blow. Ned's head snapped back. The hand holding the gun wavered. This was the opening Max needed. With one hand, he grabbed the gun, twisted the barrel away from him. The other hand groped along his own body for something he'd felt there. The other gun, still in its plastic bag, had come loose from Ned's waistband as they fell. Even as Ned regained his balance and he brought his gun back to bear, Max grabbed the plastic bag and slammed the cold hard metal into Ned's face with every ounce of strength left in his body.

At that moment, something moved in the corner of his vision, and Ned's weight was lifted from his chest. Taking huge gulps of air, Max staggered to his feet, helped by an unexpected hand. Still holding the gun encased in its plastic bag, he blinked, trying to comprehend the scene in front of him.

Three men were holding Ned. Pete was behind him, one arm locked around the man's neck in a firm strangle hold that had Ned gasping for every breath. Blood was pouring down Ned's face from a deep gash caused by the barrel of the gun. Jack North was holding one of Ned's arms. One of the miners had the other. Tia's shift boss, Blue, was standing next to him, holding Ned's gun. A couple of feet away, Sarah stood with Tia, one arm around her shoulders to comfort her. Max stared at her for several heartbeats, just to assure himself that she was all right. Her eyes, bright with tears, met his and the weight of the world was lifted from his shoulders. He could breathe again. She looked shaken and pale, but safe. That was the only thing that really mattered.

'You all right?' Pete asked Max between clenched teeth, without letting his hold slacken on Ned's neck. The gang boss's eyes were open but Max could see the fight quickly dying out of him.

'I'm fine. Blue, give me that.' He held out his hand for the gun. 'Now, can you go to my car. It's not locked. There are handcuffs in the glove box.'

'On it.'

By the time Max had engaged the safety on both guns, Blue was back with the handcuffs. Max took them.

'Turn him round,' he instructed the men holding Ned. They did and he snapped the cuffs in place. Ned flinched as the metal bit into his flesh. Max didn't care. If the cuffs were a little tighter than was comfortable, it was no concern of his.

Jack and Pete were still holding Ned's arms. They turned him around again and Max looked the man squarely in the face. He saw fear there, the bravado of the past wiped away by the realisation he was well and truly trapped. He felt a surge of anger. This man had threatened Tia; had laid his filthy hands on her. Max's hands clenched into fists as his body tensed.

'You know, if you felt the need to hit him again, we would understand, wouldn't we guys?' Blue said. 'In fact, we probably wouldn't even see you do it.'

Max thought about how good it would feel to smash his fist into Ned's face. To hurt him as he had hurt Tia so many times. And to pay him back for a colleague, shot dead while doing his duty. This man who had styled himself on a national icon was nothing but a lowlife. He would deserve anything Max could throw at him.

'No.' Max stepped back. That wasn't the person he was. There was no difference between hitting this man and the sort of brutal police behaviour he had always despised. 'That would be wrong. He'll get what he deserves. But he'll get it in a courtroom and a prison. He'll be paying for this for the rest of his life.'

Blue frowned. Then he swung a hard punch into Ned's

gut. With a grunt of pain, Ned fell to his knees, jerking forward as he gasped for breath.

'That's what you get for threatening Tia. She's one of us and we protect our own,' Blue hissed through clenched teeth.

Max laid a hand on the miner's arm. 'That's enough. All right. Pete. Jack. Can you get this guy in the car? I don't use the cells very often, but this time it will be a pleasure.'

As the men dragged the prisoner away, Max could finally turn his attention to Tia. He took one look at her tear-stained face and opened his arms. She stepped into them, as if she had always belonged there. He held her close, feeling her shoulders shaking.

'It's all right now,' he said gently. 'You are safe.'

'I thought he was going to ...' Her broken voice was muffled against his chest.

Max gently pulled her away and looked down into her face. 'That was a very brave and very stupid thing you did. Saying you would go with him.'

'I didn't want him to hurt you. I would have gone with him gladly to save you.'

Max's heart contracted as she spoke. Lost for words, he pulled her close and ran his hand gently over her face. Her emerald eyes were wide and damp. He gently kissed them dry. He felt some of the tension flow from her body. He held her for a few moments more, but that was all the time he had. He still had to deal with Kelly. He let her go, and returned to his duty.

'How did you all end up here?' he asked Sarah as they all gathered around the police car. Ned was inside, the door shut and both Pete and Jack standing guard.

'Blue saw the prowler again,' Sarah said. 'He tried to contact you. When he rang the pub, I knew you were here so we figured there might be a problem. We came to see if we could help.'

'We saw what was happening,' Pete continued. 'We waited until Tia was coming down the stairs, and we grabbed her to drag her away from him.'

'We figured maybe we could rush him ... or something,' Blue finished, looking a little uncertain.

'That was a foolish thing to do,' Max said, shaking his head. 'But I'm very grateful. Thank you.' He reached out to shake the men's hands. 'You can all be my wingmen any day.'

It was time to get going.

'All right. Jack, can you come in the front with me. Just to keep an eye on him. Pete, could you take both the women back into town. I assume you have a car here somewhere.'

'We came in Jack's,' Pete said. 'Don't worry. I'll get Tia and Sarah into town.'

He heard Sarah whisper something to her friend. The words knight in shining armour didn't make any sense, but they made Tia smile. It was a forlorn smile, but it lifted his heart.

'Blue, I need you to make sure no one goes near the trailer. I'll be back later to seal it up.'

'Got it.'

Max watched Tia walk with Pete and Sarah towards their vehicle. Just before she got in, she turned to him. Her lips moved a little. He couldn't hear her, of course, but he knew what she was saying.

Thank you.

Chapter Thirty-Three

Tia caught her breath as she saw the sign saying Coorah Creek. In a few minutes she would be home. Home? Yes, she decided. Home.

After so many years of living on the streets or sharing a place with members of a gang, she had lost touch with what 'home' really was. But she knew now. Home is where the people you love are. Home is where the people around you love you too. Home is a place where people want to help you, not hurt you. It's where you are safe. Coorah Creek was her home and more than anything in the world, right now, she wanted to be there with the community who had taken her in. With the friends she had made and the job she was proud of. And with Max.

The policeman in the seat next to her had talked pretty incessantly on the long drive down from Mount Isa, mostly about the capture of the infamous cop killer two weeks before and the evidence Tia would give later this year at the trial. And he'd talked about his admiration for Sergeant Max Delaney – the man who had single-handedly captured one of the state's most wanted men.

Tia could have corrected him and told him that, in the best Coorah Creek tradition, others had been there, helping Max even if in an unofficial and totally unexpected way. But she didn't. She'd told the story of that night more than enough times during her stay in the Isa. She had made statements and been interviewed by police both local and from Brisbane. She'd spent the first few days living in fear that she would be charged with some crime. After all, she had stolen a gun used in a major crime, and a valuable ring and a motorbike. There was also the possibility she could be charged for something she'd done in those dark days with the gang. It had taken her a little while, and a few days at a nice hotel at the police department's expense, to realise that she was a witness, not a target. And something of a heroine as well for her role in the capture. She wondered where that idea had come from. Perhaps from Max.

She hadn't seen him since that night, nor spoken to him except for one very brief phone call. She guessed he too had been giving statements and filling in paperwork. She wondered if his superior officers had deliberately kept them apart. Possibly. She also wondered if he had helped ease her way. Probably. She was grateful to him for that.

Now she was coming home and would see him again. Every part of her quivered with anticipation.

'It's not exactly a thriving city, this Coorah Creek,' the policeman next to her said as they drove slowly down the main street. 'Must get a bit boring.'

Tia felt herself bristle. 'It has its good points,' she replied. The very best of those good things was waiting for her at the police station just down the street.

'I guess so,' the constable said uncertainly. 'Still, I imagine Delaney will be glad to get out of here and back to the city.'

Tia turned slowly to look at him.

'What do you mean?'

'Well, catching Ned Kelly or whatever his real name is. That's put Delaney's career on the fast track. There'll be a promotion in it for him. And a transfer. He'll probably have a choice of assignment. Lucky guy.'

Every one of those words felt like a slap in the face for Tia. Max was going to leave? Go back to the city and leave Coorah Creek behind?

Of course he was. How could she not have realised that before? He must have ambition. He could do so much better than a small town posting. He spent most of his time in Coorah Creek taking the occasional drunk off the streets, sorting out a domestic row and booking passing motorists for speeding on the highway. The rescue of Renee Haywood and the arrest of a cop killer must have fuelled his desire for a more exciting and fulfilling career. Coorah Creek didn't have much to offer him.

And neither did she. The past two weeks of questions and statements had brought back so much of her past. Most of it was now in the police reports. The squats. The stealing. The men. Max would have read the reports. He would know all about her past. Tia lifted her hand to gently rub the skin on the right side of her chest, just below her collarbone. It was still a little sore. Three days ago, she had begun a series of treatments that would remove the tattoo. She had hated the idea that she would be forced to look at that reminder of her past every day for the rest of her life. She hated the idea that Max would look at it too. She'd seen the look of horror on his face when she had shown him what it was: Ned Kelly's brand on her. But removing the tattoo couldn't erase all that she had done. She knew that. And what would a man like Max, an honest cop with a bright future ahead of him, want with someone like her?

Her driver parked the car outside the police station and got out. He headed eagerly up the stairs. Tia followed more slowly. When she entered the station, the first thing she saw was Max. He was shaking hands with the constable. The younger man was looking at Max with something like hero worship in his eyes. In her mind, Tia saw the weeks and months ahead, as Max forged his new career. Leaving her alone at Coorah Creek.

Then Max saw her. His face lit up and he crossed the room swiftly. For one moment Tia thought he was going to kiss her. Or at least hold her. But he didn't, he stopped just out of arm's reach.

'Tia.' Her name sounded so good on his lips.

'Hi, Max.'

A heavy silence settled in the room.

'Constable, I guess you need a break and something to eat before you head back.' Max glanced across at the uniformed officer who was watching them both closely. 'Why don't you head across the road? The pub is the only place in town to eat. Tell them to put it on my tab.'

'Okay.' The young officer sounded disappointed. He had no doubt been looking forward to spending some time with his new hero. Maybe hearing more about that big night. But he left.

An instant after the door closed behind him, Max stepped so close that Tia could almost hear his heart beat.

'Are you all right?' he asked, studying her face. 'I am so sorry you had to go through all that. But in the end, it's going to be better to have it over and done with.'

'I'm fine,' she said. The words came out as a whisper.

Max hesitated for half a second and looked around him. The police station was empty, but he frowned and shook his head.

'There's something I have to tell you,' Max said in a serious voice. 'But this isn't the right place. Come on. Let's get out of here.'

He grabbed her hand and almost dragged her out the door and around the side of the station. The door of his workshop was open. He led her there and then he dragged her into his arms and kissed her. It was a hard brief kiss, then he stepped back and slowly looked her up and down.

Here it is, Tia thought. This is where he tells me he's leaving. She didn't trust herself to speak. She just waited, her eyes fixed on his face.

'Before we go any further, there's a few things I have to say. First, you need to know that I have seen all the paperwork and read all the interviews you gave.'

Tia's heart sank. If he knew all that ... Knew all the things she had done. Knew about the men. There was no way he would ever want ...

'And I want you to know that it doesn't change the way I feel. No. I'm wrong. It does. It makes me more in awe of your strength. And it makes me love you even more, if that's even possible.'

Tia's breath caught in her throat.

'I want you to know that you never have to hide any of that from me. And whatever you need to get past what happened, I am here for you. I want you to be in my life, and I won't take no for an answer.'

Tia felt the tears begin to run down her cheeks. But for the first time in a very, very long time, they were tears of joy.

'And I have a confession to make.' Max took her hands in his. 'With all the paperwork and so forth involved in the case, I did something ... well, I probably shouldn't have. But I thought ...' He hesitated as if uncertain, then continued in a rush. 'I traced your mother through the police system. I know where she is and how to contact her. If you want to.'

Tia almost staggered with surprise. 'My mother?'

'I saw the Christmas card in your bag. The one you have kept all these years. I wasn't sure how you felt or if you would want to find her, but I thought that maybe you did, and that was why you'd kept the card. She's still living in Brisbane.' His voice trailed off as he waited for her reaction.

'I don't know what to say,' Tia said. 'I think about her sometimes. But I didn't want to go back in case he was still there.'

Max smiled. 'He's not. Your mother now works with a

charity that helps troubled teens and runaways. She lives and works at a shelter where the kids can go to be safe. She's never stopped looking for you, Tia.'

'I … I don't know.'

'There's no rush,' Max said. 'I just wanted you to know that you can get in touch with her if you want to. And I'll help you. Go with you if you want me to. Everybody deserves a second chance.'

Tia was beginning to understand a lot about second chances. 'I can't believe you did that. For me. Thank you,' she said in a tiny voice.

She meant it. She was grateful to him, and not just for finding her mother. She was a different person now. She would never forget her past, but she was no longer afraid of it. She was stronger than she had ever been. She had found herself again, and she had Max to thank for that.

Impulsively, she leaned forward and kissed him gently on the lips. She pulled away again before he could react, and made as if to step back. To put a safe and proper distance between them while she was still able to.

For a long moment, Max studied her face, and then he pulled her into his arms and kissed her again. It was a long, deep kiss; a kiss designed to chase away the fears and uncertainties of the past weeks. It was a kiss filled with passion and joy. He tasted so good. She kissed him back with all the longing and love she had to give, knowing as she did that she would have to let him go.

When at last they broke apart, there were tears in Tia's eyes.

Max reached up and gently wiped them away.

'What's wrong?' he said.

It was so hard to form the words, but she'd had a lifetime of lies and half-truths. It was time all that stopped.

'The constable. He said you were leaving. It's great that

you have a promotion and all that, but I … I wish you weren't going.'

'Do you really?'

Her heart leapt as a beautiful smile spread slowly across Max's face.

'Of course I do.'

'That's a good thing. Because I'm not going anywhere.'

She struggled with the words. 'But your promotion? Your career? Isn't that what you wanted?'

'Maybe once. But not any more. Everything I want is right here.'

He kissed her again and this was a kiss filled with promise. It seemed to Tia as if their hearts were beating in time with each other.

'In fact,' Max said when he let her go. 'There is something I have been dying to show you. Come on.'

He turned to the big table in the centre of the workshop and unrolled some large sheets of paper, pinning the corners down with tools. Tia leaned forward to look at a pencil drawing.

'House plans?'

'My Inspector was here for two days, looking at the trailer and questioning people. He's a good officer, but all I wanted to do was get in the car and drive to the Isa. Then he ordered me to stay away from you while they questioned you. It was hard, but he was right. This was the only thing that stopped me going mad.' He grinned. 'I decided it was time to actually build that house I've been thinking about. This is just a rough idea. We can add or change anything you want to change. I'd like to do most of the work myself. Jack and some of the others will help me out when I need it. It will take longer than hiring builders, but it will make the place more truly ours. And look …'

He was like an excited boy. He almost bounded to the

back of the shed to pick up a large heavy wooden panel. Like the other wood that Max carved this panel was pale with age, but in places a richer colour shone through where he had been carving. In those darker shadows she could discern the shapes of birds and animals beginning to emerge.

'I spent a lot of time remembering the time we spent together during the search. What you looked like walking back into that camp with Renee in your arms. So I started working on this. It's sort of a reminder of those two days in the park. I thought it might look good over the front door. Or maybe over the fireplace.'

Her head was spinning so much, Tia focused on the one thing that jumped out at her.

'Fireplace? Max, this is Queensland. Queensland. It's always thirty degrees or more. We don't need a fireplace.'

Max stilled. His eyes shone as he looked at her in a way that made her feel like some sort of goddess, right down to the tips of her toes. 'You said "we". Does that mean what I think it means?'

She started to nod, but before she could finish the move, she was in his arms again. The kiss seemed to last forever.

They were finally pulled apart by a long loud blast from an air horn.

'What's that?' Tia said.

'Come and see. If it's what I think it is, the town is in for a surprise.'

Max took her hand and led her out of the workshop, past the police station and into the small patch of pale green grass that was Coorah Creek's tiny town square.

A large blue and white truck had just pulled up at the edge of the square. Both doors opened. Pete leaped down from one and Sarah from the other. Sarah's face broke into a grin and she darted across to wrap Tia in a hug.

'It's so good to have you back,' she said. 'Are you all

right? Max told us you were just answering questions but I was worried.'

Tia returned her hug. 'It's good to be back. And I'm fine.'

Sarah took a half step back and looked from Tia's face to Max and then back again.

'You really are, aren't you?' Sarah hugged her again. 'I want to hear details. Every single detail,' she whispered.

Tia started to blush. 'And what about you?' she said under her breath.

Before Sarah could answer, Pete appeared at her side.

'Hi,' Pete said as he too gave Tia a hug. 'Welcome home.'

When he let Tia go, he dropped an arm around Sarah's shoulders and pulled her close. There was something in that casual gesture that told Tia everything she needed to know.

'What's that?' She indicated the huge object on the back of Pete's truck. It was wrapped in tarpaulin, but that couldn't disguise the awkward shape of the thing.

'Is that it?' a voice called from across the road and within a few seconds Trish and Syd had joined them. Jack wasn't far behind, with his wife Ellen and their kids.

'It's arrived, has it?'

'Well, let's take a look at it.'

Soon the small square was crowded with people, some of whom Tia knew, and some she didn't. Sarah's parents appeared, arm in arm. They were both smiling and Tia thought they both looked so much better than when she'd last seen them.

'How are your parents?' she asked Sarah quietly.

'Much better. Mum is regaining her strength. She's been cooking enormous meals and Dad is putting weight back on. Doctor Adam says that's a good sign.'

'So are you staying here in the Creek?'

'No and yes,' Sarah answered. 'I've discovered that I really like being on the road.'

'With Pete.'

'Yes. With Pete. We thought we might travel together for a while. He gets loads that take him all over the country. There are a lot of places we could see together. We may even think about an overseas trip.'

'That sounds great.'

'Mum and Dad are talking about retiring, but not for a year or two. Maybe more. By then, I will probably be happy to come back. Coorah Creek is a good place to settle down and raise a family.'

Tia looked over to where Max was helping Pete unfasten the tarp covering the object on the back of the truck. 'You know, I was just thinking exactly the same thing.'

Tia and Sarah stood side by side as Max and Pete climbed onto the back of the truck and began to remove the tarp. It was like unwrapping a giant present.

At last the tarp slid to the ground, revealing what was underneath.

A stunned silence settled on the crowd.

Max and Pete jumped down. Max came to stand beside Tia, taking her hand in his in a way that made her heart sing. Beside them, Pete had his arm around Sarah's shoulders as the four of them examined the large bronze statue.

'What is that?' Tia asked.

'It's a gift to the town from Evan Haywood. To say thanks for finding Renee,' Max said.

'Yes, but what is it?' Trish Warren repeated.

Max laughed. A long slow chuckle that warmed Tia's heart.

'Apparently Haywood is richer than we thought. He's an art dealer, but this is a piece from his private collection. He wants it erected in the square.'

272

'Yes, but again I have to ask – what is it?' Trish voiced the thoughts that were in many of the townsfolks' minds.

The statue was made of some dark and rough metal. It looked to be lying on its side on the truck, although Tia wasn't entirely sure which side was up. To her it appeared to be just a collection of metal stripes, twisted and entwined.

'Apparently it's called "Mother and Child",' Max offered.

'Which is which?' a voice at the back of the crowd asked.

That started a vigorous discussion about the statue as laughter rose from the town square.

'So, how are we going to set it up?' Ed from the garage asked.

'Haywood sent instructions,' said Pete. 'Apparently we need some sort of concrete base to bolt it to.'

'I can help with that,' said Jack. 'And we can probably get some equipment from the mine to help build it.'

'And I know where I can get a small mobile crane,' another voice added. 'We'll need it to lift that thing.'

Tia stood listening to the voices flowing around her as Coorah Creek did what it did best, work together to solve a problem. Max stood by her side, his hand holding hers and he laughed along with the others.

Yes, she thought, it was good to be home.

Thank You

Thank you for reading *Little Girl Lost* and taking this journey with Tia and Max, Sarah and Pete … and with me.

Did I make you just a little bit misty? I hope so. The very first fan letter I ever had was from an elderly lady who had cried as she read my story. It really is an honour to be able to touch someone's emotions like that. There were days I reached for the tissues when writing this book and nothing makes me happier than to know that you and I shared the emotion of *Little Girl Lost*. It makes all those hours of hard work so very worthwhile.

If you enjoyed the book, let me know, and do tell others. If you have a moment to review the book on Amazon, or Goodreads or whatever sites you visit, please do. It would be lovely to have more people visiting Coorah Creek and meeting the characters who are so close to my heart.

There are other books set in the Creek, with Trish and Max and the rest of the gang. And who knows … maybe more to come?

I always love to hear from readers, so drop me a line, via my website or Facebook or Twitter. My details are with my author profile.

And keep reading. As you and I know, it's just THE best thing in the world.

Much Love

Janet

About the Author

Janet lives in Surrey with her English husband but grew up in the Australian outback surrounded by books. She solved mysteries with Sherlock Holmes, explored jungles with Edgar Rice Burroughs and shot to the stars with Isaac Asimov and Ray Bradbury. After studying journalism at Queensland University she became a television journalist, first in Australia, then in Asia and Europe. During her career Janet saw and did a lot of unusual things. She met one Pope, at least three Prime Ministers, a few movie stars and a dolphin. Janet now works in television production and travels extensively with her job.

Janet's first short story, *The Last Dragon*, was published in 2002. Since then she has published numerous short stories, one of which won the Elizabeth Goudge Award from the Romantic Novelists' Association. Her novel, *Flight to Coorah Creek*, won the 2015 Aspen Gold Reader's Choice Award and was a finalist for the Romance Writers of Australia's Romantic Book of The Year Ruby Award.

Follow Janet on:
Twitter: https://twitter.com/janet_gover
Facebook: http://www.facebook.com/janetgoverbooks
Blog: http://janetgover.com/

More Choc Lit

From Janet Gover

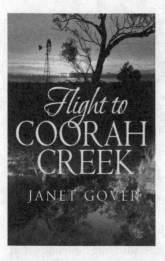

Flight to Coorah Creek

Book 1 in the Coorah Creek series

Winner of 2015 Aspen Gold Award

What happens when you can fly, but you just can't hide?

Only Jessica Pearson knows the truth when the press portray her as the woman who betrayed her lover to escape prosecution. But will her new job flying an outback air ambulance help her sleep at night or atone for a lost life?

Doctor Adam Gilmore touches the lives of his patients, but his own scars mean he can never let a woman touch his heart.

Runaway Ellen Parkes wants to build a safe future for her two children. Without a man – not even one as gentle as Jack North.

In Coorah Creek, a town on the edge of nowhere, you're judged by what you do, not what people say about you. But when the harshest judge is the one you see in the mirror, there's nowhere left to hide.

Visit www.choc-lit.com for more details, or simply scan barcode using your mobile phone QR reader.

The Wild One

Book 2 in the Coorah Creek series

Can four wounded souls find love?

Iraq war veteran Dan Mitchell once disobeyed an order – and it nearly destroyed him. Now a national park ranger in the Australian outback, he's faced with another order he is unwilling to obey …

Photographer Rachel Quinn seeks out beauty in unlikely places. Her work comforted Dan in his darkest days. But Quinn knows darkness too – and Dan soon realises she needs his help as much as he needs hers.

Carrie Bryant was a talented jockey until a racing accident broke her nerve. Now Dan and Quinn need her expertise, but can she face her fear? And could horse breeder, Justin Fraser, a man fighting to save his own heritage, be the one to help put that fear to rest?

Sometimes, the wounds you can't see are the hardest to heal …

Visit www.choc-lit.com for more details, or simply scan barcode using your mobile phone QR reader.

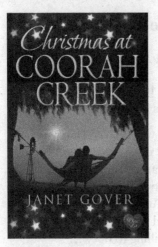

Christmas at Coorah Creek

Book 3 in the Coorah Creek series

What if you don't want to be home for Christmas?

Spending Christmas away from home is one thing but English nurse Katie Brooks is spending hers in Coorah Creek; a small town in the Australian outback.

Katie was certain leaving London was the right decision, but her new job in the outback is more challenging than she could have ever imagined.

Scott Collins rescued Katie on her first day in Coorah Creek and has been a source of comfort ever since. But Scott no longer calls the town home – it's too full of bad memories and he doesn't plan on sticking around for long.

Scott needs to leave. Katie needs to stay. They have until Christmas to decide their future …

Visit www.choc-lit.com for more details, or simply scan barcode using your mobile phone QR reader.

Bring Me Sunshine

Sometimes, you've just got to take the plunge …

When marine biologist, Jenny Payne, agrees to spend Christmas working on the Cape Adare cruise ship to escape a disastrous love affair, she envisions a few weeks of sunny climes, cocktails and bronzed men …

What she gets is an Antarctic expedition, extreme weather, and a couple of close shaves with death. And then there's her fellow passengers; Vera, the eccentric, elderly crime writer and Lian, a young runaway in pursuit of forbidden love …

There's also Kit Walker; the mysterious and handsome man who is renting the most luxurious cabin on the ship, but who nobody ever sees.

As the expedition progresses, Jenny finds herself becoming increasingly obsessed with the enigmatic Kit and the secrets he hides. Will she crack the code before the return journey or is she bound for another disappointment?

Visit www.choc-lit.com for more details, or simply scan barcode using your mobile phone QR reader.

Introducing Choc Lit

We're an independent publisher creating
a delicious selection of fiction.
Where heroes are like chocolate – irresistible!
Quality stories with a romance at the heart.

See our selection here:
www.choc-lit.com

We'd love to hear how you enjoyed *Little Girl Lost*.
Please leave a review where you purchased the novel
or visit: **www.choc-lit.com** and give your feedback.

Choc Lit novels are selected by genuine readers like yourself.
We only publish stories our Choc Lit Tasting Panel want to
see in print. Our reviews and awards speak for themselves.

Could you be a Star Selector and join our Tasting Panel?
Would you like to play a role in choosing which novels we
decide to publish? Do you enjoy reading romance novels?
Then you could be perfect for our Choc Lit Tasting Panel.

Visit here for more details...
www.choc-lit.com/join-the-choc-lit-tasting-panel

Keep in touch:
Sign up for our monthly newsletter Choc Lit Spread for
all the latest news and offers: www.spread.choc-lit.com.
Follow us on Twitter: @ChocLituk and Facebook: Choc Lit.

Where heroes are like chocolate – irresistible!